Tiger in the Night

by

L. Dawn Jackson

Tiger in the Night

Cover Art by *Rae Monet, Inc.*

The Wild Rose Press, Inc.
PO Box 708
Adams Basin, NY 14410-0708
Visit us at www.thewildrosepress.com

Publishing History
First Edition, 2023
Trade Paperback ISBN 978-1-5092-5095-0
Digital ISBN 978-1-5092-5096-7

Published in the United States of America

Malachi's tone was all respect as he addressed Pepper, his gaze never leaving Jensen. "Forgive me."

Claws slid from Malachi's fingertips. He felt the give of living flesh under the sharp tips, and then the faint resistance as he pierced skin to slice through muscle. Jensen snarled and twisted. Malachi adjusted his grip. Tendons snapped, cut by Malachi's lethal claws, forcing Jensen's fingers to release. Malachi's other hand closed behind Pepper's hip and dragged her into him as he whirled, placing himself between her and Jensen.

Her scent hit him hard, a low, wicked punch to his chest and his groin. The breath slammed out of his lungs, forcing him to inhale again, bringing her scent deep inside of him. That rush surged through him as the tiger roared recognition of its potential mate. His arms tightened to hold her to him as he struggled against his baser instincts, forgetful of both her pain and Jensen's threat until she pushed at his arm.

Something huge and heavy crashed into his back. Malachi stumbled forward, making a cage of his arms to keep Pepper safe. Nothing—not even the justice of his people—was as important as her safety. That cold, new fury took hold in his belly, cracking his control. It took all of his will to set Pepper a few feet away and take his hands off of her. Stripes appeared on his skin as he struggled to keep his fur from growing through. His teeth elongated. The tiger's roar tore from Malachi's throat, a massive sound that even shook the rain.

Dedication

To Timothy, the hero of my own romance story;
To Jen, the midwife for this story;
and to Aunt Shirley, for burning Thanksgiving dinner
over it.

Chapter One

Screams battered the muggy evening air. Pepper
Nyx straightened from her lean against the open door of
Turtle Creek Coffee. She nudged a cinder block into
place with her foot to keep herself from getting locked
out and stepped away from the brick building. The
setting sun sent streaks of fire into her eyes as she
searched for the commotion, and she lifted a hand to
shade her eyes. Along the far edge of the parking lot
was a lone car where a tall man was arguing with a
woman. The first shots of adrenaline sent her heart
fluttering against her ribs and leached the moisture out
of her mouth. Inhaling sharply, she fished under her
apron for her phone as she shouted back into the coffee
shop kitchen.

"Abby, if I'm not back in two minutes, call the
police!"

"Pepper?" the older woman called back. "Pepper,
what's going on?"

Pepper was already headed across the lot. Her grip
tightened on her phone until the case creaked in protest
as she forced her breathing back under her control. Her
worn black sneakers ground the gravel into the asphalt
with every hurried step.

"Let go of me!" a woman shouted. Pepper slowed,
picking her way by looking through the phone's
camera. She fumbled for the video setting as the sound

1

of a low growl seemed to surround the entire lot. The tall man had his back to her, pinning the woman against the side of a car. Pepper couldn't tell if he was trying to get the door open or if he was grabbing at the woman herself. The poor woman was frantically shoving at him, kicking him in the legs and beating him with her purse, but he didn't seem to notice.

"Hey!" Pepper punched the air out of her belly to make the sound carry, finally getting her phone to start recording. The man looked over his shoulder and Pepper smiled her most sweetly dangerous smile. "That's right, scumbag. Show me your face."

"Call the police!" the woman cried, still fighting to get the man off of her.

"My boss already did," Pepper said calmly, though her heart was racing. She moved around toward the front of the vehicle to get a better angle on the attacker's face. "I'm just going to get a nice close-up of this dirtbag. I'm sure the police are going to be very excited for this debut. Or maybe this isn't your first time on screen," she taunted the attacker. Slowly, he turned toward her. Her stomach churned with fear and fury, but she kept the phone steady. "Maybe they've seen you before. I bet this is the only way you get womanly attention, isn't it, tough guy?"

Pepper ground parking lot grit under the toe of her shoe to relieve the urge to run. She had the distinct impression that she was baiting something dangerous, something primal, and it made her feel overly caffeinated. The man's face should have been handsome, with a strong jawline and high cheekbones, but the hollow-eyed twist of his features sent a shiver down her spine. Dark blond hair flowed back from his forehead. He had to be close to six feet tall. His T-shirt hung off of him like he'd lost a lot of weight, but the slenderness didn't seem to be affecting his strength any. His attention shifted to Pepper as she kept circling, putting the hood of the car between them. That same low growl consumed the air again, stealing it away from her lungs. Pepper zoomed in on his face, making sure to get a good, identifiable shot, and blinked. The man had pale eyes, gray-green in color, and the pupils were clearly visible. Pepper's gaze jerked away from the screen to the man himself, to double-check what she'd seen through the lens, but he was too far away. She looked again, zooming in a little more. There. Vertical pupils, slit like a cat's even in the cloud-covered light.

"It is unwise to interfere in what you don't understand," he said quietly. It sounded like he was trying to be soothing. Pepper scoffed.

"Then tell me," she challenged. "No. Scratch that. I want *her* to tell me. Right now, on camera."

"He's trying to make me go with him. He says if I do, he won't hurt me, he'll make it good, and he's torn my clothes, and please, please help me!" Pepper's heart turned over as the woman begged between sobs.

"The police are on their way," Pepper assured her. "They'll be here any second," she added, and prayed that she was right. Pepper didn't want the situation to get any worse so she kept talking, stalling. "Hey, scumbag, you got a name? Or should I just keep making them up for you?"

That growl came again, louder this time, and Pepper realized it was actually coming from the attacker. Her heartbeat doubled in speed, but she smirked to cover it, keeping her phone up. The man turned toward her, pacing the length of the car with almost feline grace. Pepper shifted her grip to wipe the sweat from her palms. What was taking the police so long?

The attacker leaped over the hood, clearing it in a single smooth motion as Pepper jumped backward with a startled cry. She curled around her phone protectively, refusing to let the man near it. The growl closed around her. Hot breath curled across the back of her neck. He inhaled long and slow behind her ear, and chills slithered down her spine. A hand slid over her hair. He inhaled again, so close behind her that she could feel the heat of him through her polo shirt. Something scraped against the top of her head, back and forth, as a hand brushed over the curve of her hip. Pepper stomped, trying to drive her heel into the top of his foot, but she only met asphalt. Shock waves raced up her leg from impact and she wobbled. His hand tightened on her hip, dragging her backward and rumbling in her ear. There was pleasure in the sound. Pepper's stomach heaved.

As suddenly as he grabbed her, he was gone. Pepper didn't dare turn to look, instead straining her ears to listen. The sound of sirens filtered into the parking lot, quiet at first but growing steadily louder. The other woman sobbed, and Pepper finally risked a glance around her. There was no sign of the attacker. Inch by inch, she lifted her head, searching warily around her with her phone still clutched to her chest. Her knuckles ached from the tension. He was gone. He was really gone. The strength went out of Pepper's knees, dropping her against the side of the car as she struggled to slow her heart. She stared with shocked, wide eyes as the black and white cruiser pulled into the parking lot.

A door slammed in the sudden stillness and Pepper spun. Abby strode from Turtle Rock like a gathering storm as the officers got out of their car. Pepper watched one glance from Abby's keen blue gaze take in the hysterical woman sobbing on the ground, as well as her own stunned expression. Abby shouldered the aluminum baseball bat in her hand and looked expectantly at Pepper. Her friend's voice held a distinct command. "Pepper?"

Pepper had the most absurd urge to giggle. She peeled her phone away from her chest.

"I got video." Her voice was soft. A huge smile spread over her face as she danced in place. She slid into a triumphant shriek. "I actually got it on video!"

Abby stared at her. "Pepper, that was a seriously stupid thing to do." She leaned on the bat like a cane. "You got halfway through a master's degree in criminology and you don't know better than to let the police handle things? You scared the hell out of me! Just what did you think you were going to do?"

"Get evidence," Pepper said smugly. "And I did." She held up her phone and waved it. She sighed, releasing as much of the pent-up adrenaline as she could. Her hands were starting to feel shaky. The recurring urge to giggle had to be the after-effects of adrenaline, and she coughed to clear the giddiness out of her throat. She leaned her head on Abby's shoulder for a moment. "Okay, so it wasn't the smartest thing to do, but I couldn't do *nothing*. All it takes for evil to succeed…"

"I know. I know. If I didn't know it before you started working here, I've certainly learned it since," Abby said with exasperated affection. She squeezed the younger woman around the shoulders. "Go home."

"Can't. The officers will need to speak with me." Pepper made herself pause and exhale again. A shaky laugh escaped on the end of it. "Besides, I could *really* use a solid shot of caffeine right now! Just…give me a minute. And then I'll be back on the line."

"After they're done with you," Abby amended. "Get a double shot of espresso and go home. You're done for the day."

"Abby," Pepper reasoned, "we're going into the after-dinner rush and you're already a man down on the evening crew tonight. I'm fine. I'm not the one who was attacked."

"Barely." Abby's pale blue eyes stared at her hard, as if trying to read the truth. Pepper offered a reassuring smile.

"The work will do me good," she said. "Lots of people, lots of activity, lots to keep me occupied instead of sitting alone and stewing over what just happened."

Abby stared at her for a moment longer before her eyes softened slightly. She sniffed. "All right. Just…try to leave the cape in the closet for the rest of your shift, okay? Even better, the rest of the week."

"No promises on the week," Pepper said. Abby looked completely unamused, and guilt crawled through Pepper's belly for teasing the older woman. "But I promise to be a good little employee and focus on just serving the customers for the rest of my shift."

"You're always a good employee, Pepper. You're always on time, you never leave early, you have yet to call in sick, and your work is always faultless. And I still get the feeling you're too smart for your own good." Abby smiled, her hazel eyes warm with wise amusement. "Nothing time won't fix."

Pepper smiled back, ignoring the hurt that surfaced in her chest. She'd gotten good at ignoring it over the last six months, and the attack had driven it into the background. But for a moment her employer's eyes had the same knowing warmth that she'd known all of her life, until it had been ripped away.

"Miss Nyx?" Pepper looked up, grateful to be jarred out of her thoughts as one of the officers, a large man with more goatee than hair, approached her. "Thank you for waiting. Did you see what happened here?"

"Part of it." Pepper held up her phone. "I got video."

The officer held out his hand. "I'd like to take a look at it, please, if I may."

Pepper unlocked the screen and brought up the video before handing it over. Just the sound of it made her heart start pounding again, but the officer watched impassively through the entire thing, then played it back again.

"I need to take this as evidence."

Pepper hesitated. "For how long? I live alone and it's my only means of communication."

"I'm sorry for any trouble." The officer frowned in his sincerity. "We'll get it processed as quickly as possible. You should be able to pick it up at the station tomorrow."

She chewed a loose bit of skin on her lower lip, frowning thoughtfully at her phone. It was her only connection to the world from her RV, and the idea of being without it was unnerving. But if she didn't hand it over to the police, then everything she just did was pointless.

"Okay," Pepper finally said. "That's why I filmed it, after all. I just hope it helps. Let me grab a couple things from the case, please?"

"Of course. I'm sure it will be very helpful." The officer handed back the phone and gave Pepper another assessing look. "You're sure you're all right? Do you have someone to stay with tonight?"

"I'll be fine," Pepper said. Her voice was steady, almost detached, as she pulled her driver's license and debit card from the phone's case. From behind the phone itself, she slid a cracked old photograph and slipped it into the back pocket of her jeans with everything else. She flicked the phone's case shut with a snap and handed it back to the officer. The memory of the attacker in the parking lot smelling her hair invaded her mind, and she shoved it out as best she could, suppressing a shudder. "I need to get back to work."

The officer pulled a business card from its case and handed it over to her. "If you think of anything, give me a call. If you see him again, find a phone and call 911 immediately. And do us a favor, please: leave the heroics to the professionals."

The rebuke in the officer's voice made Pepper's cheeks warm. She saluted in agreement and bit her tongue against the sting in the words. The officer reiterated his warning, then he and his partner got into the patrol car. Abby raised her eyebrows at Pepper.

"That offer to go home early is still on the table," she said. Pepper shook her head.

"Nah. I won't be alone if I'm here."

"Fair enough." Abby stood with a stretch. She groaned as every joint creaked and headed back across the parking lot. Pepper followed more slowly. The man's features still haunted her mind. She couldn't stop herself from pausing to look over her shoulder, where he'd disappeared. The last rays of the setting sun slashed into the tree-covered verge between parking lots, lighting the underside of the canopy in brilliant relief. A hint of movement rustled the autumn leaves, a bit of shadow darker than the rest. Her breath stopped in her lungs as the dying light tangled in gray-green eyes with vertically slit pupils. In the next instant, they were gone. It was only an errant sea breeze playing with the leaves and shadows, and apparently her mind. Still, she hurried back inside.

Chapter Two

A small bell chimed over the door as Malachi Negrescu stepped into the coffee shop. The evening rush had left a mess of muddled scents, all crossing and re-crossing each other until it took all of his focus to sort through them. He was sorely tempted to simply let the tiger's mind sort them for him, but the beast within was currently a little unpredictable. The sheer amount of human scents was overwhelming, but it wasn't human scent he was searching for. It was Tseng Tse. The criminal he'd been hunting for weeks had attacked a woman just outside; it was possible—though unlikely—that the rogue was still hiding out, even hours later. There was another scent that drew him, too, one he could neither explain nor ignore. It had been elusive, nearly drowned in crossing scents. But it had definitely been present. It called to him on a primal level, teasing at the wild mind within his own.

He searched the room carefully, but there was almost no one in the dining room of the brick-walled coffee shop. A young man who had recently been snacking on raisins stood to one side of the door, half attempting to hide the key ring in his hand. A slightly older woman—maybe in her late twenties—sat at one of the tables, cradling her head in her hands as if holding it together. She turned at the chime of the bell, her dark eyes showing her weariness for a moment before she covered it with a bright smile. Standing, she stepped toward him.

"Welcome to Turtle Creek Coffee! What can I make for you?"

Her scent hit him hard. The beast's mind unfolded, leaping to life with such ferocity that he had to cough over the growl in his chest. He clenched his fists to keep his claws safely in his fingers. The shop popped into painful focus as his eyes shifted. He shut out the world, but not before her face was burned into his mind. He took a deep breath. Instead of calming him, it only filled him with her scent, imprinting it deeply in his lungs. His head swam.

"Sir?" she prompted. Even her voice was beautiful, slightly deeper than most women's and with an expressiveness that made every word into music.

"Malachi." His voice cracked like a youngling in puberty, and he cleared his throat to try again. He made certain his eyes were in their duller, human shape before he risked opening them again.

She was gorgeous. Her dark hair was pulled back into a practical ponytail, but a few strands escaped to frame her face, curling invitingly against her cheeks. Her skin was slightly bronzed by the California sun, a striking background to her full red lips. High cheekbones blended upward into a broad forehead, and down into a narrow chin that looked as if it could be stubborn, on occasion. But it was her eyes that trapped him. Dark eyes. Deep eyes. Intelligence and compassion stared back at him, as well as curiosity.

"My name is Malachi. What shall I call you, please?"

"Pepper." Her smile was polite and distant, and it

irritated him. "What can I get for you?"

Weariness and pain wove through her scent. He should leave, allow the shop to close, and let her go home to rest and heal while he got on with his hunt. It was clear his quarry wasn't in the coffee shop, but the thought of letting Pepper out of his sight sent a wave of desperation through the tiger's mind. He forced the primal mind under his control.

"What would you recommend?" Malachi pitched his voice low, trying not to aggravate her pain. She held his gaze, a question in her dark eyes.

"Well, that depends a lot on your tastes. What sorts of things do you usually like?"

Part of him was amused that she would ask that question. He usually preferred his women with more striking coloring, but there was no part of him trying to deny that she was beautiful. For a moment, he considered making a comment about her phrasing, teasing her, telling her about his sudden change in tastes, but he contented himself with continuing the allusion only in his own mind.

"I'm in the mood to try something new. What sort of thing do *you* like?"

She smiled—really smiled—for the first time since he'd entered the coffee shop, and Malachi felt it clear through his chest.

"One cinnamon shortbread latte, coming up!"

Pepper turned on her heel, making her ponytail fan out behind her, so close that it seemed it would hit him in the face. A vision jumped into his mind of his fingers buried in the black strands, her hair loose around her shoulders, or falling over his leg as her head rested on his lap…

Malachi focused his mind back to the present as he followed her to the counter. He was *hunting*. Jensen had left a trail of battered, abused women—both Tseng Tse and human—across two continents. Malachi was mere hours behind him, and he needed to get back out and hunt before the threatening rain broke and obliterated all scent. But the tiger's mind fought him. It wanted to stay here, with this female. She was weary. She was worried. He watched the way she stretched her neck and shifted her weight and wondered if her head or feet were the cause of the pain-scent coming from her. He reached toward her just as she turned, and he dropped his hand on the counter to cover his lapse in control. Pepper slid the sleeve onto the heavy paper cup and offered it to him.

"I'm sorry, Malachi, but we only serve to-go this late."

"Perfectly all right," he murmured absently. He reached for the cup and indulged himself by brushing his fingers over hers. Electricity shot up his hand, all the way to the base of his spine. Pepper drew her hand back with a small gasp and wide eyes as her scent changed slightly. Malachi's hand tightened.

"Is there anything else I can get you?" Pepper asked, her words slightly rushed. Malachi allowed himself a small smile.

"Your phone number, perhaps?"

Pepper laughed and his heart sped up at the sound. Even the primal mind pricked up its ears with interest.

"I have to give you points for sheer boldness, but I make it a policy never to give out my number to customers."

"I should have asked for your phone number, first,"

13

Malachi said ruefully, and sipped at the drink. The sweetness of it took him off-guard and he coughed.

"Is it too hot?" she asked, genuine worry in her tone. He shook his head.

"Sweet. Very…sweet." Malachi took another sip, better prepared for the taste, his eyes still on the woman in front of him. He inhaled again, just to feel that rush through his veins. Pepper shifted, glancing at the clock, and the thread of discomfort in her scent grew stronger. Because of him.

Her discomfort was entirely unacceptable. It was the duty and pleasure, the right and responsibility, of every Tseng Tse to put the needs of their mate first, even a potential mate. He straightened and took a step back, then another. The beast inside complained, trying to drag him back toward the female it found so interesting, but Malachi continued across the dining room.

"Please take care of yourself." The words stuck between his teeth. He refused to allow her to look away. "See to your pain."

Surprise flashed across her face. He'd said too much. Malachi backed another step, then turned away. He stalked across the dining room floor and yanked open the door with such violence that the handle groaned in protest, then allowed the night to swallow him.

****

Pepper watched him go. It wasn't just the breadth of his shoulders or way his black hair caught the lights from the bare bulbs in living streaks of deep blue highlights that held her attention. He was…odd. Memorable, in every way. Definitely the most interesting person she'd met all day, or even that month. The look on his face when he'd tried the latte still made her want to laugh. He'd just been so surprised, and with the composure he'd shown, that made it all the funnier. Her smile faded as his parting words replayed in her mind.

Please take care of yourself.

It wasn't the kind of thing people usually said as a pleasantry. He sounded like he meant it. The way he had looked directly at her, as if his deep blue eyes were seeing all of her aches and tiredness, made it seem like it mattered to him. Like she mattered to him.

"You know him?" Abby asked as she stepped forward to claim the till. Pepper startled, whipping herself in the face as she whirled around toward the register. She must have really been absorbed in her thoughts not to notice Abby coming up from the back room. Pepper shook her head.

"I've never seen him before." She would have remembered a man like that.

Abby gave a disapproving scoff, presumably for the departing customer, and took the till to the back office to count it. Brett turned the key to lock the front door and flipped off the "open" sign.

Pepper forced her feet to carry her into the kitchen for a bucket of hot soapy water and the cloth to wipe down all the tables. The familiar routine was a moving meditation, soothing her rumpled-up spirit. She needed to get home. She needed quiet and rest and a warm, purring cat. And, as much as she didn't want to admit it, something for her pounding head. Her hand stilled, leaving the cloth steaming against the table for a moment. How had Malachi known she was in pain?

Had it shown in her face? Or was it a lucky guess? Neither one would really surprise her. She'd had a pretty stressful afternoon, after all, and she might have been wearing it in her expression. It also didn't take a genius to figure out that a barista might have a headache or backache after spending all day on their feet. Pepper shook her head and scrubbed up the puddle the washcloth had left on the table. The first one was more likely; the rest was just the active imagination of a criminologist's brain.

Brilliant light flashed through the glass front of the shop. Pepper stepped back, nearly kicking over her bucket, and laid a hand over her suddenly racing heart as thunder rumbled.

"It was just lightning, Pep," Brett said. "Geez, you're jumpy. Are you afraid of thunder or something?"

Pepper laughed at herself, shaking her head. Pepper tossed down the rag and followed him to the picture windows as the lightning forked over the ocean.

"No. It just startled me." She smiled past her reflection in the glass, ignoring the sad look to it. "I like thunder storms. They're kind of a rare treat around here. When I was a kid, I used to run around the little house in Monterey with my dad, fastening all the shutters. He would lift me up on his shoulders so I could reach the catch. He was so proud of me when I got tall enough to reach it on my own."

"You had shutters? Like, actual shutters? Not just fake ones for show?"

Pepper chuckled again. "Yes, actual shutters. Dad was a general contractor and put them on himself when he bought the house."

16

"Why?" Pepper couldn't tell if Brett was more curious or disdainful. She swallowed against the lump rising in her throat and pasted on a bright smile.

"To protect the windows, of course."

"If you have time to lean, you have time to clean." Abby walked out of the back with the till, sliding it into the register with a satisfied bang. "Get it done, folks. You have lives to get home to."

Pepper and Brett exchanged guilty smiles and hurried away from the windows. Pepper scrubbed down a couple of chairs. Abby strode over. She flipped the tall bistro chairs with ease and stacked them on the table. Pepper was always somewhat in awe of the power coiled into the coffee shop owner's solid frame. Abby nailed Pepper with a look as she hauled the bucket to another table.

"I'll give you a lift home. Did you bring a jacket?" Abby asked.

"Abby, I'm fine. I can drive." Pepper dunked the cloth and wrung it out.

"You've had way too much excitement this afternoon. I want to make sure you get home without any more."

"You live on the other side of town," Pepper reasoned as thunder rumbled again, louder and longer this time. Pepper pointed upward. "And *that* is coming in. We all need to get home as quickly as possible."

Home. Suddenly an old RV on the rocky shores of northern California didn't feel so much like home. Home was supposed to be safe. The attacker's face reared in her mind again, features twisted into something terrifying. The way he'd leaped over the car's hood replayed in her mind, as well as the cat-slit eyes, and the little hairs on the back of her neck stood up. The echo of his breath over her hair sent her skin crawling. Being alone wasn't as appealing as it had been ten minutes ago.

Pepper steadied herself. It didn't have to be for long. As soon as it was light, she could come back to Turtle Creek. She'd be hours early for work, but at least she wouldn't be alone. She was fine, and she was going to stay fine. She just hoped she could convince both herself and her employer.

Abby drummed her uneven fingernails on the countertop until another bright flash of lightning illuminated the room. She glanced through the windows, then leveled a finger at Pepper. "Straight home. Eat. Sleep. Give Bunsen scritches for me."

"Yes, ma'am," Pepper smiled crookedly and dipped the washcloth into the bucket. "You spoil my cat worse than I do."

"He's a cat. That's the point. Get it done, folks." Abby's words hung in the air as the door to the back swung behind her. Pepper hurried to finish washing the tables and chairs as Brett turned off most of the dining room lights.

"Sorry," she murmured. Brett just shook his head and grabbed the handle of the heavy bucket, helping her carry it into the kitchen and dump it out.

"You're sure you're all right?" Brett asked as they turned off the rest of the lights. City lights and thunder poured in through the heavy back door as soon as Pepper pushed it open.

"Fine," she repeated. She flashed him a smile. "I'll see you tomorrow." Brett gave her a slightly disbelieving look as he locked the deadbolt. Pepper waved. Her strides ate up ground as she headed toward her car...then veered toward the far corner of the customer lot. The maroon sedan was still there. Pepper peered around the lot. Her steps slowed. It didn't seem like anyone else was around. Just one quick look. That was all. If the attacker had jumped on the hood, there had to be some kind of mark, a dent or a shoe scuff or something. But if he'd leaped all the way over it, the hood would be clean. She just wanted to check her memory. Or maybe her sanity.

The hood was hard to see, though the flashes of lightning helped. Pepper fished in her pocket for her phone but found only her keys and a couple of cards.

"No phone, no flashlight." Pepper spoke aloud, mostly to fill the void of night. "You are umbilically attached to that thing. It'll be good for you to detox from it."

Lightning split the sky, followed by the grumble of the thunder. The storm was getting closer. Pepper turned back toward her own car as fat drops of rain spattered onto her head, bringing the low background throb to sharper pain. The key was already in her hand before she reached her car. It was a relief to slide inside and lock the door behind her, just for the comfort of the familiar. She turned the key in the ignition as another bright arc of lightning lit the night.

Nothing happened. Pepper frowned. Turning the key back, she tried again. The engine cranked but stubbornly refused to turn over. With a loud groan, she dropped her forehead onto the steering wheel. Maybe if she hurried, she could catch Brett and get a ride home, or at least borrow his phone. Pepper kicked open the door and jumped out. The echo was eerily loud in the

19

night as she slammed the door. The employee parking lot was deserted. Maybe someone was hanging out around front. She set off at a jog around the front of the building, and rounded the corner just in time to see the taillights of a familiar car pulling out of the driveway.

"Hey! Hey, Brett!" Pepper rushed the taillights as the old sedan pulled into the soggy darkness.

She swore loudly, kicking the sodden leaves in the gutter between the road and the parking lot. Rain battered the branches in the little faux-wilderness area between Turtle Creek and the next set of buildings. Pepper had parked her car on the edge of it, hoping the trees would shelter her little hatchback from the storm. Cold rain dripped from the leaves to her head to run down the back of her neck and make her shiver. Snorting in irritation, she dashed to her car and yanked open the back door. She jumped inside and flopped over on the small bench seat to grope under the driver's seat in front of her. Her hand closed on the handle of a heavy canvas bag. With a sound of satisfaction, she pulled it out and angled it into what little light there was.

Lightning helped as it forked across the sky, suddenly throwing the contents of the emergency roadside kit into brilliant relief. It was too brief, though. Everything in the bag was jumbled together in a confusion of indeterminate shapes. There may have been a flashlight in there, somewhere. She felt around inside the bag, but there were too many objects with similar shapes to pick out anything for sure. With a sigh, Pepper upended the bag onto the back seat beside her. It was a little easier to see the contents in the bit of light that wandered in from the parking lot. She picked across the selection of screwdrivers, the jumper cables, the road flare, the tow strap, a couple of batteries, and a thermal blanket. Not a flashlight in the lot.

"Well, that sucks," she muttered. She debated for a moment, then grabbed up the silvery thermal blanket and tore it from the package. It might be some help against the rain, anyway. Pepper wrapped it over her head and shoulders as she slid out of the hatchback. She squinted up at the sky, then dragged the makeshift hood a little farther forward for a small brim. Carefully, she locked the doors and started off on foot. It was only a couple of miles to the RV park. Bunsen would grumble about her getting home late, but he was a cat—he grumbled about everything.

Lightning lit the streets better than the streetlamps as she wound her way along the concrete paths. The wind was picking up, tugging at the edges of the thermal blanket and tossing them around her. Poor Bunsen. He never liked it when the wind blew around the RV. Even that slight rocking motion would make him yowl and hunker under the driver's chair. One of these days, she'd get a proper place for them to live, even if it was just a little studio apartment. The RV had been one of the few things left of her parents' estate after the expenses were paid. Working at the coffee shop paid for gas, food, and a place to park the RV. If she was careful, she would have enough left over soon to put toward a deposit on a real apartment. The RV lot catered to tourists on a small budget, with little more than electricity and other necessary hookups, but it was right on the ocean. The amazing view and the comforting sound of the waves made up for the spartan conditions, for now. Only for now.

She slid her fingertips into her back pocket. Safely wedged between her driver's license and her debit card was the photograph. She just had to check that it was still there. Still safe. She didn't pull it out. She didn't want it to get wet or blow away, and it wasn't as if she needed to see it. She had it memorized. Her mother, a beautiful woman Pepper didn't remember, in a pretty floral dress and a bright smile, dark hair flowing over her shoulders. Herself, of course, the chubby baby on her mother's lap, with downy hair sticking up inside a rosette headband, two teeth peeking through the wide smile. And her father, standing behind her mother with his hands on her shoulders, smiling from under his heavy mustache. Her fingertips brushed over the edges of the cracked photo.

"I'm trying, Dad," Pepper murmured. "I know this isn't what you wanted for me, not yet, but I'm trying."

A dog barked. Pepper's heart beat too hard as adrenaline tipped into her system. It had to be after midnight. The street was deserted, except for the dog still barking somewhere ahead of her. Fat drops of rain spattered on the pavement like overripe grapes. They beat on her head, exacerbating her headache and doing nothing for her mood. She knew the statistics of being attacked on the street by a random stranger in the middle of the night in this area of the country, and they really should have reassured her. The trouble with statistics is that they don't mean a thing to the individual who became the statistic. Pepper hunched up her shoulders and walked faster.

The sound of the ocean struggled to rise through the clamor of battering rain and mounting thunder. The buildings became fewer and farther between as she moved away from the town center. Worse, she ran out of sidewalk. That was something she was still getting used to: the sidewalks occasionally just stopped in this town, abandoning any pedestrians to walk on bare dirt on the shoulder of the road. Or, in this case, mud. The trees and other shrubs dwindled out away from the town center, too. The wind drove the rain at her in the open space nearing the river. It never made sense to her that there were no trees growing down by the river. Stream, she mentally corrected herself. Where she was from, the water that ran through town on its way to the ocean was large enough and deep enough to be called a river, but they called it a stream, here. It was definitely smaller than the Sacramento River.

Pepper reached into her pocket for her keys, just to reassure herself that they were still there. Her skin felt battered as her whole body tightened. This was the part of the walk that made her the most nervous. It was too dark. There were no streetlights between the flood plain and the RV lot, and very few cars came by after dark. She started running the statistics through her head to steady herself.

A flash of lightning threw the road into bright relief, showing a large, dark shape a hundred yards in front of her. Pepper stopped. The teeth of her keys dug painfully into her palm as she gripped them in her pocket, then shifted them to bring them out, wedged between her fingers. A car laid on its horn behind her, warning her away from the road as it sped closer. She skittered out of the way, glancing reflexively over her shoulder. Headlights—high beams—caught her straight in the face and she flinched away. Spots danced behind her eyelids as she screwed her eyes shut to recover her vision as something cold and slick drenched her legs. Scrubbing at her eyes, she looked back down the road. Headlights illuminated the empty shoulder clearly as the car passed.

The figure was gone.

Pepper slowed her pounding heart. Her gaze raked from side to side, trying to cut through the rain to find the figure again. This wasn't some major urban thoroughfare, people going back and forth constantly. This was the edge of a middle-sized town on an old scenic highway, strung like a jewel on a necklace for tourists to follow from one to the next, spending lots of money on the carefully cultivated Americana charm. Its crime rate consisted of a few burglaries and some drug-related charges, embarrassments to local citizenry that they were quick to clean up before any outsiders took them too seriously. It was a safe little town, one of the reasons she'd stayed here. That, and she'd run out of gas.

Her jeans were soaked. The oil-slick grit on the very edge of the asphalt shifted constantly under her sneakers, making traction unreliable, at best. Her foot shot out from under her, slamming her hip into the guard rail and jolting a cry of pain out of her. She steadied herself on the slick metal and tried to catch her breath.

Something warm and solid knocked her from her feet, sending her rolling down the embankment toward the river's edge. The blanket tore away long before she reached the bottom. Rain battered at her eyes as she struggled to her feet.

"You shouldn't be out in this storm."

The masculine voice shot frigid needles of fear

through her entire body. She knew that voice. That roughened voice with its attempted suavity was still fresh in her mind. Pepper rubbed her hand over her face trying to clear her eyes as she slowly backed up. If she could pinpoint where he was, she might have a chance at getting back up to the road.

"Carefully. Carefully," the same voice continued, sounding genuinely concerned. "If you slip, you'll fall in the water, and I'm not sure I could reach you before you were swept out into the waves."

Pepper searched the drenched darkness until she found the slightly darker patch that hid him, and she kept her gaze fixed there. There was not a doubt in her mind that he was the attacker from the coffee shop.

"I'm not going to harm you," he continued in the same low, coaxing voice. Deliberate footsteps carried him through the storm. "My name is Jensen. They called you Pepper. Is that your name or a nickname?"

Pepper kept backing toward the bridge, turning so that she could start up the hill again.

"Nickname," she lied. "You must have been hiding in the trees."

"I was. I have very good hearing." The amusement faded from Jensen's voice. "I also have a very good sense for when people aren't telling the truth, Pepper. Don't lie to me again. I don't like it, and it isn't good for us."

"Us?" Pepper choked on the word. Her head was shaking before she was even aware of it. "There is no *us*. I'm going to go back up to the road and get out of this storm, and you can go…wherever it is you go, and you and I are never going to see each other again."

Jensen clucked his tongue, shaking his head.

"Another lie, Pepper. You have every intention of seeing me again."

Pepper opened her mouth to deny it, and then realized he was right. She had been planning to see him again, at his trial. But how did he know that, even before she did?

There was a flash of movement. Jensen stood in front of her, so close that she could feel his warmth. She fell backward with a gasp. His arms snapped around her like steel coils.

"Careful," he cautioned again. This time, Pepper could see the gleam of teeth as he smiled. "It's a good thing I was here to catch you."

"Let go of me, right now," Pepper demanded, struggling to keep her voice steady. Her heart was beating so hard that she felt sick to her stomach. Her hand worked along the set of keys in her palm. Jensen kept one arm around her as the other hand stroked her dripping hair. Pepper heaved against him, freeing her arm enough to drive the key between her fingers toward his eyes. His hand snapped around her wrist. Sheer strength held her arm perfectly still, midway to his face, as she struggled to reach him.

"Let go of me!" she shrieked. She slammed her heel down on the top of his foot and tried to peel away from his one-armed grip around her waist, but he was too strong. She might as well have been fighting the steel girders of the bridge. Jensen bent low and inhaled deeply near her neck, then again in her hair.

"It's the rain," he murmured. He smiled down at her. His pale greenish eyes met hers, and something about their expression made her feel sick. "If not for the rain, I could smell it. Come." Jensen released her wrist to wrap both arms around her again, pinning her arms to her sides. His arms tightened, simply lifting her feet off the ground to carry her into the darkness under the bridge.

A roar shattered the night.

Chapter Three

Malachi couldn't hold back his roar. Fury surged hot through his blood, cracks in his control that had begun the moment he caught Pepper's scent. It had teased him in the open air behind the coffee shop, but once he had been inside with her and been able to draw her deep into his lungs, it had unlocked the well of emotions sealed in the deepest parts of his mind. That pitiful excuse for a man had no right to put his hands on Pepper.

Malachi crouched on the guard rail of the highway bridge, rain soaking his clothing to his skin as the blood ran hot in his veins.

"Let go of me!" The words were almost lost in the rumbling thunder. He sprang off the railing to drop down through the driving rain. His eyesight was excellent in the dark, far better than human, but even he failed to pick out the struggling figures until he was far closer than he liked. Fortunately, the struggling woman had all of Jensen's attention as he carried her toward the bridge. Toward Malachi. Pepper screamed, a sound of fear and rage that made Malachi's blood run hot and cold with fury. His shoulders bunched as he loomed out of the driving rain like some dark destroyer on the side of angels.

"Jensen." The single word was spoken gently despite Malachi's raging emotions, a caress of sound rolling through the trembling air. The other male looked up, dragging Pepper between them. She still struggled frantically, though she had to have figured out by now she had no hope of breaking her attacker's grip. Malachi fought the urge to show his teeth; there was still a growl in his voice as he enunciated each word. "Let. Her. Go."

"Malachi." Jensen sounded mildly surprised, as if he'd happened to run into an old acquaintance unexpectedly. "I had no idea you were in the area."

"Clearly." Malachi's voice was flat, unamused. He ignored the taunt as Jensen addressed him by name alone, disdaining to use Malachi's proper title. His hands flexed as he worked to keep control of himself. "Release the woman and come with me."

"We can catch up soon," Jensen said. His hand smoothed over Pepper's hair. Malachi watched the shudder ripple through her, and his gut twisted. "Right now, I must see to my chosen mate."

"*What*?" the woman shrieked, her voice cutting through the storm as her struggles redoubled. "I am not your mate!" Even through the dark and storm, Malachi could see Pepper look to him. Her dark eyes demanded as much as pleaded. "Help me!"

"I will," Malachi said, controlling his voice for her sake. There was no way he could deny her. He expected her to be terrified, but she merely looked furious. An unexpected feeling of pride filled him—pride and pleasure—that she was such a courageous fighter. But with all of her courage, she was only human. She didn't stand a chance of stopping Jensen from hurting her. That was *his* job. Cold steel crept into Malachi's tone as he glided forward, never taking his eyes off of Jensen.

"Release her."

"Will you take her from me by force?" Jensen showed his teeth, part smile and part snarl. "I'm still Tseng Tse. I'll still fight for my mate."

"She isn't yours for me to take from you." Malachi advanced a few more steps, stopping when Jensen backed a step in response. "You're going to let her go. You're going to come with me, and we are going to put an end to this madness."

Jensen's arm tightened around Pepper, squeezing the breath audibly out of her lungs.

"Malachi, my prince," Jensen nearly purred. "We are about to mate. My chosen mate may object to your presence."

Pepper shrieked. The furious sound shattered the night, and possibly Jensen's eardrum; he bared his teeth as he jerked his head away. The sound rang painfully in Malachi's sensitive ears as he leaped. Twisting in midair, he landed facing Jensen's back. Malachi slammed his fist into Jensen's kidney. Jensen grunted as the force of the blow loosened his grip. Malachi grabbed his wrist, wrestling it behind him. Jensen spun, his other arm still pinning Pepper to his side. Malachi could see her struggling for breath as she was dragged through the mud. Unaccustomed anger lashed through him, but he didn't have the luxury for such emotions at the moment. Jensen twisted his arm in Malachi's grip. The forearm swelled, muscle and sinew bulging in Malachi's hand. Malachi growled, squeezing hard.

"Don't do it," he warned, just loud enough to be heard over the storm. "I won't have any choice if you do."

Jensen stared hard at Malachi, his mouth twisted

into a strange smile. "There's an exception for mates, my prince."

Thick black stripes rippled over Jensen's arms. Coarse hair grew over the skin. Milky white claws glinted as the lightning flashed. Jensen twisted his hand and Malachi was forced to let go or have his tendons cut by vicious claws. He didn't have time to heal that kind of damage right now. He lunged forward, turned sideways to wedge himself between the other man and his captured prey. Pepper cried out just as the coppery scent of blood hit the air. Malachi worked his fingers around Jensen's wrist.

"You have drawn her blood, Jensen." Malachi's voice was cold, an ice flow held in check by sheer will. The depth of fury coiling in his chest shook him, but he had to push it out of his mind. He couldn't afford the distraction.

"No Tseng Tse would draw his mate's blood. You are lying to yourself, and you are trying to lie to me. Woman," Malachi's tone was all respect as he addressed Pepper, his gaze never leaving Jensen. "Forgive me."

Claws slid from Malachi's fingertips. He felt the give of living flesh under the sharp tips, and then the faint resistance as he pierced skin to slice through muscle. Jensen snarled and twisted. Malachi adjusted his grip. Tendons snapped, cut by Malachi's lethal claws, forcing Jensen's fingers to release. Malachi's other hand closed behind Pepper's hip and dragged her into him as he whirled, placing himself between her and Jensen.

Her scent hit him hard, a low, wicked punch to his chest and his groin. The breath slammed out of his lungs, forcing him to inhale again, bringing her scent deep inside of him. That rush surged through him as the tiger roared recognition of its potential mate. His arms tightened to hold her to him as he struggled against his baser instincts, forgetful of both her pain and Jensen's threat until she pushed at his arm.

Something huge and heavy crashed into his back. Malachi stumbled forward, making a cage of his arms to keep Pepper safe. Nothing—not even the justice of his people—was as important as her safety. That cold, new fury took hold in his belly, cracking his control. It took all of his will to set Pepper a few feet away and take his hands off of her. Stripes appeared on his skin as he struggled to keep his fur from growing through. His teeth elongated. The tiger's roar tore from Malachi's throat, a massive sound that even shook the rain. Reaching over his shoulder, he grabbed the back of Jensen's skull with one hand while the claws of the other dug into the soft spot under the man's chin. With a twist and a bend of his back, he sent Jensen hurtling over his shoulder to slam into the ground several feet from Pepper. Real fear shone in the other man's eyes. Malachi snarled. The beast was riding him hard, giving his human brain little chance to control himself, let alone the situation. His hands tightened, aching to crush the other male's skull.

Jensen rolled on his shoulders, moving enough to grab Pepper by the ankles and pull. She crashed face-first into the ground. Grasses tore loose by the roots as she clawed at the muddy embankment. Horror twisted Malachi's gut as she dug into the steep earth, only to have it slide alongside her and plunge into the storm-churned stream. He needed every bit of his enhanced vision to pick out her dark head bobbing out of the water as the current swept her away between the steep banks.

There was no debate. No internal clash between the man and the tiger. Before he consciously made the decision, Malachi sprang away from Jensen. Some part of him was aware his prey would escape him, but he couldn't care about that, not with his potential mate caught up in the swollen current. He angled toward the river at a run, as fast as he could keep his feet on the treacherous bank, until he couldn't wait any longer. He detested the time it took to kick off his shoes before plunging into the water. Violent currents tugged at him, but he refused to be dragged off his course. He had never been as grateful for his incredible strength as he drove himself through the waves with powerful strokes.

Her dark head broke the surface scant feet ahead of him. Storm-capped waves crashed into her, and she disappeared. His heart seized. He couldn't lose her. He dove under the surface, eyes wide open against the stinging salt. Her shadowy shape sank rapidly, twisting in the currents in her struggles. Clothing coiled around her. Malachi almost forgot to hold his breath, choking back a warning not to tangle in her clothing. He kicked hard to follow her drifting shape, willing her to reach out for him. Another powerful kick brought him close enough to one of her flailing arms to get a hand around her wrist. Her arm turned in his grip and he tightened it. She might wrench herself away from him in her panic. Then her fingers clamped around his wrist with desperate strength. She wasn't panicking; she was looking for him. Power surged through him at the realization. He pulled. With all of his great strength, he kicked for the surface, dragging her with him.

Malachi's head broke through the foam-tipped waves, gasping down air as rain slashed against his face. He kept pulling until her dark head appeared beside his. His gut loosened as she coughed, sucking in great lungfuls of air. Sliding his arm around her collarbone, Malachi struck out for shore. Pepper gripped his forearm with both hands and relaxed, letting herself float. Now and then, he felt her kick to help propel them toward the shore. He didn't need it. The unfamiliar but undeniable need to protect her, to see her safe, gave him even greater strength. He would see them safely to the shore because he had no other choice. No matter what, she *had* to survive.

Chapter Four

Water crashed over Pepper's face. She tried to inhale between waves, but the rhythm was hard to catch. The rain beating on her face didn't help, either. Her lungs and throat burned as she coughed. Relief loosened the awful knot in her chest when the water fell away. Her rescuer drew her against his chest, strong arms cradling her close as he carried her easily. The heat radiating from his solid body was dizzyingly welcome after the frigid coastal water. The battering on her face stopped. She scrubbed salt from her eyes to crack the lids apart. The man from the coffee shop— Malachi—hunched over her, using his own shoulders to shield her from the rain. Lightning splashed over the chiseled planes of his face, turning them to warm stone. Droplets of water clung to the stubble on his strong jaw, and dark hair coiled against his neck and clung to his forehead. She was fascinated by his face. Like she had to learn every plane and angle by heart. At a safe distance from the water, he knelt and laid her on the ground. One large hand pushed her sodden hair back from her face. Even that simple gesture made her skin tingle.

"Are you all right?" he asked. His voice was deep, rolling with the waves and the thunder. Pepper squeezed her eyes shut hard, and her jaw, too. Her stomach coiled tighter, only this time it had nothing to do with him. She turned her head away and prayed the nausea to pass. It would be just her luck to throw up on the most gorgeous man she'd ever seen just after he saved her life.

"Woman?" he prompted, his low tone filled with concern. Pepper bit her lip, panting hard. Rolling suddenly away from him, she heaved. Sea water streamed out of her mouth and nose, burning the entire way. She was suddenly glad she hadn't had dinner yet. Her hands gripped the grass in tight fists, and her arms shook with the effort to keep from falling face-first into the dirt.

Gentle hands gathered up her hair, holding it back from her face as her body rid itself of a dangerous amount of water. Confusion warred with wonder. Was he really holding her hair out of her face while she vomited? Another tearing heave shoved everything else into the shadows of her mind; she couldn't think about it now.

It felt like half an hour before the retching cough let up. She felt appallingly weak. Her arms and belly trembled so badly, she had to be careful they didn't give out on her. Her hands shook as she pulled her hair out of Malachi's hands. Pepper couldn't even remember when her ponytail had come loose. Her hair was a tangled mess around her shoulders as she turned her face away. She tried to wipe her mouth subtly, but she had no doubt that Malachi saw it, anyway. She struggled to catch her breath, but her side burned, stabbing her every time she inhaled or exhaled deeply.

"Thank you," she croaked out. Her voice was harsh, like an old crow, and she coughed again. Slowly, she managed to roll to sitting and wrapped her arms around herself, drawing her knees to her chest. She was shaking too badly to stand up. It did let the pain in her side ease, at least for a little while. Pepper finally lifted her gaze to Malachi's face. "For everything."

Malachi bowed slightly, still sitting beside her. The movement was so odd that Pepper wanted to laugh. His steady gaze was filled with worry.

"Are you all right?" he repeated.

"All right enough," Pepper answered truthfully. Her head pounded. Nausea swept through her, leaving weakness in its wake. Her side was on fire, and she was pretty sure she didn't want to know why. And she could not stop shivering. It took an annoying amount of effort, but Pepper managed to push herself to unsteady feet, careful of the pain in her ribs and hip. Malachi rose swiftly and smoothly with the grace of a great cat uncurling. His hand closed around her elbow as he stood close. He loomed over her, a solid bulwark against the storm. Her heart beat against her ribs, making her all too aware of the fact that he was a man and she was a woman. She gave herself a solid shake. "I need to go."

"I'll walk you home." Malachi made it a statement of absolute fact, not an offer. Pepper's belly tightened at the thought, but she shook her head.

"No," she said, then added, "Thank you."

"Pepper." Malachi turned her name into a caress that slid across her skin like warm silk despite the sound of steel underneath. "Jensen may still be close. I will not risk him attacking you again. I am walking you home."

The very thought of Jensen made Pepper's stomach turn. Tears stung her eyes, but she refused to let them fall. Ocean water still streamed down her face, and she wished she could cry. It would make her feel better. But not right now. She needed to get home. Exhaustion swamped her. Every muscle and bone ached, and her throat was raw fire. Her knees threatened to dump her back on the ground but she forced her will through them, demanding they hold her. Her spine straightened until her head was held level. Malachi's hand tightened as he stepped so close she could feel his warmth.

"You're injured," he continued in that low voice. His gaze never left hers; she felt the force of it down to her aching bones. The man wore power like a second skin. Pepper felt like a butterfly pinned to a card and backed up a step. It didn't help.

"Malachi." She managed to force his name through her raw throat, though the effort made her cough. Stabbing fire flared through her, racing up her side and down into her hip. Frowning, Malachi stepped toward her again. She put out a hand to warn him back, shaking her head. Her palm met his chest. Common sense demanded she pull it back, but she let it linger for a moment, just long enough to feel the strong and steady heartbeat beyond the hard muscle.

"Malachi," she all but snapped his name. She tried to calm herself with a deep breath, but it only reminded her of all the places she hurt. "I've had the day from hell. I've dealt with that…that *rapist* twice today. The police have my phone, my car is dead, I nearly drowned, and my side is killing me. I'm soaked to the skin, I passed exhausted a long time ago, and I am just not dealing with one more thing tonight, and that includes you!" Pepper pressed one hand to her mouth and the other to her belly as her stomach rolled in outright rebellion again. She retched, but there was nothing left to come up.

Malachi growled as he stepped around her, angling himself to shelter her from the rain with his own body. His warmth seeped through her sodden clothing and into her skin, driving out the chill. He seemed so strong. Invincible. It was a stupid thing to do, but she leaned into him, giving in to weakness, physical and emotional. He caught her chin in his palm and lifted her face. Pepper let her gaze drag over his features before finally finding his eyes. The unbroken intensity trapped her, her breath stuttering in her raw throat.

"I will help you." Malachi's voice was a calm command. "Come. I will take you home."

He was too tempting. Too warm. He smelled of seashore and leather, and something else she couldn't name but it made her want to smell it again. It made her feel safe and wanted. It made her think of *home*, a real home with family and friends and laughter.

"Fine." Her voice was little more than a croak. She coughed against the rawness of her throat as she forced herself out of his embrace. She could only blame her fright and exhaustion. She needed to put a little space between them to clear her mind. Her head swam, making her stumble, but Malachi's chest was right there, his arm around her. She could feel the muscles rippling against her back as he silently urged her forward.

Pepper hated to admit it, but she needed his help. The thin strip of sand that counted as a beach soon gave way to rain-slicked stones and grasses. Her balance was shot. Every step jarred her side and sent stabbing pain through her abdomen. Several times, stones turned under her feet, and twice she would have fallen on the way up the grassy slope if Malachi hadn't caught her. The adrenaline had completely abandoned her. Not only was she drained and chilled, but her side burned with every movement. She refused to think too much about that; it raised questions she didn't have the strength to face.

Chapter Five

As soon as they were up the slope and on the pavement, Pepper stepped away from Malachi. Irritation rumbled in his throat. He choked it off, but she glanced at him, as if she'd heard it. The thunder had passed, leaving only the wind and a battering rain behind. Malachi kept her close to his side, blocking as much of the rain as he could. Her constant shivering worried him. She seemed so small, pressed up against him, but she had shown so much courage, facing Jensen. Twice. She had fought like a tigress to save herself, even though she must have known that Jensen was not only much larger, but stronger than her. It amazed him that so much strength of spirit could be housed in such a fragile, *human* body. He had never felt any particular attraction to human women, but his body was reacting to hers. Her soaked clothing clung to every curve, giving him a tantalizing outline as she walked slightly ahead of him. The sight of her hips swaying stirred his blood, making him think of things he should *not* being thinking about when the woman before him had just been attacked and nearly drowned. The tenacity of his reaction shocked him. He had never been unable to put a woman out of his mind. Even in his youngling years, when urges were new and powerful, he had never had much trouble mastering them. Yet in the space of a few hours, Pepper had started making herself an obsession.

Pepper turned to the right, wincing as she stepped over the stone border to a large parking lot. A few RVs dotted the asphalt, as if trying to get as far from each other as they could. Strips of grass sprouted between each painted space, with a single small post in the middle. Malachi realized the pole held the water and power hook ups. Pepper led the way to an older RV, parked near the far edge of the lot and overlooking the ocean. The grass nearby was stunted, showing pale in the orange halogen lights that cast weird shadows on the pavement and the tiny strips of grass between. Malachi didn't trust his eyes and inhaled deeply. Her scent invaded his system, and he inhaled again. The other scents that rushed his brain weren't nearly as pleasant. Alcohol and urine were pervasive, and rotting food was far too present. The scents of gasoline and sun-baked metal were unpleasantly strong. Even the scent of the grass seemed sick and weak. The RV was as exposed to the elements as it was to more human—or Tseng Tse—risks. The sheer vulnerability made his hands tighten. Pepper sneaked a look back at him, as if trying to gauge his reaction. Her teeth scraped her lip. Heat sparked in his gut, a sudden desire to feel her lips against his, soft and warm and surrendering to his kiss. Malachi forced himself to focus on the matter at hand: Pepper's safety.

"This is where you live?" he asked, appalled. Pepper shrugged as she fumbled the key into the lock. Her face was pink, even under the sodium lights.

"Rent's cheap. You take what you can get on a barista's wages."

Malachi shook his head over her living conditions

and settled his hand over hers, stilling her. Heat poured through him from the simple contact. From the change in her scent, she wasn't immune to his touch, either. Satisfaction and hope soared through him, but he had to stay focused. Her safety came before all else.

"Wait." He deliberately weighted his voice with command. He leaned close to the door handle and inhaled. Straightening, he inspected each of the windows, slowly circling the RV. Every door, every window, anything that could be an entry point had to be inspected. Around the other side of the large vehicle, he dropped to the ground to search under the RV. Only when he was certain there was no trace of Jensen—or anyone else—did he allow himself to stride back to the door.

Pepper still stood with her arms wrapped around herself. Even soaking wet, she was the most beautiful woman he'd ever seen. Her long lashes were spiked with rain, black crescents against the curve of her cheekbones. Her features were delicate, combining with her slightly upturned nose to make her look a bit puckish. Dark hair hung in loose, wet coils around her shoulders, clinging to her neck in fascinating little patterns. Her polo shirt and slacks still clung to her body, showing every womanly curve with such detail that Malachi dragged his gaze back to her face. He made himself see how pale she was, and how badly she was shivering. He forced himself to smell the weariness, pain, and blood rolling off of her, and encouraged the tiger's mind to rise. It *needed* to see her safe and comfortable, and Malachi used the tiger's instincts to steady him.

He nodded to her. "The area is clear. Go on."

Pepper's hand shook as it slipped on the wet doorknob to tug open the perilously thin door. A piteous meow hit the air just before a black-and-white missile streaked out of the open door. Pepper's keys clattered to the pavement as she caught the small cat. The scent of pain increased as she grunted, but Pepper insisted on clinging to the purring little creature.

"Crazy cat," she crooned, burrowing her face in his fur. The tenderness in her voice was almost maternal, and it made Malachi's heart turn over.

"I know. I know I'm late. I'm sorry, Bunsen." Pepper peered around the ball of fluff in her arms, searching the ground. Malachi flicked her keys onto the toe of his boot and kicked them into the air. He snatched them before they could start to fall again and held them out in his palm. Pepper flashed him a grateful smile. The look in her eyes was answered with a rush of his blood.

"Thanks. Ever tried to bend over without dropping a cat?"

"Something like it, yes." Malachi chuckled. A sweet ache brushed through his chest. He suddenly missed the nieces and nephews back in his homeland, Tseng Tse or part-Tseng Tse cubs who loved to swarm all over their elders. He wanted to reach for the little cousin in Pepper's arms to comfort his homesickness but stopped himself. If Bunsen were like most domestic animals, it would only make matters worse.

Malachi watched as Pepper reached for the balance bar bolted to the side of the RV, and clearly saw the wince as she lifted her foot to step up. He frowned. One large hand cupped her backside. She whipped her head around to stare at him with wide, shocked eyes, but before she could form a protest, he simply lifted her into the RV. Careful to keep downwind so he wouldn't upset the little cousin, Malachi gripped the balance bar—her hand looked perfect just above his—and swung into the RV behind her. He crowded her inside with his much larger body, forcing her away from the door enough for him to shut it. Bunsen kept up a running commentary, purrs punctuated by piteous mews and grouchy yowls. Wrapping his paws around her neck, the cat rubbed his mostly black face along her jaw, his rough tongue occasionally dragging over her skin. She petted the little black-and-white head as she moved through the narrow space between the eating area and the cooking area, dripping the entire time. For some reason, that trail of wet footprints both amused and distressed Malachi.

The inside of the RV was as shabby as the outside. Cabinets hung loose on their hinges, barely closing. Some were warped by water damage. The old linoleum floor in the kitchen area was discolored with use and showed several places where it had been glued back into place. The carpet was threadbare and peeling up at the edges. Through a tiny doorway, Malachi could glimpse a tinier shower door and sink, with a stained mirror on the wall. Half hidden by a door was a short bed, meticulously made, with too many flat pillows and a coverlet with a pattern at least twenty years out of date. The entire place smelled of cat, ramen, and *her*. Malachi's hands closed into fists to contain his outrage. This was *wrong*. Human standards were different—he knew that, as did all his people—but to see how Pepper had been abandoned by all community to scrape out an existence made his fur stand on end. She was worse than alone. Isolated. Exposed. Endangered. And the fact that she was *his* potential mate only made the outrage that much more volatile.

"Hungry, baby?" Pepper crooned to the cat. She reached for a cabinet to one side of the sink, still juggling the cat, and winced. Scowling, he bent around her to flick open the thin veneer door and grab a can of cat food. Pepper backed away from him, holding Bunsen in front of her like a talisman.

"Care for your cat." He tried not to snap out the words, but even to his own ears, he wasn't very successful. It still sounded like an order. "I'm going to take a more thorough look around your perimeter, and when I return, we will tend your injuries."

Malachi ignored the disbelieving, mutinous expression on Pepper's face as he backed out of the RV doorway. Being inside was a mistake. The whole interior was filled with her scent, and he needed a moment before confronting her injuries. Closing the door behind him, he leaned against the side of the big vehicle with his head back. The rain pelted down on his upturned face. He welcomed the coolness of it. His blood had felt too hot for too long, ever since he'd first caught Pepper's scent.

All the members of his species knew that, when they found someone with whom they were genetically and psychologically compatible, the attraction would be intense. Everything would feel more powerful as his instincts jumped to the fore. He could feel the beast pacing inside his mind, watchful, constantly attempting to assert itself. It demanded to hunt, but, worse, it demanded its mate. He would have to be careful. He could lose control far too easily. He had already shown

Pepper too much. It didn't really matter that Jensen had forced his hand, giving him no choice but to show his own claws. Malachi would still be held responsible for that action, and so would Pepper.

Malachi dragged his hand through his wet hair and let himself snarl. He had known it was possible for a human to be a potential mate for his people. He just hadn't expected to find a potential mate while hunting down a fugitive from justice. Powerful strides carried him away from the RV with its precious occupant, and then carried him right back as the beast within roared at him. With that fugitive still out there, there was no way he could leave her unprotected. He couldn't leave her without claiming her, but he couldn't claim her without her choosing him, and there was no time to woo her in the middle of a hunt. Some Tseng Tse spent their entire lives without ever meeting someone with whom they could have that connection. Malachi snarled his frustration, more loudly than was wise, and dropped to one knee to slam his fist into the pavement. It gave a little under his strength, reminding him of the immense power he had to control. He breathed and rose. Now was no time for a tantrum. Pepper needed him.

Chapter Six

"There," Pepper said as she set the dish of cat food on the floor beside the table. She had to sit at the kitchen bench to do it. Bunsen immediately stuck his head in it, mumbling wetly to himself with each bite. Pepper ran her hand down his back, all the way to the end of his sleek tail. Bunsen arched his back into the touch, purring for just a moment. The quiet moment should have calmed her. It usually did. Instead, she just felt...wound up. Jittery. There must have been some adrenaline still in her system or something. Pepper stood and went to the window over the little kitchen sink. Her fingers parted the blinds, just enough for her to peek through them. Malachi paced on the pavement outside. Dark hair clung to his face and neck in shadowy stripes. The rain slicked his shirt to his skin, defining every muscle. And there were a lot of them. The orange glow of the parking lot lamps made him look surreal, like some kind of dark angel formed of night and power. She shivered with the awareness of it.

Or just with cold. She wasn't getting any drier standing and dripping on the floor while drooling over a man. Slipping into the bathroom, she stripped out of her soaked pants and wadded them into the sink. She'd have to visit a laundromat sometime tomorrow. Around figuring out what was wrong with her car and somehow managing to get to work on time, and, hopefully, to the police station to get her phone back. She didn't like being out of communication with the world. If she'd been able to call the police tonight, Jensen might have left her alone. If Malachi hadn't been there…She wasn't going to think about it. She had enough on her mind without adding the horrible "what if" on top of it. Malachi *had* been there, and she was safe inside her own home.

Pepper shifted to take off her shirt and winced, sucking in air against the pain in her side. She really didn't want to know, but she needed to. Gritting her teeth, she steeled herself for the pain and yanked off her shirt. Her side knocked against the edge of the sink. Bright lights sparked in her vision, and she had to hang over the sink for several seconds as the pain-induced nausea subsided. Still shaking from it, she balanced one hand on the sink edge as she turned to examine herself in the mirror. She had to stand on her toes to see it; air hissed out between her teeth. Four neat gouges that ran from her side and up into her ribs and back oozed thick blood, leaving bright stains down her skin and onto her underwear. She had a first aid kit under the seat in the kitchen. That would have to be enough.

Pepper toweled off her sodden hair then wrapped the big terrycloth towel around her to step out of the bathroom. The pain in her side was a deep, steady throb, occasionally jumping into sharp stabs. Giving Bunsen another pat as she stepped past, she bent to lift the kitchen seat and swore. That *hurt* and she was tired of pretending it didn't. She had been calm, cool, and collected all night, and she was done. Just for one moment, she was going to be scared and hurt and pissed off.

The RV rattled as the exterior door popped open. Her heart jumped into her throat. One hand clutching the towel to her as she whirled, the other hand struck out for the knife block. She yanked a long chopping knife out of the block as Malachi stepped into the RV. Instantly his eyes were on her, leaving a hot trail as he took in every curve, every inch of skin. Pepper swore again as she exhaled.

"Malachi! Don't scare me like that!" She slammed the knife into the counter, under her palm, as she dropped against the solid surface to catch her breath. Her side hit the edge. Fiery pain blossomed in her side, and wet warmth trailed down her hip. Again. She'd swear, if it didn't hurt so much.

Malachi loomed too big for the tiny living and eating area, his head almost brushing the ceiling, and his shoulders only inches from each wall. He frowned, concern filling his handsome features, despite the edge of irritation around his mouth. Something dangerous and almost feral radiated from him. Pepper was all too aware of it, and the way it made heat flood through her skin. She shifted awkwardly, struggling to keep her gaze on his. She gestured toward the bathroom without looking at either.

"The bathroom is a little small, but there's a dry towel in there. It's better than nothing."

"Thank you, but no." Malachi's voice was rich, with the faintest trace of an accent. "I must see to your wounds."

Pepper clutched the towel tighter.

"I'm okay," she said hurriedly. She even put out a hand to stop him. Malachi caught it, bringing her body to his. His other arm wrapped around to the small of her back as his eyes burned down at her.

"I need to see," he insisted. "I need to know that you're okay. Grant me this."

Pepper bit her lip and winced. She was turning it into hamburger, at this point, and it was starting to hurt. Malachi watched her, his entire being still. All of his focus riveted on her through those impossibly blue eyes. He watched her so intently, she felt as if the towel weren't even there. But there was something there, something she couldn't name, that made it seem like her wellbeing not only mattered to him but mattered intensely. She rubbed the towel between her fingers, picking at the fraying edge, and gave in.

"Let me get some clothes on."

"Hold the towel against your side to absorb the blood." Malachi glowered, as if it were some great concession for him to allow her to get dressed. He turned Pepper toward the bedroom and, reluctantly, released his hold. She was far too aware of him behind her and the lack of coverage from the towel. She refused to let him see that he might be having an effect on her. She shook back her hair and strode through the bedroom doorway.

Pepper shut the door and sagged against it. Just being around that man was exhausting. He was far too intense, and so was her reaction to him. He was...fascinating. Fascinating, mysterious, powerful, and ridiculously gorgeous. And exhausting.

Pepper pressed the towel against her side then peeled it away with a wince. The blood wasn't nearly as bad as she expected. To hear Malachi talk, she was bleeding to death on her feet. She might even be able to salvage the towel, if she could get to a laundromat soon enough. She held out no hope for her shirt, however, which meant replacing it, which meant that much longer before she could get into a *real* apartment—

Focus. One thing at a time. She had to focus to function, and that meant keeping her mind on the next right step: dress the wounds. An image of Malachi popped into her head, offering to help. Insisting on helping. She could just imagine the way his large hands would slide across her belly—

"Focus!" Pepper made herself say the word out loud, though quietly. Thinking about Malachi was the wrong focus. She shoved the towel under the door to wedge it shut. There. That would make it easier for her to resist opening the door to get another look at him, or, worse, go out to him. He didn't need to know how much she was hurting, or how he affected her. He could just wait until she was better under her own control.

Pepper allowed herself the luxury of limping as she moved to the tiny closet beside the bed. A grunt escaped as she reached up for an old, soft flannel shirt. Instantly, there was a knock on the door.

"Pepper?"

"I'm fine," she answered, though her tone was breathier than she liked. She hurried into the shirt as much as possible with her side on fire. The blood wasn't bad, but it still needed bandaging before she could go to bed, and this day was in her top three choices of days that just needed to end.

"Do you need help?" Malachi's voice sounded tight, like he was putting out a lot of effort. She could just imagine him on the other side of the door, looming, his shoulders bunched and his hands tight.

And dark stripes across his skin.

"No!" Pepper called too loudly as she forced the image out of her mind. The soft tails of the shirt brushed over her thighs as she grabbed at the pants neatly folded in the bottom of the closet. Pain stabbed through her side, stealing her breath as she lurched into the wall to keep from toppling over.

The bedroom door rattled. "Pepper, woman, open the door. Please." It sounded like an afterthought.

"No," she gasped out. The door rattled again. There was a loud pop, and Malachi stood framed in the doorway, his hand dwarfing the doorknob still in his palm. He blinked, looking just as surprised as she was.

"Did you just break my door?" Even the reproach was breathless with pain. "Get out!"

"Possibly." He looked chagrined for a moment, then his eyes fixed on her side. They turned hard as sapphires, implacable, and his voice echoed it. "No."

Setting the first aid kit on the bed, he took her by the arms. His hands were hot and immensely strong as he backed her onto the bed and made her sit. Pulling the bloodied towel from under the door, he pulled it over her legs to mop up the blood. His touch was surprisingly gentle. Pepper could only stare until he lifted her legs onto the bed and covered them with the blankets. Malachi flicked on the overhead reading lights and knelt. He bunched up her shirt in one hand; Pepper grabbed at it, determined to keep her breasts covered. Malachi ignored the movement, pinning the shirt to her skin against her ribs, as if that were precisely where he wanted it. He cleared the blood from the gashes on her side with firm, careful presses of the towel, leaning in until his nose nearly touched her skin. Pepper held her breath, hoping it would steady the fluttering in her belly. He sniffed. His broad shoulders dropped as he exhaled. The dark tension in his face eased until he almost smiled up at her. Her heart double-beat.

"They aren't as deep as I'd feared, thank the ancestors. You won't need stitches."

"This would be pretty awkward to explain at the hospital, wouldn't it? I bet you have plenty of practice at those kinds of lies." Pepper had to distract herself from his nearness, from his scent wrapping around her like a heated embrace, filling her with comfort and nearly forgotten desires. She couldn't remember ever feeling this way toward a man before, and certainly not a near stranger! It was disconcerting, to say the least.

Malachi didn't answer. He had already opened several sterile gauze bandages to press against her side. His mouth hung open slightly, like he was trying not to breathe. The thought felt like a bruise. Granted, she had just taken a head-long dive down a muddy riverbank and dunked in saltwater to wash it off, and she probably smelled like it, but he'd just done the same thing. Though he didn't smell like it. She probably stank like seaweed and muck and just couldn't smell herself.

His fingertips brushed over her skin as he taped the gauze into place. Malachi's face was impassive, clinical. The simple touch of his fingers sent bright sparks of lava into her blood. Her nearness wasn't affecting him at all. It wasn't fair.

Taking an elastic bandage from the kit, he began to wind it around her torso. Pepper's belly tightened, quivering, and he paused with his palm near her navel. She bit the inside of her lip hard to keep from squirming away. He had to feel the way her heart was pounding. Malachi inhaled and looked up at her sharply. The sudden impact of his gaze froze every movement. Pepper's mind stuttered to a stop with his hand on her belly like that, unable to get a breath. She swallowed, lost in the fierceness of Malachi's eyes.

Chapter Seven

Malachi *had* to inhale. He had been breathing through his mouth in order to minimize his exposure to her scent, but when Pepper began to tremble under his hands, he had no choice. He had to know what was making her shake. He filled his lungs with the rich, spicy-sweet scent that was *her*. His senses swam. Colors without names and music without form chased each other through his mind in a maddening dance, miring his ability to sort through the scents. The bedclothes were thin under his palm as he steadied himself with one hand on the bed. The fingers still on her abdomen twitched with the desire to find her soft skin once more.

"What is it? Pain?"

"What is what?" Pepper blinked at him in confusion, looking as if she was having a difficult time focusing. He couldn't help hoping he was the reason for it.

"You're shaking, Pepper. Why are you shaking?"

Pepper shook her head but refused to give him her gaze. That irritated him more than it should have.

"I'm just cold."

Malachi inhaled. She *was* cold, but she was also lying. He could smell the stressors of a lie on her exposed skin. His thumb brushed a caress over her belly, the movement almost unconscious. Even irritated with her, he needed to reassure her. Especially as he was about to demand answers from her, and he wasn't known for being especially diplomatic.

"Tell me the truth, please, Pepper. Whatever it is, we'll deal with it. Why do you shake?"

Pepper bit her lip and turned her face toward Bunsen, who was still dedicatedly scraping every last molecule of food out of his dish as he purred wetly to himself. Her expression softened. He wished the look were directed at him, but as long as the little cousin gave her whatever she needed to speak, he could deal with it.

"I'm cold. I'm hurt. I've had more adrenaline today than is good for any three people. I'm allowed to shake," Pepper said, obviously exasperated.

Malachi inhaled again; she was still telling part-truths, and it irritated him more than it should have. Why couldn't she just trust him to hear the truth? He had to draw on his years of control to simply close the elastic bandage. His palms literally ached for the heated satin of her skin. His hand splayed over her belly again, this time reveling in the tremors running through her. He sat on the bed, so close that his thigh rubbed against hers. Heat filled his blood. Resting his forehead against the side of her head, he gave in to temptation and pulled her scent deep into his lungs. It wrapped around his brain, settling into every tiny crack and corner, filling him up from the inside out.

He was starting to learn her baseline. Threaded through the other scents was a streak of arousal. A rumble sounded low in his chest as his other hand slid into her hair, letting the wet strands curl around his fingers. He could feel the sudden pounding of Pepper's heart, and the way she tensed at his touch. That was wrong. Entirely wrong. His potential mate should never stiffen at his touch. He had to release her. Closing his eyes, he forced himself to peel away until only one hand touched her, his palm cupping her cheek.

"Never be afraid of me. You're safe." He kept his gaze on hers, willing her to believe him. His thumb slipped over her lips, brushing gently until her mouth fell open in an enticing little movement that captivated him. "You cannot be safer than in my arms, including from me." Leaning forward, he kissed her forehead as he allowed his hand to trail downward to rest against the side of her throat. He lingered, not entirely voluntarily, before he managed to pull himself back. "You need to rest, Pepper."

She stared up at him as if in a daze. Her pulse thundered under his palm, her heart beating almost in time with his. She wet her lips, and he felt her throat work as she swallowed. The thread of arousal in her scent thickened, strengthened, until it became a solid rope. Malachi found himself fixating on her mouth, on the small, reddened blot that showed where she'd been chewing her lip. He had the most ridiculous urge to kiss that blotch away, to give her full lips another reason to be sensitive and plump that had nothing to do with injury.

A sharp meow punctured his thoughts. Pepper gasped, blinking as if she'd been shocked back into reality, as well. She shoved his hand away from her face as she peered right past him toward her cat, but she couldn't hide the way the blood rushed into her cheeks or the restless movement of her fingers over the tails of her shirt. Malachi fought a scowl as he reined in his exasperation at the interruption. He couldn't quite keep it out of his voice.

"Your small protector will object to my presence soon."

"Oh, don't worry about him. He's the biggest love sponge ever born," Pepper assured him, with such a warm smile toward her furry favorite that Malachi felt a surge of jealousy. He shook his head, as much at himself as at her words, and rose to his feet.

"I'm sure he's very friendly," he began.

"Are you allergic?"

"No." Malachi answered. "Some animals—"

Bunsen slinked through the bedroom doorway, licking his whiskers as he purred at himself. Malachi stayed very still as the little cat stuck his head out to sniff Malachi's bare feet, gray nose twitching. At one sniff, Bunsen's ears flattened to his skull as his eyes went round. The cat turned on one hind paw and sprinted through the RV. Malachi winced at the sound of Bunsen hitting the dashboard.

"Bunsen!" Pepper called out as she struggled to her feet. Malachi put his arms out to steady her.

"Will you be still?" he demanded. She ignored him, and instead hurried through the RV. He followed her as far as the door. He sighed.

"Some animals don't like me much." Malachi finished his interrupted thought. "I'm truly sorry that I frightened him. Poor thing."

Pepper called to the black-and-white cat again, bracing her hand on the driver's seat to peer under it. Malachi's frown deepened, his voice hardening.

"Pepper, you're going to start the bleeding again. He'll come out when I've gone. Get back into bed."

She sat up and returned his glare. If he hadn't been worried about her side bleeding again, he would have found it an adorable challenge. "They say to trust animal instincts when it comes to judging character."

Malachi scrubbed his hand over his jaw and did his best not to sound as exasperated as he felt. He didn't have much success, even to his own ears.

"It isn't his fault. It isn't mine, either. It's just the way things are. Do you plan to leave the...house tomorrow?"

Malachi almost managed not to stumble over the word. The RV hardly qualified as a *house*. Any wind made it rock on its wheels. The walls were perilously thin. Not only did he worry about her surviving even a mild California winter, but Jensen would be able to tear through the walls, if he really wanted to. The thought made his chest tighten and tiny pricks start where his claws would sprout.

Pepper tossed her hair with a defiant lift of her chin. Somehow, it combined with the damp hair and the over-large shirt to make her look even more vulnerable. And adorable. Everything protective rose up inside of him, reaching for her. She steadied one hand on the seat as she shifted to stand. He reached out to help her without thinking about it.

"Yes. Don't work, don't get paid. Don't get paid, don't feed the cat." She raked a hand through her hair. "And I've got to find out what's wrong with my car." She shook herself just as the scent of worry started on her skin. "Why?"

Malachi's gaze never wavered from hers.

"I'm concerned that Jensen has fixated on you." If the aberrant Tseng Tse had decided that Pepper was a potential mate, he wasn't going to walk away just because Malachi interfered. If anything, the perceived threat would only make Jensen more determined. Mentally, Malachi swore.

"The police still have my phone," Pepper said, sounding very weary. Her dark eyes lifted to his. The silent plea there twisted his heart. "You'll call them, won't you? I mean, you know this guy, right? You can tell them where to find him and everything?"

"It's not that simple."

"Why not? Is he, like, your brother or something?" Pepper frowned. "He talked like he knew you."

"As I said, it's not so simple as calling the police." Malachi closed the few steps between them, until her scent surrounded him. He kept her gaze, refusing to allow her to look away. "I need you to trust me, Pepper. Jensen will see the justice he deserves, I promise you. But you need to trust me."

Malachi found himself holding his breath. He needed her to trust him, not just because it would make it much easier for him to get his work done, but for himself. Her pale face showed the exhaustion of the day. He wanted nothing more than to wrap her up in his arms, where he could warm and protect her, and insist that she sleep herself out. His fingertips twitched with the desire to touch her soft skin, to feel her silken hair between his fingers once more. Her scent became so distressed that he couldn't stop himself from leaning into her, one hand on the wall behind her as the other lifted her hair back from her face. She held her breath but didn't move away.

"I know you're worn through. I know you're frightened by Jensen, and by me. I know your world

61

feels upside down." He spoke very softly, barely stopping himself from chuffing to her. "Trust me, beauty. I will protect you. I will help you. You need to be warm and rested. Sleep. No one will disturb you tonight."

"How?" Her voice was angry, betraying the tears that she scrubbed from her eyes so brutally that he grabbed her hand to stop her.

"Don't worry about how. I can, and I will. Sleep." He backed up enough that he could guide her from the wall and turn her toward the bedroom. An image flashed through his mind of joining her in the bed, finding ways to make sure she slept, but he forced it out. That was one of the last things she needed. He urged her through the small space with a gentle tug on her hand, but he stopped at the outside door. "I'll see you tomorrow, Pepper."

She paused in the doorway to the bedroom, looking vulnerable and sleepy and sexy. He waited with his hand on the doorknob, more to delay his moment of leaving than because he had a good reason to stay.

"Okay."

The word was enough. Malachi smiled and nodded deeply, almost bowing as he stepped out of the RV and listened until he heard the lock click behind him.

Chapter Eight

The cold rain battered down on Malachi's head and shoulders. He lifted his face to it, letting it wash away the heat from being in such a small, enclosed space with Pepper. His potential mate. His body was on fire, aching from being so close to her. His fingers still burned with the memory of her silken skin under his touch. A shudder slid through him. The tiger was close. He hadn't had trouble controlling his shift since his youngling years, but it was to be expected. The scent of a potential mate made everything more intense, battered on one's control, like learning it all over again, or so he'd been told since cubhood. Everything inside of him demanded that he get back inside that RV, where he could watch over her as she slept. Where he could ensure that she was safe and warm and fed. He had his doubts that there was food in that tiny fridge or the equally tiny cupboards. He glowered into the night. It was wrong that she should suffer any kind of deprivation while he was in the world and perfectly capable of caring for her and her cat.

Malachi forced himself away from the flimsy wall behind him long enough to tug off his sodden shirt. Carefully, he slid out of his jeans. From his pocket, he took a small, cone-shaped pouch and tugged on the cord that cinched it shut. A practiced flick of his wrist turned it inside out, giving him a waterproof bag just big enough to hold his clothing. Shoving it all inside haphazardly, he tugged the cord and cinched the bindle shut again. A hiss slid through his teeth as the rain continued to beat on him, then a short chuckle. It was almost as good as a cold shower. He needed one. Pepper was frightened and injured and had no idea what he was. He had to take things slowly, give her a chance to get used to him. The Tseng Tse weren't the easiest people to live with, and princes were often the worst of all.

Glancing over his shoulder, Malachi made sure Pepper wasn't peering through her blinds. Good. She should be resting. If he couldn't be curled beside her, at least she had his tiny cousin to comfort and warm her. Jealousy rippled through him at the thought, making him chuckle and shake his head. Jealous of a *housecat*. His family would never let him live it down, especially his brothers.

He stepped into the rain, uncaring of his nudity. One hand pushed his hair out of his face as he focused entirely on his surroundings. Not a sound came but the storm. He didn't care if people saw him naked—it was a natural state of being—but he did care if they saw this. He closed his eyes and reached for the beast.

His shoulders bunched as stripes shimmered on his skin. The hair on his body quickly thickened and turned white. The world sharpened into clear focus, despite rain and darkness, as his eyes changed, giving up the round pupil for a vertical one. Then the pain started. He welcomed it, reached for it, embraced it as a part of him and a part that he needed. Claws tore out of his rapidly shifting fingers and toes as his face bulged to make room for the long and lethal teeth. Bones shifted, growing longer and thicker, sometimes changing entirely. His spine grew as he dropped to all fours, adding bones to create a tail. Black and white fur covered it to the tip just as he lashed it through the air. Nearly a thousand pounds of muscle shook from sensitive whiskers to the tip of his tail as he felt his new body.

The need to roar gathered in his chest. There was a stranger in his territory. His female had been injured by another male, and the need to drive off the usurper boiled hot in his blood. He snarled, his claws scraping the soft stone under him as he freed them for battle. His great head lowered toward the ground. The rain had washed away much of the scent but there was a chance he could find the scent on the water, if the intruder had been near the den. *Her* scent was still there, fresh and bloodied and deliciously female. He inhaled again, just to get more of her scent. He could hear her voice, bravely roaring out against the intruder, and shaking after he pulled her from the water. He could feel her skin under his hands. Human skin. And human hands.

With a sudden rush, Malachi's human brain resurfaced through the tiger's instincts. He shook his head rapidly. Rounded ears twitched as he listened for any sound from inside the RV. Nothing. He hadn't roared, then. Relief flooded him, a strange emotion to his tiger brain but not entirely alien. Hearing him roar would only have frightened his potential mate more, and made things more difficult in the future, for her and for him. Pepper would need to see his shift eventually, but not like that, and not tonight.

The cold rain still poured over him. He shook out his coat, puffing the black-and-white fur against the wet. The rain was cold compared to his homeland, but it was welcome. The chill would help to cool his blood, both against fury and against desire. He felt both in abundance, and that was far too dangerous. He needed his head clear, not clouded with need. Jensen was insane, but he was strong and cunning. If Malachi couldn't stay calm and calculated, Jensen could out-maneuver him.

His claws bit into the asphalt as he stretched, working through every muscle. The tiger's body felt *good*. Powerful. Fast. An apex predator in his absolute prime. Carefully, he leaned against the RV wall. The metal caved slightly as he rubbed his head against it, drawing a wordless grumble from his chest. It was unacceptable, but she wasn't going to agree to leave tonight. Malachi worked his way around the vehicle, rubbing against it often to make his scent strong. Let Jensen know that she was under *his* protection. Let all of the preternatural world know. She was *his*. He would accept no other outcome. The chances of finding another potential mate in his lifetime, no matter how prolonged, were just too small. Now that he'd had the tiniest taste of what it could be like, he wasn't sure he could go back to simple sex, companions for a time before parting ways, as many of the Tseng Tse did. Pepper's scent would haunt him for the rest of his life. Every woman would be compared to her strength, her fire, her courage, her gentle, loving care. For the first time in his life, he could imagine himself having cubs. No other woman—human, Tseng Tse, or part-blooded—had inspired such thoughts in him.

The growl sounded in his chest again, softer. A sound of desire, of need, rather than anger. Malachi slowly widened his protective circle around the RV. He needed to run, to calm the fires in his blood, but convincing himself to leave her alone was proving harder than he anticipated. His brother had tried to explain to him what it would be like to find a potential mate, how his control would be taxed just by the thought of her, how everything would be more intense, how the entire focus of his world would shift to that single woman. He had never been able to appreciate it until now. Obsession wasn't a strong enough word. And the timing couldn't be worse. Jensen had already raped several women, leaving a trail of ruin from their homeland in southeast Asia to the California coast.

The rage bubbled up again. He barely remembered to grab the bindle in his mouth before breaking into a lope. The tiger wasn't designed for all-day runs, but his body had to keep pace with his emotions or he'd roar, and he was still too close to Pepper's den. The challenge might draw Jensen to her. Part of him wanted to do just that. At least then he'd be there to protect her. The thought of any male putting his hands on *his* potential mate was almost too much to take, but to have her taken against her will, to have her *raped*, was utterly unthinkable. Jensen's victims had never been faceless, but, somehow, after having seen the fear in Pepper's face, smelling it on her skin, the magnitude of Jensen's crimes fully hit him. He *had* to stop him, before he hurt anyone else.

It gave Malachi a reason to stick close to Pepper. The other male had fixated on her; he wouldn't turn his attention elsewhere until he had destroyed the object of his fixation. Malachi veered away from the softer ground at the edges of the parking lot for fear of leaving footprints. Pausing, he looked back at the RV. It wasn't the only one in the lot, but it was isolated, a little distance from the few other vehicles that crowded closer to the road. He didn't like that, either. He sighed, his flanks heaving with his displeasure. He needed to get back across town to his own vehicle. Pepper was determined to work the next day, and there was no way he was going to allow her to go alone. If the rain continued, he didn't want her walking, either. He'd spend the night in the parking lot, dozing in his truck where he could watch her RV, and then drive her to the coffee shop the next day.

First, however, he needed to investigate her car. It was a little too convenient that, after she'd disrupted Jensen's plans, her car had suddenly stopped working; he was certain Jensen had had something to do with it. His mind settled somewhat at the idea. Yes. He could keep close to her, protect her, and still complete his hunt. The night would be long, his body and mind slamming him with the need to be beside her, but with the promise of seeing her the next day, he could soothe himself. He would be able to see her tomorrow. Until she accepted him into her life, that would have to be enough.

The long strides of the tiger covered the distance quickly, and that was worth the risk of being caught. This late in a rainy night, very few vehicles passed by. Whenever headlights punctured the darkness, he slipped onto the shoulder of the road and hunkered down in the shallow ditch until they passed. For some time, Pepper's scent kept to the shoulder and it was easy to retrace her steps. At the edges of the neighborhoods, however, he had to pause. Humans prized the white coat in tigers, but they had no understanding of how impossible it made camouflage, especially in the dark. He would have to be very careful. Straining his senses to keep watch for humans, he stepped into one of the carefully cultivated faux-wilderness areas that dotted the small city. It was better someone stumble on a track and wonder what they had found than for someone to look out the window and know.

The scent trail brought him back to the parking lot surrounded by small shops and specialty restaurants. The trail was growing faint in the continued rain, and Malachi had to search the edges of the lot twice before finding what he was looking for. Even then, it took a bit of luck, as a puff of breeze drove Pepper's scent to him, along with cold drops of rain. A small blue hatchback was still parked in the mostly empty lot, close to one of the wilderness areas. Malachi closed his eyes and remembered being human. Touching Pepper's hair. Binding her wounds. Looking into her deep eyes. The sound of her voice as she crooned to the little cousin, Bunsen. Pain flowed through him, but it was familiar. It was *right*, and he breathed through it. Rain dropped onto naked skin as he shook himself against the weariness that dragged at him. The cold and wet helped to drive back the exhaustion. He wouldn't be able to shift again until after he slept, or he would simply pass out from exhaustion wherever he was, in whatever form he was.

Working quickly, he pulled his clothing from the bindle and dressed, then stuffed the collapsed bag back into his pocket. Malachi strode from the shadows of the trees. Even in human form, he could smell Pepper around the car. And Jensen. He snarled, the sound tearing the night.

Something pale lay plastered against the windshield, tucked under the windshield wiper. Malachi took it between his fingers, almost gingerly, and held it to his nose. The stench of the aberration filled his nose, but there was another scent, as well. Malachi snorted to clear his nose as he unfolded the paper. A dark, brownish-red heart ran slightly, still wet on the paper. Horror and anger filled him, but he had to be sure. He bent his nose to the paper and sniffed again. Blood. Human blood, female, of age to bear cubs. Very carefully, Malachi folded the paper again, before his furious trembling could rip it apart.

He worked to control his breath, but it still came in shallow puffs, heavy with anger. Malachi circled the car, inspecting it carefully. The doors, windows, and locks seemed to be whole, as did the tires. Why, then, had his woman chosen to walk in the rain? Circling back around to the front of the car, he searched for the catch to the hood. He felt it behind the front grill, but it was one of those models with the release in the cab. He ground out a Tseng Tse curse. Clenching his jaw, he gripped the hood firmly, and tugged hard, pitting his anger against the catch. The hood flew up with no resistance, and he had to make a fast grab to keep it from tearing off entirely. Malachi allowed his eyes to shift back to those of the tiger. The light from the parking lot was more than enough to immediately illuminate the problem: the sockets where the spark plugs should have been were empty, with the wires dangling where they dropped. He reached in to lift one, bending his face close, expecting to find Jensen's scent all over them. He wasn't disappointed. His roar shredded the night, startling birds out of cover despite the storm. The hood slammed back into the car, hard enough to bounce back up again. He caught it before it could damage the windshield and inspected the catch. It had been torn off by sheer strength. Still snarling, he pressed the hood back into place. It was slightly dented, but it would close. He would have to have it repaired, as well as the spark plugs replaced, before he allowed Pepper to drive it again. From the age of the car, there was likely more work that needed done as well, in order to make it safe. The realization didn't help his mood.

He could do no more to secure this area for her. His scent was here, and that was the best deterrent she could have against Jensen. As for humans...Malachi almost wished thieves would take it, and then Pepper couldn't argue with him about it being unsafe.

He took off at a run. It was several miles to the temporary den—hotel—where he'd left his truck. He would be calm and able to control his instincts by the time he reached it. He hoped.

Chapter Nine

Pepper stepped off the verge of the RV lot with her breath stuck in her lungs. She was fine—except for the four nasty gashes in her side and the persistent soreness in her throat. Every step stabbed through her as she jogged across the small highway. A pale disc of dirty-cotton gray showcased the sun's futile effort to shine through the storm. The thunder-and-lightning excitement had passed, leaving only the steady drone of rain. Every third drop shattered as it struck Pepper's umbrella, so that a fine mist hung perpetually beneath the faded black cloth. Still, it was better than arriving at the coffee shop soaked to the bone.

Pepper eyed the bridge as it loomed up at her. Jensen wouldn't be bold enough to attack her in the light of day, with vehicles passing every few seconds. He wouldn't.

Didn't he attack that woman in the parking lot yesterday? The voice in her head sounded suspiciously like Malachi. He had no business being there, even if he was ridiculously gorgeous. The way his soaked clothing had defined his body rushed back into her mind, and her breathing stuttered. He'd saved her. First from Jensen, then from the water. Her hand went to her side. Even through the rough fabric of her polo, she could feel the bandages. He hadn't *had* to see her home or stay to bandage her wounds. These were all perfectly valid reasons for her to feel a strong attraction to him. There was nothing at all unusual about it.

"There's nothing at all unusual about a man who can leap over another man from standing," she muttered. "Which isn't possible. You missed something in there, Nyx, or the hysteria is messing with your memory. It didn't happen."

It *couldn't* happen. Her mind raced for logical reason after logical reason, but every explanation she attempted fell short. What about the gouges in her side? Where had those come from if not Jensen? The image flashed in front of her again, of Jensen's eyes in the zoom of her phone's camera: vertical, cat-slit pupils.

As much as she wanted to, there was no denying it: something strange was going on around Malachi Negrescu. And it only made him all the more interesting.

Pepper groaned. She let her head fall back, just in time for a rain drop to shatter through the umbrella and scatter a fine mist over her face. The cool water made her flinch slightly.

"I know, Dad," Pepper murmured to the underside of the worn fabric. "I promised you I'd live a safe and happy life, even after you were gone. Nothing about this Malachi Negrescu is safe. I know this can't be a good idea."

A large gray pickup slid to a stop across the two-lane highway, still shiny despite the rain. Pepper's heart rocketed into her throat, her hands tightening on her umbrella. She dug her sneakers into asphalt, her weight on her toes as she bunched to run. The driver's window lowered; through the space she caught sight of a familiar—and uncomfortably welcome—face.

"Pepper, you're getting soaked," Malachi called through the open window. Pepper relaxed her stance, determined to keep herself from reacting just to the sight of him. Even at this distance, she could see his frown. It only made him look dangerous and sexy, instead of just regular sexy. "Get in."

"No, thanks," Pepper called back, lifting her umbrella in salute. "I'm good."

His expression darkened. Pepper took an involuntary step backward, more to escape her reaction to him than to escape him. A slow burn ignited in her blood just looking at him. The close confines of her RV had been hard on her hormones last night, or at least her self-control. The cab of the pickup would not be an improvement.

The slam of a car door echoed through the rain. Pepper blinked to bring her eyes back into focus to see Malachi striding across the highway. His smooth movements made her feel like he was stalking her.

"Good morning." Malachi's voice was as smooth as his stride. His eyes held a diamond-bright glitter as he held out his hand, clearly expectant.

"Morning." Pepper forced her lungs to inhale. The subdued light was gentle on his features, and he was far too handsome. A faint breeze wove through his hair, bending the tips, and her fingers itched to join it. She made herself find somewhere else to look, like his hand. "I need to get to work."

"That's the idea, Pepper." His voice was a purr as he said her name. The sound curled low and delicious in her belly, and she put her hand defensively over her stomach. Malachi's gaze didn't leave hers but from the sudden flare of heat in his blue eyes, she knew he saw it, and that he knew exactly what it meant.

Pepper shook her head. "Thanks, but I can walk. It's such a beautiful day and all."

"I don't want you aggravating the wounds in your side." His face darkened. "Nor am I willing to risk your safety with Jensen out there."

"And it's so much safer for me to get into that monster of a truck with you?" She gestured to the big pickup idling in the far lane. She couldn't keep the admiration out of her tone as her gaze lingered on the truck. "That thing could take off over the scrub and you'd hardly notice. You could just forget the roads and just cut straight across country."

"Of course." His voice was filled with humor, though still with a dark undertone. "Just in case we need it."

"We?" Pepper echoed. She liked the sound of that a little too much. He tipped his head, his gaze never wavering.

"I'm not leaving you without proper protection." His tone left no room for an alternative. "Jensen is out there, and he's hunting you. The rain isn't going to stop, either. Please, Pepper." It sounded like a formality.

"Are you seriously going to stand in the middle of the highway and argue this?" Pepper shook her head in disbelief, irritated and amused at the same time. A car rumbled down the blacktop, sliding to a stop too close to Malachi for Pepper's comfort. She started forward with her hand outstretched. Malachi merely turned his head and looked at the driver. Pepper saw the man reach for the horn, but he never completed the movement. Pepper didn't blame him. She wouldn't want to be on the receiving end of that look, either.

Malachi turned back to her, his hand still outstretched. "Are you coming?"

"Malachi, you're going to get run over."

"Then you had better come with me before I do."

"Are you even taking this seriously?"

His attention snapped to her, sharpening like a laser. "Quite the contrary," he said, his tone a quiet, precise counterpoint to her scattered thoughts. "I am taking this entire situation very seriously."

Pepper shifted her weight. Another car had pulled up behind the first and a truck with a horse trailer stopped behind Malachi's idling vehicle. Someone laid on their horn.

"Will you please get out of the middle of the road?" Pepper demanded. "This is a highway!"

"I am well aware of that." Amusement lurked behind the intensity of Malachi's gaze. Realization hit: he was going to stand in the middle of the highway until she went with him. Slow heat churned low in her belly as the thought warmed her. She hadn't had anyone care about her like that for a long time, not since her dad died. Pepper slammed the door on that pain in her heart and focused on the gorgeous man staring at her with such intense expectation.

"Malachi, you're being absurd," Pepper said. "You can't expect me to get into a truck with a stranger."

"*Are* we strangers, beauty?" The low purr of his voice was far too intimate. In the low light, his eyes seemed to glow a deep, brilliant indigo. Raindrops clung to his hair like stars scattered in the night sky. The sudden hammering of Pepper's heart wasn't due entirely to the cars lining up. Her fingers worked along the handle of her umbrella, betraying her restlessness. And Malachi saw it all with those deep, penetrating eyes.

"Are we?" he prompted, his low voice cutting through the sound of rain and idling vehicles. Before she could answer, the truck with the trailer laid on its horn, making her jump. "Settle. We're both safe."

"You're standing in the middle of a highway!" she reminded him, her adrenaline mounting. "Just get in the truck and go, okay?"

"Not without you."

"You're being stubborn."

"Only because I need to be." His fingers twitched and he took another step toward her. All she had to do was lift her hand and her fingers would find his. Her skin itched to feel his again. His tone was coaxing over steel. "Get in the truck."

"Let me drive," Pepper challenged, her expression openly daring him. A shrug rippled through his powerful shoulders.

"If you'd like."

Pepper blinked, tipping her head. "Are you serious?"

"Yes. It's an excellent idea. It gives you the means to escape if I should need to fight off Jensen."

Pepper gave him an appraising look. He didn't *sound* sarcastic. She took another step closer to him, asphalt under her feet as she got close enough to stand on his toes. Her heart raced at his nearness, and at challenging him.

"I'll drive," she said. "And you can ride in the bed."

Malachi raised one eyebrow. Pepper tipped her

head in return and refused to look away.

"It's the only way you're getting me into that truck, Malachi." She did her best to sound nonchalant. As if it didn't matter what he said next. It would matter to her.

A bar of warm steel wrapped around her back as he dragged her against his body. She hadn't even seen him move. The strength in his arm was incredible. His scent wrapped around her, making her brain short out. She put her hand on his chest to push him away but found her fingers stroking over the fabric of his shirt instead, sculpting the hard muscle underneath. He bent his head.

"I *could* simply pick you up and put you in the truck, beauty." His warm breath skittered over her ear, sending goosebumps over her flesh that had nothing to do with the rain. His jaw rubbed against hers, the rough rake of his stubble against her softer skin highlighting the marvelously attractive maleness of him. He lifted his head just enough to capture her gaze again. He was so close she could feel his breath moving across her lips. "I will, if I have to. Choose me, Pepper. Choose to come with me, and trust me."

Pepper's heart fluttered, fast and strong. There was something vulnerable in his eyes, as if some part of him was pleading with her. That shook her.

"Malachi, I—"

A horn suddenly blared, cutting her off and making her jump. Malachi's arm tightened. He raised his head and grimaced at the line of vehicles, looking like an animal baring its teeth. A deep growl rumbled in his chest. Instinctively, Pepper rubbed her hand over his chest to soothe him. His hand covered hers, his thumb stroking over her knuckles to send little sparks of heat skipping through her blood. Malachi slowly turned his attention back to her. Her gaze caught on his, and that heat surged through her in a wave, robbing her of thought. His head inched toward hers, and she lifted her face in unthinking response.

A police siren blipped in warning. Malachi ignored it but Pepper glanced around, guilty. Heat flamed her cheeks with embarrassment. Malachi chuckled, a low sound of masculine amusement. She grabbed his wrist with her free hand and hurried toward the pickup, wincing at the pain in her side. Malachi took the umbrella and lifted her through the open door before slamming it behind her. Pointedly, she locked the doors, and stared through the window with one eyebrow raised in an open dare. Malachi was laughing. He winked and sprang into the bed of the truck, folding the umbrella as he settled. That ridiculous man was actually going to do it. Pepper bit her lip against the laugh that wanted to bubble out of her, put the truck into gear, moved the seat forward six inches, and pulled back into the road.

Chapter Ten

The chatter of the coffee shop died as Malachi opened the glass door. His other hand pressed into the small of her back, and she felt it deeply, like a brand. Pepper's cheeks were hot, despite the cool of the rainy day. She kept her eyes firmly fixed on the "Specials" board above the bar. The weight of stares was heavy on her skin, and the worst were the startled, impressed expressions from her coworkers. As she hurried behind the bar, she caught a glimpse of Malachi looking around the street before stepping into the building. Low murmurs started as she yanked open the closet and shoved her rain-slicked jacket inside. Maybe she was being paranoid. Maybe everyone would think she had simply arrived at the same time as Malachi, who had courteously held the door open for her. A couple of people had irritatingly speculative expressions, but she met their gazes steadily. Nothing had happened…except him saving her life once or twice. She shut the door with enough force to rattle the hinges.

"Pepper." Malachi's low voice held an intimate note as it carried over the counter, making her fumble with her apron strings. "You promised you'd leave me your keys. It will be much more difficult for me to take a look at your car without them."

Pepper closed her eyes as she willed the wall to fall over on her and hide her from everyone's view. Either that, or give the man a solid kick to the shin. She turned with red cheeks and lifted her chin, waiting for the retort to jump out of her mouth. It never came. His blue eyes shone with laughter. Heat lurked behind the amusement, and she had to press her lips together tightly to keep from biting them. Pride and defiance swelled in her chest. Digging into her pocket, she fished out her keys and dropped them into Malachi's waiting palm. His hand trapped hers, bringing the back of it to his lips as he held her gaze. Time stalled. Her lungs forgot how to work as the world fell away behind those indigo eyes.

A bang from the kitchen door jarred her back into reality, making her jerk her hand away. Abby stepped through the door and Malachi looked at her with mild annoyance. He allowed Pepper's hand to slide from his with apparent reluctance, but he retained possession of her keys.

"Wait for me."

Pepper refused to turn and see Abby's face. The feeling of disapproval emanating from the owner was palpable on the back of her neck. The silence of the shop had given way to the oceanic murmur of many hushed voices, all talking over each other at the little drama unfolding in front of them.

"I never agreed to meet you during break," Pepper reminded him. She tried to be firm, but the best she could manage just sounded stubborn.

"I still need to speak with you," Malachi said in that low, coaxing voice. His eyes never left hers. A slow, sexy smile tugged up on one side of his mouth. "Since you made me ride in the bed of the truck."

"I wasn't about to trust you in the cab of it," she

retorted. Her chest felt tight under the weight of that steady gaze, like he was a predator and she was the prey.

"Of course not. That doesn't change the fact that I need to speak with you."

"About my car?" Pepper focused on drawing air into her lungs. Each breath came with his scent, mixed in with those of the coffee shop. She found her fingers actually twitching to touch him again. Malachi shrugged one shoulder with casual elegance.

"Among other things." A smile hovered around his lips for a moment. His beautiful, sensual lips. "Say yes, Pepper." His voice dropped several notes, a low, intimate sound that made her belly tremble. She swallowed, catching the inside of her lower lip between her teeth where he couldn't see it. The truth was that she wanted to see him again. She simply would have preferred to be more discreet about it.

"Okay."

Malachi straightened from his lean on the bar with a smile in his deep blue eyes.

"Thank you, beauty. I'll see you then." He nodded deeply, an old-world gesture that bordered on a bow. Every head turned as he walked out. The bell on the door shattered the near-silence with its jubilant chime.

A tide of whispers and giggles swept through the room as the sound faded. Feeling like she was waking from a daze, Pepper hurried to the back to clock in and wash her hands. She'd only pulled back the top half of her hair that morning, so the lower half was free to fall around her, obscuring her features as she passed by her unusually quiet coworkers. Shutting the bathroom door behind her, she snapped the lock into place. Cupping cold water in her hands, she splashed it on her still-flaming face. And then left her hands there to support her whirling head.

How could he do this to her? How was it even possible? No one got under her skin like that. He saved her life. He saved her from Jensen. He had given her a ride to work this morning, offering to take a look at her car. It was really more like insisting but...he was sexy. She could pretend all she wanted that, after all he had done for her, she was allowed to feel something for him, as well as allowed to feel completely awkward about it, but it wasn't true. The reason she felt awkward was because the man was flat-out sexy.

And dangerous. She hadn't seen much of the fight on the riverbank, but her side still ached. Sharp pains shot through her if she moved just wrong. One hand went to her side. She could feel the bulk of the bandages under her shirt. His touch had been so gentle, so at odds with the strength and power that radiated from him.

He still hadn't explained the claw marks. Gently, she traced her fingers over the burning marks on her side. They were spaced just a little wider. Because Jensen's hands were bigger. He had left distinct claw marks—large and clear, but, thankfully, not deep—even through slashing her shirt.

Something strange had gone on by the river last night, and Malachi knew exactly what it was. He was dangerous, powerful, and he was paying far too much attention to her. She shouldn't trust him.

But she did.

The door handle jiggled, and adrenaline shot through her system.

"Pepper?" A muffled voice came through the door, and it was both feminine and familiar. Before she could reach the lock, it turned. Abby poked her head in, key still in her hand. One look at the younger woman's face, and the coffee shop owner stepped into the room. Shutting the door behind her, she locked it again before propping one hip on the counter and crossing her arms. Her salt-and-pepper hair was pulled back in its typical low ponytail, with its typical three pens and a coffee stirrer stuck in it. Pepper felt a sudden rush of affection. "You okay?"

"Yes." Pepper smiled, though she could feel the weariness and trepidation in it. Abby raised an eyebrow.

"You've been here for, what? Six months now? I've never so much as heard you mention a man before."

Pepper sighed. "Because there hasn't been a man before. There still isn't, so don't go reading more into that scene back there than there actually is."

"Maybe you'd better tell that to him," Abby said, her tone deceptively mild. "Where did you meet him?"

"On the riverbank on the walk home last night."

"You walked home last night? Pepper. Why didn't you call me?" the older woman demanded.

"Because by the time I discovered my car wasn't going to start, everyone was gone and the shop was all locked up. The police still have my phone."

Abby sighed. "Okay. You're forgiven that one. So what were you doing down on the riverbank?"

Pepper hesitated. Lying never felt right to her. Abby had always been an understanding boss and a reasonable person. But something gave her pause.

Jensen's hands had turned to claws; she had the gouges in her side to prove it. Malachi had jumped clean over their heads without even a running start. The strength with which he'd fought the current had been unreal. And then there was Bunsen's reaction to him.

"I slipped down the embankment on the wet grass." It wasn't entirely a lie. She just omitted the part where she'd had help slipping. "I ended up in the water. Malachi pulled me out and made sure I got home safely. When I started for work this morning, he was out there and offered me a ride."

"Holy moons, child! Are you all right?" Abby's face was filled with shocked concern. "What are you doing here? Take the day off. You've seen a doctor? The answer is 'yes,' and it better be true."

"I'm fine, Abby. I promise." Pepper warmed at Abby's maternal concern, tears stinging the back of her eyes. She had to swallow hard before she could free up her voice again. "Malachi got there quickly enough to pull us both out of the water before anything happened."

Abby snorted softly. "I don't know about *anything*. But if the man saved your life, it's little wonder you're besotted with him."

"Abby!" Pepper protested. It would have been more convincing if her cheeks hadn't been heating again. "I am not besotted with him."

"He's besotted with you," Abby pressed, then sighed. "Look, honey, your personal life is your business. I'm not trying to pry. But I didn't get these gray hairs doing nothing. I've been around the block, and I've seen men like him before. Smooth. Sophisticated. Worldly. Gorgeous as sin. That air of mystery and danger and excitement. Believe me, the only part that's real is the danger. He's going to chew you up and spit you out."

Pepper looked at her hands, still on the counter, the skin still dried out from their dip in brackish water. She could almost see Malachi's strong hand still wrapped around hers, like he'd somehow branded her with that simple touch. Or maybe it was the way he'd looked at her in front of the entire shop. Or still feeling his hands on her side, almost tender as he cleaned and bandaged her wounds.

"I know," she said quietly.

"If you need help, ask me. I don't like the thought of you being beholden to that man for any reason. There's something…off about him."

"He's really kind, Abby. He's not, like, pushy or anything." That wasn't quite true. Malachi could be pushy, but so far, he'd only pushed her to allow him to care for her. Sweet flutters started in her stomach at the thought, and she struggled not to press both hands over her belly in order to quell them. She could only imagine how the coffee shop owner would interpret *that* gesture.

"Yet." Abby's tone was dire. She sighed again. "Finish washing up. I'll see you behind the cash drawer in ten minutes."

Steady rain drizzled down the coffee shop windows all through the day. The spectacular thunderstorm of the night before was a constant buzz of conversation as customers kept the staff running. It seemed like most of the town put in an appearance at one time or another, some more than once. Even a few late-season tourists stamped their way through the door, shaking off the wet cool. Pepper smiled and nodded and made the same comments about the wild lightning over and over again as the clock ticked a metronome into her brain. She refused to look at it, mostly because she was convinced if she did, it would be going backward. She could pretend to everyone else that she wasn't waiting, that she didn't jump every time the door opened, but she knew better. Several times she caught Abby watching her with that same maternal concern, and her cheeks went pink.

By the time midday rolled around, Pepper was so used to her heart double-beating at the chime of the door that she almost didn't feel it anymore. It was a relief; it had been an exhausting morning. Something uncomfortably like bitter disappointment curled in her stomach, filling it so she didn't feel hungry. The CPA from down the street was in for his usual lunchtime latte, and Pepper was only half listening to the threadbare come-on lines he used on all the girls at least once a week. Part way through the rehearsed schmooze, he suddenly stopped talking. The coffee shop fell silent. A small shiver rippled up Pepper's spine. Even before she turned around, she knew it was him. He'd come. Her hand was shaking when she handed over the paper cup. The CPA slid to one side, like he could feel he was in the way. Pepper caught at her breath and lifted her gaze. Malachi stood at the end of the bar, rain tangled in his hair. The shoulders of his leather coat were wet, as were his boots. His eyes were heated as they met hers over an expectant smile. His expression alone made her body come alive, every nerve aware of him as a man and herself as a woman.

"Abby," Pepper called to the woman at the register. "Is it all right if I take my break now?"

The older woman looked from her to Malachi, her lips pressed thin. With a brief snort, she slammed the drawer into the machine and nodded.

"One hour. No tardiness."

"Thanks," Pepper found herself muttering. Fumbling with her apron strings gave her a good excuse to not look up, and she kept her gaze averted as she pulled her jacket from the closet. A large hand closed over the collar of it. Malachi had moved around the end of the bar. His gaze never wavered as he took the jacket from her hand and held it by the shoulders. Pepper reached to take it back, but he only raised an eyebrow, almost as if he were daring her. Lifting her chin, she turned around and allowed him to help her into the sleeves. The usual activities of the shop had ceased. Malachi's hand was hot on her back as he guided her out into the parking lot. A shiver went up her spine that had nothing to do with the weather.

"Are you all right, beauty?" he asked softly, as soon as they were outside. He stayed close, angling his body to take as much of the rain on his back that he could, keeping it from falling on Pepper. Picking up an umbrella propped beside the door, he opened it, holding it over both of their heads. "Is your side bothering you? It must hurt."

"I can ignore it, unless I move wrong. You really don't need to worry about me so much."

Malachi smiled. One hand reached out to trail his fingertips through the loose strands of her hair.

"Your boss doesn't seem to like me. Is she making things difficult for you?"

His tone was solicitous, but there was iron underneath it that made Pepper look long at him. Her voice was just short of defensive.

"She worries."

"I'm glad that she worries about you. You need more than just a housecat in your life."

"She thinks you're just out for a good time," Pepper said. She risked a look at him. Malachi's eyes were blue flame, and for one heart-stopping moment, she thought he was angry. Curling his hand around hers on the umbrella, he backed her into the railing. His large body blocked the weather, and she could feel the warmth radiating from him. His face was only inches from hers.

"I will happily assure her that my intentions are entirely honorable," Malachi said in a low, heated voice. His gaze lowered to Pepper's lips. She returned the compliment, staring at his mouth. He had such a tempting mouth. His free hand cupped her cheek, his thumb tracing tiny little lines near the corner of her lips. She still stiffened, and Malachi inhaled deeply, as if bringing her scent deep into his lungs. He kept his body close to hers, his voice low and carefully controlled. "What troubles you, beauty?"

Pepper shook her head a little, taking deep, deliberate breaths to steady her racing her heart. It didn't work; it beat too fast. Malachi breathed deeply, in and out. Pepper found her lungs trying to sync her breath with his as he gradually slowed his breathing. His thumb kept up the steady little caresses to her cheek as if waiting for her answer.

"I don't believe you," she finally murmured, keeping her gaze on his.

"About what?"

"That your intentions are honorable. Whatever that

even means. No one uses that phrase anymore," Pepper said crossly.

"I do." With a sweep of his hand, Malachi cleared water from the railing behind her. Leaving her with the umbrella, he placed his hands on her hips and lifted her easily onto the railing. Pepper steadied herself with a hand on his broad chest. He kept her close, his arm around her back to keep her steady, leaned against her legs, intimately close. Pepper lowered her gaze to his mouth again. A quiet sound rumbled from Malachi's chest, something like a growl but far more pleasant. His voice was low, intimate, rolling through the gray day to bind them together. "Pepper. I'm not the kind of man who plays around. If all I wanted was sex, you would have given it to me by now."

Something rebellious flared up in Pepper, making her lift her chin. Her gaze met his square on, blazing with defiance.

"You wish." Her voice broke on the words, and she coughed. Malachi rubbed her back as he chuckled.

"I think I shall be insulted," he said in that rich, low tone, his amusement shining through it. He leaned down to whisper into her ear. The warmth of his breath so close sent sparks through her blood. "If I wanted to seduce you, beauty mine, I could. You could no more resist me than I could resist you."

"I'm the one who needs to feel insulted." Pepper managed to put some spice into her tone, despite the breathlessness. Malachi looked as if he was trying not to laugh. "You have a very high opinion of yourself, Mr. Negrescu."

"Don't *you* have a high opinion of me?" His gaze held weight, pressing against her chest. The playfulness had gone from his voice. Malachi seemed to be willing her to answer. She could feel the tension vibrating through his frame. Without looking away, Pepper nodded.

There was command in his tone, however he tried to gentle it. His eyes were hot stone and his voice was red steel. "Look at me and say it out loud."

Pepper's jaw ground tight, pride warring with truth. She lifted her chin, throwing back her hair as if daring him—or herself—to make something of it.

"Yes, Malachi. I *do* have a rather high opinion of you."

One arm kept her tight against him, sheltering her from the storm in his warmth, keeping her safely perched on the railing. The other slid up her throat leaving fire in its wake. The heat followed his touch over her cheek as he buried his fingers in her hair. His large hand cupped the back of her head, holding her still as his mouth descended on hers.

Chapter Eleven

Fire shot through him. It was all Malachi could do to keep from dragging Pepper's body fully against his, wrapping her legs around his waist, and carrying her off to somewhere more private. Her lips were soft and hesitant, as if unaccustomed to such use. He might have been as hard as a rock, but she was still getting used to him, to being with a man. The thought cooled him. He had to go slowly, or he'd frighten her away. He coaxed her through the kiss, urging her to follow his lead as his mouth worked against hers. His tongue brushed against the satin of her lips, bringing a quiet moan from her. His hands tightened involuntarily.

Pepper's heart hammered against his, slamming blood through her body. A tiny whimper escaped her throat. He couldn't have said if it was need or fear.

Malachi broke away. Pepper tried to follow but he pinned her in place on the railing. He needed to catch his breath, to put some distance between his taxed control and her intoxicating responses.

"Malachi!" Pepper demanded. He leaned his forehead against hers, eyes closed, as he slowly stroked his hand through the loose ends of her hair.

"Shhh." Malachi might have been talking to himself, the sound was so quiet. "Just breathe with me, beauty. I have you."

A shudder ran through him, making his skin ripple.

The scent of her arousal was pushing his control too far. Only his fear for her had allowed him to pull himself together again. For the first time in his life, Malachi understood—on a deep, visceral level—why the Tseng Tse drilled their cubs and younglings on self-control so relentlessly. If he wasn't careful, he would place not only his people in danger, but Pepper as well.

He focused his mind on Pepper's scent. Her breathing. Her heartbeat. She was aroused, far too aroused for the middle of her workday. The scent of it nearly drove him into his fur. He slowed his breathing. His heart rate slowed; hers followed. Malachi allowed himself to steal a kiss near the corner of her mouth before raising his head and opening his eyes. It only took a moment before Pepper lifted her gaze to his, a question in her liquid-dark eyes.

"I'm sorry," he said simply. "I shouldn't have gotten you worked up like that."

"As long as you aren't apologizing for kissing me." Even now, she was trying to be tough. The desire to laugh welled up in his chest, as did the need to keep her sheltered and safe beside him.

"Never," he answered with a smile. His expression sobered a little, trailing one fingertip over her cheek. "I could get addicted to kissing you, Pepper. You should know that right now."

Her hand slid up his chest, wrapping her chilled fingers around the back of his neck. He gritted his teeth against the sensation, forcing himself to remember that the gesture was innocent. She was probably attempting to warm her hands, and nothing more.

"That doesn't seem like such a bad thing to me." The soft haze of pleasure faded from her face as she frowned. "Except my cat doesn't like you."

Malachi sighed. Taking her hand from his neck, he cupped it in his warmer ones and gently blew.

"I'm afraid that's going to be a problem, and there's very little I can do about it." Frustration and regret tinged his voice. He had to find a way to work with his small cousin's natural fear of a large predator—himself. Pepper would never leave her cat behind, nor put him in a position where he was constantly stressed. Nor would Malachi ask it of her. He wouldn't make her choose between him and the one companion she had in her life. He would leave her first.

The thought shot fear through him. What would happen to Pepper? Who would care for her and protect her and Bunsen? Images of the flimsy RV by the sea washed through his mind. She was so vulnerable there, both to the elements of nature and to predators, human and otherwise. If anything were to happen to Pepper, he could never live with himself.

Pepper must have felt the sudden tension under her hand. She began to rub Malachi's neck, small, little strokes to soothe the straining muscles.

"Were you able to learn anything about the car?" she asked. She was trying to distract him. It worked, but not the way she had intended. His arms tightened around her like a cage, a solid wall to keep everyone else away from her. Malachi didn't allow himself to speak until he could keep his voice calm and steady, for her sake.

"The spark plugs were removed."

Pepper frowned. "The spark plugs?" Hurt and confusion filled her face and her scent. "But who would do that? How? You have to release the hood from inside, and it was locked. I know it was locked. How…?"

"Jensen."

Fear sharpened Pepper's scent, stinging in his nose. He fought the urge to roar a challenge, or to crush her to him and kiss her, over and over again until she forgot to be afraid. Malachi shifted, indulging himself in bringing her closer, and rubbed his stubbled jaw over her hair.

"Are you sure?" Pepper's voice wobbled, despite her brave attempt to keep it clinical and steady.

"Yes." He couldn't tell her that the other Tseng Tse's scent was all over her car, though he longed to do just that. Longed to tell her everything and have her accept him just as he was. Pepper shook her head, bumping it gently against his jaw.

"But *how*? And why? What reason would he possibly have for sabotaging my car? There's no way he could have known it was mine."

"On foot, you were vulnerable to him." Just the thought made the rage boil up in Malachi's throat, threatening to choke him. He buried his face against her hair and breathed her in. He had to be calm. Protecting Pepper was going to be difficult enough as it was. He couldn't guard her and hunt Jensen; he was only one man. The nearest group of hunters was a hundred and fifty miles away, at best, and he had no guarantee the streak was available to come aid him in his hunt. Even if they did…He was a solitary hunter for a reason. What of Pepper? How would she tolerate being invaded by an entire group of tiger shifters, each hunter in the streak as arrogant and bossy as himself? He wasn't sure how well *he* would tolerate it. If there was, perhaps, another solitary he could call on…

Like Israel. His brother was in Arizona, working a hunt of his own. Israel was a powerful, capable hunter. He would come, if he possibly could. Between the two of them, they could keep Pepper safe and bring Jensen to the justice of their people.

Pepper peered up at him with an expression in her eyes like dark fire.

"You have no proof. For all you know, it could be some random prank." Pepper pushed against him to hop down from the railing. Malachi didn't release her. He kept his arm tight around her, shielding her against his body as the rain fell on his back.

"You want proof?" Malachi tried to keep the impatience out of his voice. He reached into his pocket. He'd been hoping he could protect her from it, but if she was going fight him every step of the way without it, he would give it to her. He handed her a small piece of paper, folded in half. Gingerly, she took it between her thumb and forefinger and opened it. On the inside was the heart in thick, reddish-brown blood. Her brows drew together as she looked up at him again.

"I don't understand," she said, waving the paper in the air. "What is this supposed to mean?"

"It's a threat," he answered. "I found it on your windshield."

"A heart is a threat?" Pepper scoffed. She tried to draw away again. Malachi caught the paper and held it where she couldn't help but see it.

"That's blood, Pepper. A heart drawn in blood," Malachi wanted to shake some sense into her. He should tell her the heart was in blood from a young, human female, just to make her see the danger she was in. "How is a heart drawn in blood *not* a threat?"

Pepper looked from him to the paper and back again. All color left her face as she slowly shook her head. He could tell she was fighting it, but she began to tremble, anyway, hard shudders running through her until it felt like she was rattling in his arms. Instinct overwhelmed him. The need to comfort her swamped his self-preservation instinct, and even the duty to protect his people. He chuffed against her hair.

"Pepper." He made his voice as soothing and reassuring as he knew how. "You're going to be all right. I'm going to protect you and stop him. You're safe."

Pepper shook her head, the denial vehement and reflexive as real fear threaded its way into her scent. "The police. We need to take this to the police. They need to know everything that you know about this Jensen."

Malachi cupped her face in both hands, bringing her gaze back up to his. His thumbs feathered across her cheekbones. "I told you, Pepper. There's nothing that they can do."

"What do you think *you* can do, then?" Pepper spat the words at him. "You keep saying you'll protect me, but if the police can't do it, what makes you think *you* can?"

"I don't *think* I can. I *know* I can." Power filled his voice, both the strength of the tiger and the authority of the prince. There was no doubt in him that he could defeat Jensen. There couldn't be. "I need you to trust me. Can you do that?" Malachi found himself holding his breath. Time stretched taut as he forced himself to wait, still, unmoving, and outwardly calm.

It took too long for Pepper to relax a little. She dropped her head wearily against his sternum. "I don't know. I think I do trust you and it—"

Pepper cut herself off. Unaccustomed softness curved his mouth into a smile. He stroked her hair as he cradled her close, warming and comforting himself as he warmed and comforted her. He breathed deeply, chuffing again. Pepper lifted her head.

"What was that?"

Malachi blinked. It took a moment for him to realize what she was talking about, and he swore mentally. Keeping his voice steady, he continued stroking her hair. "What was what?"

Pepper pulled far enough away from him to glare up at him. "Really? Now you're going to insult my intelligence? What was that sound you just made?"

Malachi smiled his most charming. Taking her hand, he kissed her knuckles. "Your break is going fast, beauty, and you haven't even had anything to eat. Where would you like to go?"

"I'm not hungry." Pepper shrugged it off. Malachi raised a disbelieving eyebrow.

"Now who is insulting whose intelligence?" he teased.

Pepper's stomach rumbled audibly as the color rushed to her face. Arm still around her, he scooped her off the railing to tuck her under his shoulder.

"I'm buying." He kept his tone light but made it clear he wasn't in the mood to accept an argument. Pepper dug in her heels against him, anyway.

"Seriously, Malachi. I'll be fine. I'm not going to take advantage of you."

"It's now taking advantage for a man to take a

woman he admires out for a meal?"

Pepper stared at him. The cautiously hopeful expression on her face made him want to laugh.

"That's a date."

Malachi laughed. "That's exactly the idea, beauty." He moved down the sidewalk, checking his stride to bring her along with him. Laughter came as easily as growling. Everything about her got under his skin, and it filled him with awe.

Pepper refused to look up at him, but a sweet smile curved her lips. His heart turned over. He couldn't help but stare in wonder. He needed to see that expression on her face as much as possible.

"So you're intentionally taking me out on a date?" Her tone was somewhere between shy, sly, and proud.

"You doubt it? I *did* say my intentions are honorable, didn't I? I do believe that going on dates— including meals—is included in honorable courtship." His arm tightened around her, and he lowered his voice to a playful growl. "I could forego the honorable courtship, if you prefer. I could simply throw you over my shoulder and carry you off to my palace. That *is* an option."

Pepper's eyebrows flew up, laughter finally returning to her eyes.

"Palace? Seriously?" Amusement filled her voice. Malachi just grinned and winked at her. She laughed and shoved playfully at his arm. It wasn't enough to make him move, but she didn't seem to notice.

"You're so ridiculous."

"Oh, you think so?" Malachi opened the door to his truck and helped her in, closing the door carefully. He stepped up into the other side and inhaled. Her scent in an enclosed space was heady. Sliding over the seat, he leaned into her, trapping her against the door. His hand found the side of her face again, urging her to look at him as his thumb stroked along her jaw. It was a little too easy to fixate on her tempting mouth as she smiled up at him.

Pepper scoffed playfully. "Who has a palace? Unless, you know, you're secretly a millionaire or something. Oh!" Pepper snapped her fingers. "I know! You're actually some foreign dignitary in disguise, traveling to add American women to his harem!"

"Not a harem, beauty. There's only one woman that I'm after, American or otherwise." Malachi's voice was a low, rough sound. Pepper seemed to be struggling to catch her breath, and the thought was oddly pleasing to him. She wet her lips, making them glisten in the muted light. Malachi groaned softly. His hand slipped from her cheek to catch her chin.

"You shouldn't have done that," he said, his voice barely above a whisper. Her heart rate spiked up several notches, and his followed right behind. Heat coursed through his body. He was intensely aware of every place his body touched hers, as if their clothing was far too thin. Anticipation filled him as he leaned slowly into her. Pepper's eyes drifted closed as she shifted closer, as if in invitation. Her breath skittered over his mouth, sending heat waves through his blood as he hesitated on the very verge of kissing her. She had one last chance to pull away. She didn't take it. His tongue flicked against her lips. Her whole body tensed beneath him. Malachi rumbled once, then his lips were on hers. Slow. Lingering. Savoring the taste of her just because he could. His hand cupped the back of her head, his fingers buried in the silken strands of her hair.

Malachi allowed the kiss to end, slowly easing away from her. The pad of his thumb traced the full curves of her lip, sending shivers through her. His voice was rough with the raw desire etched in his eyes.

"I'm picking you up from work tonight," he said. As quiet as it was, his voice sounded unnaturally loud in the cab. He nudged the side of her jaw with his nose, urging her to tip her head. His mouth left a hot trail over her throat. Her pulse thundered under his lips and he scraped his teeth over it, making her jump.

"I need—" Pepper's voice was a breathless stutter. "I need to get my phone from the police station."

"I'll take you." His hand cupped the other side of her throat, protective and possessive.

"Malachi." Pepper pressed her palms against his chest in protest; he slid his arm across the back of the seat and around her shoulders in retaliation. "Malachi, I can't keep taking from you. I can't even remember your last name half the time."

"Negrescu. What time do you get off work?"

"No."

He scraped his teeth over her skin again, making her squirm.

"Yes. How am I supposed to report the note I found on your car or the missing spark plugs unless I talk to the police?" Reluctantly, he lifted his head from her throat. His thumb stroked over her pulse as he pinned her gaze. "What time do I pick you up?"

"Four."

Malachi smiled. "Thank you, Pepper." His eyes warmed with humor. "Now…where am I taking you for lunch?"

"How am I supposed to think with you hovering over me like that?" Pepper pushed against his chest, and Malachi laughed. The sass in her voice—part pout, part accusation—was so beautifully human. He stole one last kiss, then allowed her to push him away, at least long enough to take her to lunch.

Chapter Twelve

Malachi listened to the phone on the other end of the line ringing as he strode through the streets, the speed of his steps kicking up water.

"Speak." He smiled at the comfortingly gruff greeting, as well as the familiar deep voice.

"You first," Malachi said with a hint of humor. "Your manners haven't improved, Israel. You should set a better example for your younger brothers."

"You are long past the age when you heed an elder brother's example, or advice, or anything else." The affection was heavy in Israel's tone. "So why do you call me?"

Israel tried hard to sound casual, but there was a sharp alertness to his tone that betrayed his worry. Malachi hesitated for a moment. It would be easier to explain in their native language, but the chance of being overheard was too great.

"I found her."

"Her?" Malachi heard a car door slam, then quiet surrounded Israel's voice. "I thought you were hunting Jensen Coburn. What has changed?"

"Everything." He paused to look out over the landscape, raking a hand through his hair. Israel inhaled to speak, but Malachi beat him to it. "It's exactly like Josiah said. Her scent. It is the most amazing, most powerful thing I have ever encountered."

The line was silent for several seconds.

"A mate?" Israel finally asked. "You have found a potential mate?"

Malachi nodded, though his brother couldn't see it. The unbelievable joy that Pepper brought to him shone so brightly it colored his voice as he grinned like a fool, and he didn't care.

"Her name is Pepper. She's...everything." He suddenly sobered. "And she's in trouble."

"Tell me," Israel commanded.

"She filmed Jensen attacking another woman, and he knows it." Malachi's voice turned grim, a low growl in his throat. "He attacked her. The filthy traitor was going to force himself on her! A *human* woman!"

Israel snarled. "I will come to you. Protect your woman."

"She isn't my woman yet," Malachi said. "I can't protect her and hunt Jensen at the same time, but I can't allow him to escape justice, either. My potential mate isn't the only woman he's hurt. He must be stopped."

"He will be."

"I won't ask you to leave your hunt." Malachi's voice was almost a warning.

"There is no need. I have my prey in sight. Two days more, at most, and my hunt is over. Protect your woman," Israel repeated. "I will find Jensen's scent when I arrive."

Malachi hesitated. Jensen was *his* hunt, but if he insisted on finishing it alone, Pepper was in danger. His pride could suffer, for her sake.

"Thank you," he said stiffly.

"If you wish to truly thank me, introduce to me my new sister." Israel's tone was only partly teasing.

Malachi rubbed his fingertips together, wishing he had a tail to twitch; it was more satisfying.

"I haven't won her yet, Israel. She doesn't even know our people exist, and now isn't a good time to tell her."

"You *must* tell her," Israel insisted. "You cannot accept a commitment from her until she understands to what she is committing."

"Do you think I don't know that?" Malachi snapped. "I learned our laws right alongside of you. My mind may be addled with her scent, but I still know that much."

"Then tell her."

"She's terrified. She's terrified, and vulnerable, and alone. The only companion she has in this world is a housecat. That traitorous aberration has her so afraid of our people that she would bolt the moment I revealed that I am Tseng Tse."

"*Your* potential mate is that easily terrified?" Malachi could almost see Israel shaking his head, even from hundreds of miles away. "Impossible. She is no fit match for you, then. Your nose is broken."

Malachi swore, loud enough to send nearby birds into flight. The words were ground out between bared teeth.

"He put his claws in her."

The line grew deathly quiet.

"Say it again," Israel demanded.

"Jensen put his claws into Pepper's side. I witnessed it myself." The memory bobbed in his mind of her satin skin horribly marred by four parallel gashes, taunting him. He couldn't even protect his own woman, the one person in the world who would mean the most to him, if he could convince her to accept him. If he were to reveal his whole self to her before Jensen was brought justice, then she would bolt, and he couldn't blame her.

A Tseng Tse oath tore through the phone, loud enough to make Malachi jerk the speaker away from his ear.

"Tomorrow," Israel vowed. "I will run my prey to ground tonight and be on a plane out of Sun City before noon. I will pull rank if I must, Malachi. Leave your hunt and focus on protecting your woman."

"You're only the Second Prince," Malachi said drily. "You don't have the authority to call off a hunt ordered by the First Prince."

"I do have the authority to tell my younger brother to stand down until I can reach the First Prince and tell him to assign someone else to the hunt."

"Don't you dare."

"Do not force my hand. Wait for me. Stay with your woman. I will hunt this son of a she-bear and he will pay for every drop of blood, every bit of sweat, and every tear he brought from your potential mate and my potential sister."

Malachi smiled, his heart softening. "Thanks, Israel."

"I will call you when I arrive. I mean what I say, Malachi: *protect your woman.* I have no desire to suffer the emotional disaster you would become if anything happened to her."

"Thank you...I think," Malachi said in the same dry tone. With a shake of his head, he ended the call and pocketed his phone. Somewhere out past the ocean, a few determined patches of blue sky showed through the relentless clouds. Streaks of sun traced long lines over the dark underbelly of the storm, a promise of light to come. The air was thick with the smell of wet garbage. The ever-present scent of gasoline assaulted his nose and for a moment he longed for his homeland and the clean scents there. Malachi slipped his phone into his pocket. Turning his face toward the ocean, he rested his palms on the salt-worn wooden fence in front of him. Even the water smelled different, here. Colder. Of course, California on the whole was cooler than the dense jungles where the Tseng Tse had made their palace, so many generations ago. The only access was still by way of the river that ran through the palace gates. It had been nearly a year since he had been home, traveling from one hunt to the next as duty called. He rarely spoke their native language, though he knew that he still carried the accent. Like his brother Israel—and many of the other Tseng Tse living in diaspora— Malachi tended to cling to the language and traditions of their homeland in order to remember who he was. At least *he* could travel home from time to time. Israel's duties as the Second Prince kept him traveling for years at a time. The last time Malachi could recall Israel returning to the palace had been for the birth of their eldest niece—the daughter of the First Prince and First Princess, Josiah and his mate Ana—and that was a full ten years ago. Or was it eleven years, now? She would be entering her youngling years far too soon, and he had missed most of her cubhood, as well as the cubhood of her younger siblings.

Malachi pushed away the homesickness. His work was here. Pepper was here. She needed him to do his job. He glanced at his watch. She wouldn't be done with work for several hours yet. He'd promised to take her to the police station for her phone, despite her objections, and he refused to be late. She would be far too vulnerable to Jensen, once she was outside the relative safety of the coffee shop. He couldn't just sit on his tail and do nothing, waiting for his big brother to swoop in and save the day. Malachi walked the short distance back to the front of the coffee shop and peered through the large plate-glass window. Pepper was in the dining room, her dark hair falling in gentle waves over the shoulders of her deep green work uniform. Her dark eyes were warm as she laughed with an elderly customer. His heart turned over. She was more than beautiful. Her bravery, her humor, and her intelligence all attracted him, but it was the warm heart underneath that held the most appeal. If anyone could love him, it would be her. She had so much capacity to love, and only one small cat to return it to her. He could give her love. He could give her the love of an entire race. As his mate, she would be the Third Princess, and there was not a single doubt in his mind that the Tseng Tse would all adore her as soon as they met her. But that meant making sure she survived long enough for him to win her.

Malachi inhaled deeply. Jensen's stink troubled his nose. He indulged in a low growl as he bared his teeth. His reflection growled back. He looked feral. Dangerous. Absolutely deadly. And he was. His hands worked and released with the need to hunt this strange male and kill him, tear out his throat for putting claws into his woman. If Malachi was being brutal with himself, his need for revenge wasn't even for hurting Pepper; it was for being anywhere near her. Tseng Tse weren't very far removed from the jungle. They were possessive, violent, territorial. Over centuries, they had developed a social system that allowed them to live and work together, but he'd never appreciated before just how necessary that system really was. Without his lifetime of training, he would have removed Pepper to the safety of the palace, where he could afford the time to woo her properly. Where he could show her everything he could offer her, convince her that she was perfectly safe with him, despite his wildness.

But he didn't have that time. Jensen was out there, too close but nowhere he could be found, and he was targeting Pepper. Israel had said to wait for him, but Malachi couldn't afford to lose that time. His instincts screamed at him to drive the interloper out, protect his mate, defend his territory, and there was only so much he could do to mitigate them. Pepper would be safe enough, surrounded by her coworkers and patrons at the coffee shop. As long as she stayed inside, the witnesses would protect her. His shoulders bunched up toward his ears. He could feel the prickling sensation spreading over his skin, the presage to his fur sprouting through his flesh. His feet didn't want to move him away from this spot and the vibrant, beautiful woman laughing behind the bar. He peeled one foot away from the pavement, then the other, keeping his eyes on his woman as long as he could. As if she felt his gaze, Pepper lifted her head. Her dark gaze found his heated blue one. Everything about her went still. That unnamed connection sizzled between them. Color rose to her cheeks as he held her in his eyes. She broke the long look, dropping her gaze to the side, and desire surged through him with the triumph.

Malachi made himself move, long strides eating up the pavement. He was too close to the tiger. For Pepper's sake, he had to put some distance between them. He circled the building, running his hand over the rough brick. At the back door, he sculpted the metal jamb, the door, and the handle with both hands. If Jensen came sniffing around, he'd scent Malachi there, a Tseng Tse prince in his prime, and very, very angry. Malachi marked the periphery of the building before heading back to Pepper's car. Running his hands over it, he refreshed his claim on the little hatchback as his territory as well. It was a dangerous gambit. It would let Jensen know that Pepper was *his*, that she was under *his* protection. Any healthy Tseng Tse would step in to protect and care for their prince's potential mate, but Jensen was far from healthy. There was the chance that the fugitive would take it as a challenge, but it was a chance Malachi was willing to take.

He inhaled deeply, swinging his head slowly from one side to the other. Jensen's scent overlaid the rain-soaked city, but it was too muddied. It was impossible to tell if the other male had been hunting, or simply wandering. Malachi feared it was the former. It had taken a couple of weeks to catch up to him, after following his trail of shattered lives and battered bodies across two continents. Six victims. Six victims too many. Fury raced through him as he paused at a corner, leaning close to the wall. The only sentence possible under Tseng Tse law was death, and Jensen knew it. Like a coward, he had run from the palace as soon as his crimes were discovered.

Malachi pushed off the wall. Picking a street that headed into a more residential area, he began hunting again. A thread of fresh scent caught at Malachi's attention. He inhaled deeply. Stripes flickered over his skin: Jensen's scent was filled with adrenaline and lust. The other male was hunting. Malachi turned hard left and leaped into a jog, water slapping up from under his feet. The wail of sirens broke the air, coming nearer with every step.

He smelled the green before he saw the trees and open lawns, a fresh swath winding through the unending city. He could smell fresh water and ducks, and as he grew nearer, traces of the bats that patrolled at night. And blood. The scent of human blood burned in his nose, setting all of his instincts to an agitated buzz. The hairs on the back of his neck stood up as his fingernails stretched into claws. Feeling his way, he slipped in among the trees. Silence shrouded him as he followed that awful burning scent to a quiet section of the park.

A young woman lay in the edge of the water, her half naked body partially obscured by cattails. There was no scent of death, yet. The body was too fresh. Fish and birds and other scavengers had yet to start picking it apart. Blood smeared her thighs. The otherwise-smooth flesh was torn by ragged gashes, and deep punctures still spilled precious fluids, leaving a grotesque map to the last minutes of her life. Her dark hair bobbed with the gentle rhythm of the water, twining itself into the duckweed. Glassy dark eyes stared at nothing as her head floated, almost onto her shoulder. Her neck had been brutally snapped. There was very little blood on her face, only a small trickle from the corner of her mouth, but the color was a painful scarlet in his mind. Her legs were splayed on the shore, cast at unnatural angles. A ragdoll tossed aside by a heartless child. The unmistakable scent of aroused Tseng Tse male clung to the cattails; the smell of pain, and blood, and terrified human female saturated the verge grasses, even floating with the duckweed.

Sharp pain sparked in Malachi's hands. Blood dripped down his skin as his claws dug into his palms. Swearing under his breath, he wiped his hands on his shirt sleeves. Leaving his blood at a murder-rape scene would be disastrous. He had to get control of himself, or he would be in no fit shape to hunt. Letting his eyes lose focus, he inhaled and exhaled through his mouth, deeply, rhythmically, falling into a meditation pattern. The image of Pepper filled his mind, soaking wet and retching into the sand after her spill into the ocean. The feel of her slender body shivering in his arms, desperate to warm itself. The sound of her terrified, furious scream echoing under the bridge, surrounded by the crash of thunder and the battering of the waves. A growl vibrated his chest. Stripes rippled over his skin, his fur pricking against the inside of his skin.

He focused again on his breathing, this time allowing the scent to travel through his nose as he shook himself. A faint whiff of delicious, perfect scent fluttered off his shirt. Tipping his head nearer, he inhaled more deeply. Pepper had rested her head on his chest, leaving her scent more strongly there. His Pepper, aroused. His Pepper, calmed. The way her eyes shone when she laughed. The tender sound of her voice when she crooned to her cat. The heated satin of her skin under his hand, and the sweet taste of her mouth against his.

The prickling stopped. The tightness in his face

eased as his claws retracted into fingernails once more. His woman. Just the thought of her could drive the beast within back under his control, even when faced with something so unnatural, so unthinkable as the scene before him.

Malachi brought his eyes back into focus. The skin on his palms had already knitted itself together, marred only by the fading pink of newly healed skin, but he was still careful to touch nothing as he crouched. There was no sign of footprints leaving the water's edge, and no trace of Jensen's scent, either. Inching forward, Malachi inspected the duckweed. There. Small pieces floated free, torn from the main plant as something passed through them. He would bet his life that Jensen had shifted before swimming across the large pond in order to avoid leaving further tracks, including for him.

Red and blue lights swarmed over him as sirens stung his ears. Malachi hurriedly slipped from his shoes and tied the laces around his neck, the socks balled into the toes. The anger made the shift easy, but it took some concentration to funnel the change into his feet. The toes and ball flattened, broadened. He stopped it before it got too far. The shape should be odd enough to confuse any officers who looked into the print. Crouching low, he circled the edge of the water as swiftly as he dared. He couldn't afford to miss the place Jensen exited the water. He kept his gaze and his nose focused on the bank, but his ears strained for any sound of the authorities. Human police would only be a liability, at best, hindering his hunt and putting him at risk of outing his people. The Tseng Tse couldn't afford it, and neither could he.

Malachi rounded the far end of the pond and

headed back toward the poor girl's body without finding any sign of Jensen. The sirens had stopped, but the police lights still flashed. Car doors echoed as they banged shut. The eager snuffles of a tightly restrained dog broke through his concentration. Malachi risked a quick glance. The police were crossing the large grassy field far too quickly. He couldn't be seen here. He would have to come back, after the police had finished their work. Silently, he slipped away into the trees, leaving almost no trace behind.

Chapter Thirteen

Malachi pulled his truck into a parking spot near the front of the coffee shop and slammed it into park. He slid from the seat, scanning the area continuously as he shut the door. His hair was still damp from his quick dip through the shower to wash away any traces of the crime scene. His instincts were insistent: he needed to see her, touch her, hear her voice. He needed to fill his lungs with her scent and know that she was well.

The hinges creaked a protest as he pulled open the door with a little too much force. Everyone looked up suddenly with varying degrees of alarm.

"Welcome to—" Abby started. Her friendly expression cooled when she recognized him. "Oh."

Malachi couldn't help but smile. The older woman may have taken something of a dislike to him, but it pleased him that someone was looking out for his Pepper.

"Abby, isn't it?" He made himself as friendly as he could while scenting for his potential mate. "Pepper has spoken highly of you. It's a pleasure to meet you."

The older woman regarded him steadily for a few seconds before answering.

"I'd love to say the same," she finally replied. "Just a moment."

She stepped from behind the bar, drawing down the window shades against the afternoon light. Abby turned to him with her brows lowered and crooked her finger.

"Come with me. Please." The word was obviously an afterthought. A prickling sensation ran up his spine, tingling in the back of his neck, as his hackles rose under his skin. His gaze was steady, almost predatory, as he flowed behind her like a stalking cat. She must have felt the hunter's air, because she turned to look over her shoulder uneasily. It was only once, however. The older woman had an unusual amount of courage for a human. Relief moved through him that such a woman was Pepper's friend and protector. He was calm, even indulgent, as he stepped into her office and closed the door behind him. Almost. He left it open just a finger's width.

"I'm guessing that you would like this closed for privacy, but perhaps not all the way?" His offer was genuine, to put the coffee shop owner more at ease.

"Close it." Abby leaned on the desk in the small office, never taking her eyes off of him. Malachi stood near the door, hands in front of him, and waited. Abby simply stared at him for a few heartbeats.

"I don't want to be a beast about this, but someone has to be, and it certainly isn't going to be Pepper. You may be able to fool her with your tailored clothes and smooth talk and magazine-cover looks, but I'm not nearly so naive. She isn't as vulnerable as she looks to a man like you."

Malachi chose to ignore the insult, and simply allowed himself to enjoy the older woman's protectiveness over her young employee.

"Excellent. I'm very glad to hear it. I'm glad she isn't as alone in the world as she seems. The more friends she has around her, the better." His expression grew more earnest. "Please believe me when I tell you that my only intentions toward Pepper are the most honorable."

"She's not in your league. Or even the same ballpark."

That caused Malachi to raise an eyebrow. "She's a grown woman."

"But she's a young one, and not...experienced. Certainly not with men of the world like you. That girl is going to fall in love with you," Abby accused. His heart swelled with the thought of it. He bowed slightly, as far as the small office would let him, and his tone was of the utmost respect.

"Woman, I pray that you are more right than you know. You believe that I'm a predator, out to steal Pepper's innocence and break her heart for my own amusement." Malachi allowed the full weight of his gaze to fall on Abby for the first time. Even as formidable a woman as she was, she backed a step. He was careful to keep his voice low, though he poured the power of his heritage into his voice. "You have it backward. Pepper is the one who could break my heart, while she has every defense against me." He smiled, breaking his hold on her gaze. "Including an employer who is willing to stand in the very tiger's path to protect her."

Abby blinked and shifted, her hand going thoughtlessly to the collection of pens in her ponytail. She finally cleared her throat.

"Pepper's worth it. You here to pick her up again?"

"Yes. Her car is still not working, and it isn't safe for a lady to walk alone at night."

"You taking her straight home?" Abby was starting

to get her wind back, strictness coming back into her tone.

"No."

The older woman's gaze sharpened. "Where are you taking her?"

"To the police station." Malachi fought the desire to laugh at the stunned expression on Abby's face. "They're holding her phone as evidence in yesterday's attack. She was told she could pick it up today. I'm sure no one wants her to be out of communication any longer than absolutely necessary."

"Well, no." Abby sounded a little less certain. "There's no arguing that."

"I'm glad we agree." Malachi made a show of looking at his watch, for Abby's benefit. "We don't want to miss our opportunity to get Pepper's phone back today. I should let her know that I'm here. I'm sure she's ready to clock out by now, wouldn't you say?"

His tone was mild, but nonetheless a strong suggestion that Abby allow Pepper to leave. The older woman pressed her lips tightly together and checked the clock on the wall.

"I'm not in the habit of allowing other people to run my coffee shop, Mr...?"

"Negrescu."

"Mr. Negrescu. I'm most certainly not in the habit of allowing slick strangers to run *me*." She straightened from her lean, rearranging the pens in her hair. "Pepper's free to clock out when she's done with her work, as always. If you'll excuse me."

Malachi opened the door and stepped into the tiny back hallway in order to make room for the business owner to step past him. Abby swept past with a regal air that made him smile.

Even before the door to the front end opened, Malachi was looking for Pepper over the top of Abby's head. She was bent over a table in the main dining room, wiping it down, laughing over her shoulder with one of her coworkers. Her coworker, a young man who barely looked old enough to be working, tossed the cleaning cloth at her face in a teasing gesture of exasperation. It startled a laugh out of Pepper as she ducked away, batting it away from her face. Malachi tensed. His human mind knew that she was in neither danger nor distress, but the tiger's mind only saw another male throwing something at his mate. Potential mate. She hadn't agreed to be his, or to take on his life. Israel was right. He couldn't afford to wait too much longer, or it would be impossible for him to walk away if she were to reject him.

"Pepper, scrub out," Abby said without preamble as she walked to the drawer.

Pepper turned with a look of confusion. She looked from her employer to Malachi, looming behind the woman, and Pepper's gaze stuck to him. "Abby? Is everything all right?"

"You have a date at the police station." Wry humor underlaid Abby's tone. "Call me when you have your phone back. I want to know you've got it."

Malachi retreated to a corner of the dining room where he could watch the entire room, especially the doors. He soothed the ripple of unease that ran up his spine when Pepper disappeared to wash by cataloguing the items in easy reach that he could weaponize and calculating how fast he could cross the room. If he wasn't worried about anyone knowing he wasn't human, he could be across the room in three seconds, at most. That was a comfort. The big windows to the sidewalk would be a nightmare to defend, but they made it practically impossible for Jensen to sneak up from that direction. Customers trickled in and out. There would be more as the standard human workday came to an end. He'd have to find out what shifts Pepper was scheduled to work. It would be easier to protect her during the somewhat busier daylight hours. Once Israel arrived, it would be easier still.

The door to the back swung open again and Malachi gave it his full attention. Pepper hurried to the closet with her apron in her hand and took out her jacket.

"Bye, Brett." Her tone was teasing even in good-bye. A shaft of jealousy stabbed through Malachi's chest. Her young coworker was treated so comfortably but she was uncomfortable with him. He stepped forward, opening one arm to guide her from the room. Pepper lifted her chin with a proud expression, as if stepping into the circle of his arm was her right. The gesture pleased him immensely.

He watched her steps as he guided her into his truck, even as he kept eyes and ears tuned around them. The last thing he needed was to be surprised by Jensen, still aroused from a kill. Malachi didn't push Pepper to talk. She smelled tired, more interested in the world outside the window than conversation. He turned on the heater, aiming the center vents toward her, and let his hand fall to her knee. She stilled slightly, then smiled as her cheeks turned pink. Her hand drifted onto his. Malachi's heart thudded too hard twice before settling into a regular, if fast, rhythm. Her skin was cold. He twined his fingers with hers, bringing her hand to the warmth of his mouth and breathing over her fingers. She didn't look at him again, but she smiled deeply out the window.

Pepper's scent hit him on a level nothing ever had, dragging both man and beast into a world of heat, of sensation, of fantasy that he had no hope of truly controlling. He didn't want to. He wanted to indulge in every fantasy his overactive imagination was concocting. He wanted to spend all night adoring her body, then spend all day doing the same thing with the sunlight shining over her satin skin. He wanted to run with her in the woods, only to catch her and show her the meaning of the word "mate". He wanted to bathe her in the heated springs of his homeland, drowsy and sated, then tuck her into bed beside him to sleep in his arms where he could protect and care for her. Every breath drew her scent into his lungs and drove it straight into his groin. Only the knowledge that, if he lost awareness of their surroundings, his Pepper might be hurt or even killed kept his focus on the road.

Malachi already knew where the police station was. He made it his business to keep tabs on human law enforcement, military forces, or anything like them whenever he was on a hunt. He turned into the parking lot and turned off the ignition. Pepper's nervousness suddenly saturated the air.

"You don't like police?" Malachi asked. He would have guessed such a little crusader would be on friendly terms.

"It's hit and miss," Pepper confessed, opening her seat belt. Sadness tinged her scent, a soft echo of the emotion in her eyes.

"Wait," Malachi commanded. He stepped from the pickup and walked all the way around it before opening the passenger door. Almost instinctively, he checked the vehicles, both civilian and fleet. Had any of them been at the park? The memory of the murdered girl flashed into his mind, a taunt suspended in his own thoughts. Her ghost would never let him rest until her killer was brought justice. The dark hair, the dark eyes...so like his Pepper. He didn't want to tell Pepper that her stalker had killed her lookalike, and hopefully he wouldn't have to. Hopefully, he and Israel could bring Jensen to justice without Pepper getting any more upsets. Malachi opened the passenger door and offered Pepper his hand.

"Why do the police make you nervous?" he asked, restarting the conversation.

"The last time I really dealt with the police, they were investigating my father's death." Her voice was distant as she refused to look at him, instead staring at the reddish brick building in front of them. She took his hand and braced herself to jump from the truck.

"How did he die?" Malachi asked. His arm slid protectively around her, keeping her close to his side. She shivered once and leaned into his higher body heat. His heart swelled along with the fire in his blood.

"A heart attack."

Malachi frowned. "Why would the police investigate his death?"

"It happened at work. He was a carpenter, and he fell from the rafters of a building when the heart attack hit. They had to investigate, to be sure." She smiled crookedly, sour humor in it. "I've dealt with them briefly since, of course. Living in an RV, that tends to happen. They like to knock on the door a lot, ostensibly to make sure everything is okay but really to tell you to move along." She stared at the low but intimidating brick building. "And then there's filming an attempted kidnapping."

"It was a brave thing to do." His arm tightened, fear stabbing his heart at the thought. "Don't ever do it again."

"What makes you think you get to tell me what I can and can't do?"

"We'll talk about that later." Pepper looked instantly mutinous, both of her eyebrows rose, but Malachi simply pointed to the large digital clock on the front of the bank across the street. "We're running out of time to get your phone. After that, we can talk all night, if you'd like."

Pepper grew quietly thoughtful, her cheeks turning a lovely shade of pink. Malachi maneuvered them across the lot, leaning low.

"I would love to know what you're thinking right now, beauty."

Pepper glanced up at him, waiting another half a breath before smiling a bit. "I was thinking that I *would* like that."

Malachi opened the door to the station, smiling like a fool and not caring. He kept close beside her as they made their way to the heavy desk that dominated the crowded room. He leaned close to her, partly against her side and partly against her back, rubbing her arm soothingly.

The woman behind the desk looked up with the clipped curiosity of practiced competence.

"What can I help you with?"

"I'm Pepper Nyx. I gave my phone to some officers yesterday so they could get some video off of it. I'm here to pick it up."

She presented her license dutifully to the sergeant, who looked at it thoroughly before handing it back. The sergeant had to shift three stacks of papers to unearth her keyboard. Several seconds of typing produced only a frown.

"I'm sorry that you were misinformed, Miss Nyx, but I'm afraid we won't be able to release your phone to you until after the trial ends. I assure you that we are doing everything in our power to arrest this man, and when we do, we'll need that video in order to convict him. I'm sorry."

Chapter Fourteen

Pepper stared at the woman behind the desk, her hand gripping the worn wood.

"The...end of the...trial?" she repeated. It was an effort to blink. "How long will that be?"

"It's impossible to say, at this point." The sergeant's voice was very kind. "An ambitious estimate is six months, and that's if we find the man in the video in the next few days. Realistically, you're probably looking at a year, at least, before we're able to release it to you."

"A *year*?" Pepper's voice cracked on the word. Malachi shifted closer, his arm tightening around her. She wanted to lean into him, and it irritated her. "I need my phone. It's the only communication I have!"

Something choked off her voice. It was too much. She was too tired for this nonsense. Her hand tightened until her knuckles went white. The sergeant looked sympathetic.

"I'm sorry. But I'm afraid your best option is to get another phone."

"With what money?" Desperation made her rude enough to blurt out the words. "If I had that kind of cash, I'd just hire a lawyer to get my own phone back!"

"Ma'am, I understand that you're upset," the sergeant began. Pepper scoffed.

"Damn right that I'm upset!" she snapped.

Malachi's hand tightening on her shoulder was a reminder to watch herself. She took a deep breath to calm herself, and then another. It wasn't working. Biting the tip of her tongue, she shoved off Malachi's arm and stalked out of the building. She didn't even get the satisfaction of the door slamming shut after her; the air stops caught the door and eased it gently to a close.

A sound of utter frustration ripped out of Pepper's throat, somewhere between a growl and a scream. Both fists slammed into the brick exterior of the police station. Her hands burned at the abraded skin and her side tugged painfully. Turning her back to the building she threw herself against it.

Her head hit something soft. Malachi stood beside her, looking exasperated and sympathetic, with his hand between her head and the wall. Pepper tore herself away from him. Malachi followed, catching her hands in his and tugging her against his broad chest. His arms wrapped around her. It wasn't fair. None of it was fair. The weight of the last twenty-four hours crashed down on her and she lashed out at the nearest focus: Malachi. Her fists beat against his chest. His hands rested lightly on her shoulder blades, keeping her close but making no move to stop her. He was so solid, so steady. The little shrieks of frustration started to sound too much like sobs. She threw herself against his arms, but Malachi refused to let go. He lowered onto the uncomfortable bench beside the door, cradling her in his lap.

"It's not so bad as all that." His voice was low in her ear, his warm breath moving across her skin.

"What is wrong with you!" Pepper shouted, slamming her elbow into his chest to push herself away.

126

She might as well have been pushing against a wall. Malachi kept his arms close about her. "My phone is not coming back and there's no way I can buy another one, my car is never going to move again, and I have a psychopath stalking me that you say the police can't do anything about, even if they happened to believe me! How the hell is it 'not so bad as all that'?" She was shaking. Anger warred with despair in a potent mix, and she shoved at Malachi again. "Let go of me!"

"No. Pepper," he said, his voice roughened as it grew hard again. "You aren't alone." Pepper scoffed. His arms tightened. "Your employer will help you as much as she can. I have no doubts about that. And"— Malachi settled his hand on the back of her neck—"you have me."

Pepper laughed, and it wasn't a pleasant sound.

"And you're going to do what? Kiss me until I forget that my life is a disaster?" The instant the words were out of her mouth, Pepper regretted them. Malachi's face was far too close, his deep blue eyes as hot as flame. Once he had her gaze, he refused to let it go. His hand tightened on the back of her neck.

"That," he said in the same low voice, "sounds like an excellent place to start."

He drew her toward him. Pepper felt her anger rising along with her anticipation. Oh, she would kiss him, all right! If he wanted to make her ignore her life by distracting her with sex, she might let him, but she would make him feel her anger, too. Suddenly, he stopped. His hand slid from the back of her neck to her jaw, and his thumb grazed over her lips.

"But only after you've calmed down a bit." He allowed her to back up a little bit, still feathering the

127

pad of his thumb at the corner of her mouth. It was distracting. "You mentioned three distinct problems. Let's break them down. Pick one."

"What?" Pepper tried to get her thoughts back together and catch up.

"Pick one of the problems that is weighing so much on your mind," he repeated.

"My phone."

"What about it?" Malachi sounded like he was coaching her, like he had some experience working through anger.

"I can't get it back!" Upset was starting to creep into her tone again. She inhaled, but it only seemed to increase the pounding in her skull. He massaged her neck gently.

"We'll talk to a lawyer. I'm sure Abby can recommend someone. Many lawyers give a small assessment of their ability to help you before they take on a case and start charging."

"How do you know so much about lawyers?" Pepper eyed him. Malachi's enigmatic smile did nothing to satisfy her curiosity. If anything, it only made it worse.

"Next problem," Malachi prompted.

"My car." The words were almost a groan. "I know nothing about fixing cars. I guess…I guess I try looking up a how-to on replacing spark plugs."

"Excellent idea." Malachi leaned in close to her ear, and she leaned in to meet him. "Or you could ask me."

Pepper glanced at him, and he winked. He was serious. He would fix her car for her, if she asked. Something sweet and beautiful curled low in her belly, rippling outward until it filled her. She let herself lean more against him, fitting her shoulders under his to get more comfortable. And closer.

"Next problem," Malachi said, his voice lower. Pepper exhaled deeply and scrubbed her face with her palms.

"The psychopath."

Malachi's hand against her jaw urged her to turn her head until she was looking at him. His eyes were intense, determination bordering on obsession in their blue depths.

"You will be aware and alert and listen to me." His thumb slid over her lower lip again, sending little shocks all the way through her system. "I *will* protect you and see that justice finds Jensen. I swear it."

Malachi's gaze dropped to her mouth. He held her still as he closed the small gap between them. His mouth worked against hers, taking away the feeling of trembling and giving her his strength. His tongue swept into her mouth, pulling her into a haze of pleasure. He teetered on the edge between coaxing her response and demanding it.

Pepper's capitulation was sudden and complete. One moment she was trying to stay firm, to keep some degree of control over her own body as he poured heat through her. The next instant, she was boneless against him, demanding more of everything he was giving her, everything he was. Her hands slid around his neck to pull herself closer to him, and his hand tightened, curling his fingers into her hair. She *needed*. She needed his strength to lift her, and his amazing heat to burn away the fear of Jensen and the soul-crushing exhaustion that too many years alone had battered into her. Her body was on fire, her mind melting down until nothing existed but Malachi. He abruptly broke the kiss but refused to release her. His forehead resting against hers, he kept her against him.

"Say it."

Pepper struggled to scoop her brain back together after the savage beauty of that kiss. Her thoughts kept swirling back to Malachi, his mouth just a breath away from her, his arms keeping her tight against his chest, his scent surrounding her, filling her, until she felt half crazy. Confusion crashed down on her. Fascinated, she looked into his face. His deep blue eyes swept her under like the ocean's waves. He shifted to take her mouth again, and she moaned. Instantly, she softened into him as every part of her reached for him. Malachi's mouth hovered a breath away from hers, but he refused to close the distance.

"Say that you're going to let me help you," he repeated, his voice a low, sexy sound that sent sparks skipping down her spine. His hand slid from her hair to massage her neck. "You're going to let me help you with your phone, and your car, and you're going to let me protect you without fighting me at every turn."

His hand stroked down her back in an intimate, connecting gesture. Despite the command in his voice, there was a tenderness in his touch that threatened to seduce her from the soul outward. His blue-diamond eyes held an emotion she had never seen before, a depth of worry and concern that she could barely fathom. Her hand rose to touch his cheek. He nuzzled into her touch like a cat, though his gaze never left hers. It would be such a relief to let him take over, to just let him worry about everything for a little while and take care of her.

He was hot as sin, and the way that man kissed—! Every time he touched her, her brain short-circuited and her body took over, demanding long nights tangled up in nothing but each other.

"No!" Pepper almost shouted the word, startling herself and Malachi. She pushed hard against his chest, determined to get off his lap, out of his embrace, away from those entrancing eyes and hypnotic voice. She needed to get some distance from him.

"Pepper." Her name rolled off his lips with perfect rhythm. He made an odd, soothing sound in his throat. "What's frightened you?"

"You have," she answered without thinking. He tensed. Shaking her head, she tried to force her thoughts into a coherent order. "Not you, exactly, and I'm not scared, exactly."

"Then what is it, *exactly*?"

She scowled at the touch of humor beneath the exasperation in his tone. "This. You're like a force of nature. And this chemistry? It's amazing and it's out of control, and it's making me want to do stupid things. Let me go."

"What kinds of stupid things?" His voice was back to that low, intimate sound that seemed to draw her to him with an invisible golden cord and bind her to him, just a little tighter each time. And he didn't let her go.

"Like sitting here in your lap, bawling like a baby, when there's work to be done. Problems to be solved. A cat waiting at home to be fed and cuddled. Let me go, or, so help me, I will scream until every cop in this place storms out here with guns drawn."

Malachi sat still for too long, taking his time considering her demand before finally allowing his arms to drop.

Pepper shot to her feet, immediately retreating against the wall to put something solid at her back while she waited for Malachi's spell over her to fade. Even in open night air, Malachi filled the entire space. He rose from the bench with the grace nature reserved for great predators, and all of it was focused on her.

Prey, she thought suddenly. *I'm his prey, and he's stalking me with every weapon at his disposal, including his wealth and that gorgeous body and sexy voice. Like he's...he's hunting me, driving me into bed with him.*

The thought sent a little thrill through her, leaving her feeling aching and empty in its wake. What was *wrong* with her? She had legitimate problems to solve and all she could think about was the way his shirt slid over his defined chest, and the way his jeans perfectly sculpted his hips and thighs. Apparently, she'd left her self-preservation instinct by the bridge last night, or it had been washed away in the waves.

"Look. Mr. Negrescu," she started again, reaching hard for any kind of distance.

"Malachi," he corrected, his eyebrows twitching with annoyance.

"Mr. Negrescu," she repeated, very firmly. She leveled her chin and met his gaze. "You saved my life last night. There's no doubt about that. And I'm grateful, more so than I can ever express. And..." She had to breathe deeply one more time to clear her mind, though her face flushed hotly. "And you are seriously sexy, and insanely good at kissing, more than any man ever should be."

"Thank you," he said gravely, though she swore

there was laughter in his voice. She ignored it.

"But." Her voice was very firm. "But I really can't accept any of those things from you. I'll come up with something. I'm a big girl, and I'm quite capable of taking care of myself. I've been doing it for a long time now."

Malachi closed the distance between them. One palm lay flat on Pepper's belly, pressing her back into the wall as his other hand cupped her cheek. Pepper's mouth fell open, her breath growing shorter at his nearness. His scent enveloped her, and she inhaled unconsciously.

"That, beauty mine, is precisely why you will let me help you." His thumb feathered over her cheekbone. "You have been taking care of yourself for a long time, longer than you ever should have had to, all by yourself. It's my turn now." His hand slid from her belly to her low back. Cautiously, Pepper allowed him to guide her off the wall. "We'll discuss it over dinner."

"I need to feed Bunsen," Pepper insisted. She tucked her hair behind her ear only to bring it back into her face again. Malachi smoothed her hair back for her, tucking it into the elastic band with large, surprisingly agile fingers.

"Very well," he said with a small smile. "It doesn't do to keep a majesty waiting."

Pepper gave a little scoffing laugh. "Spoken like a man who has been owned by a cat."

"Something like that," he answered vaguely, suppressing a smile. Arm still around her, Malachi shepherded Pepper away from the building. He handed her into the truck and carefully shut the door as Pepper sank wearily into the seat.

Chapter Fifteen

Pepper's scent drifted between anger and worry, but she slowly relaxed as she stared out the window at the autumn darkness. The night was soft and sweet, cradling them in calm, easing Pepper's scent toward weariness.

"You still need to eat," Malachi said, his voice breaking through the stillness. "Your cat won't starve for waiting another hour, two at the most."

"Bunsen first." Pepper was adamant. Malachi frowned. The cat had been her only family. Of course she would focus on his needs first. The way she cooed and purred over the little cousin only proved her maternal instinct, and the thought made Malachi want her more. He inhaled deeply. Even after so short a time, he was starting to gain a baseline for her scent, her heartbeat, her breath rate. He would know if she were in distress and the thought gave him as much pleasure as it did relief. He needed it.

The parking lot was entirely too dark. He glanced at Pepper. She was still staring out the window, looking quiet despite the scent of worry enveloping her. He let her scent guide his shift, just enough to change his eyes from the round pupil of a human to the vertical slit of the great cat. Light flooded his vision. The dismal parking lot turned a muted gray, like the sun struggling to shine through thick clouds. Dropping his speed, he crept through the nearly empty asphalt, ignoring the lines to quarter every visible inch, from indifferent surf to slinking delta to hulking oleander verge.

"Stay here," Malachi ordered. Pepper raised both eyebrows at him. He ignored it and pulled alongside the RV. Kicking open the truck's door, he instantly opened his mouth to taste the evening air.

The scents of sea and river washed through him, garnished with greenery. The smell of asphalt was also heavy, releasing its peculiar acrid scent after a day of rain and sun. Other scents teased at him, but they weren't heavy enough to be more than a hint. He slid from the cab, making no more noise than the warm mist that lifted from the parking lot. Something made his hackles stand on end, even in human form. He took two cautious steps and tasted the air again. Shaking his head, he stepped back toward the truck just as the passenger door opened. Malachi whirled, already tensed to spring over the cab. Pepper casually dropped onto the pavement. The flick of her gaze dismissed him, and she turned her back. He raised his lip. Without bothering to close his door, he rounded the front of the pickup, clearly stalking her.

"I asked you to stay in the truck." He enunciated every word with painful clarity, biting down on each consonant. His shoulders bunched toward his ears, his hands already flexing toward the change that would bring him claws.

Pepper flicked another look over her shoulder, pretending that his obvious displeasure didn't have the slightest effect on her. Her scent said otherwise, but he did his best to shove it out of his mind. He didn't have the luxury of time, at the moment; dealing with her emotions would have to wait.

"No, you didn't." Pepper splashed straight through the puddles, getting wet halfway to her knees. "You ordered me to stay. Like a dog. Since I'm *not* a dog, I decided *not* to listen."

"Pepper." Malachi married warning and exasperation into the single word. Pepper hesitated. Her feet were part way turned around when she jerked herself back on track toward the RV, like she was denying that he had a pull on her.

"Stop," Malachi said in a low, coaxing tone, a sound designed to draw out her cooperation rather than demand her obedience. She slowed, still resisting him. She dug in her pocket for her keys and drew them out like she was moving through molasses. "Is it really so much to give me to just stay in the truck for a few minutes while I look around?"

Pepper gave herself a solid shake and lurched toward the RV door. Malachi managed two steps after her before the scent of violence and lust hit his nose, tangled with illness: Jensen. Fear launched through him. A snarl tore from his throat. Using his full speed, so fast he blurred, he ran after Pepper. Her eyes were still widening and her jaw going slack as he slammed into her, wrapping her tightly against his body.

"Malachi!" Pepper protested. One hand braced on the side of the RV, he kept the other arm tightly around her, an iron band forcing her against his side.

"Quiet." Malachi snapped off the command. His gaze was on the parking lot around them, sharp and careful, as he tucked her head against his shoulder. He swore. Shifting in front of her would put him at risk of treason and her at risk of being imprisoned in the ancestral lands of the Tseng Tse. Jensen wouldn't observe any such niceties, however.

"Malachi, let me go!" Pepper pushed against him, her voice largely swallowed in his shoulder. He cupped her cheeks in both hands, holding her still as his blue gaze burned cold.

"Jensen has been here."

The blood drained out of Pepper's face. She stared into his eyes. Fury and fear filled him in equal measure, though his deep voice remained steady.

"Get back in the truck. Lock the doors, start the engine, and wait for me."

"I can't leave you out here." Her voice was small, but her bright eyes held a protectiveness that went straight to his heart. It had been a very long time since a woman had wanted to protect him, and it warmed him.

"You can, and you will. I'll be fine. Go." He kissed her swiftly on the mouth then drew back to meet her gaze again. Pepper was still for a moment, then nodded once, and Malachi eased his hands from her face. Immediately she ducked around him, half running to the open driver's side door of the pickup. A pleased growl rumbled in his chest. She was brave, but not foolish, and not so proud as to endanger her life. Good. He waited until she had shut the door and he heard the lock click into place. Pepper looked at him again through the windshield, hesitating, though her hand was on the ignition. He kept her gaze, pinning her with the command of it, willing her to take that next step in trusting him.

She didn't look away. She turned the key with a sudden, decisive motion, and the engine roared to life. Malachi grinned, showing his teeth. That was his woman. Pride and heat shone in his eyes, and from the sudden flush in her cheeks, Pepper could see it, even across the distance. He nodded once, then forced himself to turn away. Instinct screamed at him for losing sight of his potential mate when there was a threat in the vicinity, making his shoulders bunch up and his hands flex. He allowed the claws to slide from his fingertips, embracing the sting as his birthright, his calling. Never before had he been so grateful for his heritage, for the gifts that would allow him to protect his woman, for the instincts that guided his power, and for the lifetime of constant, intense training to use them well.

His back to the truck, Malachi's face bulged outward as he shifted toward the tiger's form. He wanted that nose and those ears, as well as those eyes. His barbed tongue scraped across his nose as he wet it to gather more scent. Jensen's stench surrounded the RV. An inaudible growl vibrated in his throat as he leaned against the flimsy side of the trailer. Jensen had touched it…had actually put his hands on the sacred den of Pepper and her cat. The familiar prickling sensation of fur slipping toward the surface of his skin felt like a thousand needles along his spine as he crept toward the back of the vehicle. The stench was more concentrated there, by the back tires. Malachi stooped slightly as something odd flashed in his gray-lit vision. The rear tire had a clean slice a few inches long, half hidden in the tread. He pressed his palm against it and pushed; the rubber gave way easily. His lip curled in a silent snarl. Malachi glanced over his shoulder. Pepper was still in the truck, door locked and ready to make an escape. Only then did he slip around the end of the RV.

Jensen's stench lifted off the roof access ladder, almost like a physical slap. The rungs had been ripped from one of the supports. If Pepper had put her weight on that, not only would she have fallen to the pavement and been seriously injured, but the jagged metal would have torn her badly on the way. His hands flexed. Fur sprouted from his skin as his fingers thickened. The second rear tire was slashed as well. Malachi's growl was a constant threat in the darkness as he stalked along the far side of the RV. He knew what he would find when he reached the front tires: both slashed, completing the threat to his woman.

Jensen was a dead man.

****

Pepper's hands tightened convulsively on the steering wheel of the big pickup as Malachi turned the corner of the RV. She hadn't realized how much his presence was keeping her fear in check until he stepped out of sight. She couldn't even comfort herself in denial, that this wasn't happening, or ask the universe why it was happening to her. She knew. If she could go back, she would still record Jensen attacking that woman in the parking lot. She just wouldn't draw attention to herself in the process.

The roar of the truck was comforting. At least if the crazy man jumped out of the bushes at her, she could run him down. She checked the gas gauge: almost a full tank. She had Malachi's keys. Her driver's license was in her pocket. She *could* just go. People abandoned jobs all the time, especially ones like a barista. There were other towns where she could hunker down for a mild winter, even milder than in California. Like Arizona. Wasn't that where everyone went to avoid a harsh winter? She had a little bit of money set aside, enough to keep the gas tank filled for a bit. She could sleep in the truck and get a job as a waitress so she could eat at work, and there was always somewhere to snag a shower, even if it was in a gym. She could just start driving, leaving Jensen and this terror behind her.

Malachi. Unbidden, her mind whispered his name. The thought of leaving Malachi was a punch in the chest, and it hit her hard enough to make her wince. The stitching on the wheel cover dug into her palms as her heart raced, until she could feel an answering throb in her hands. Her mind rebelled against it. She'd only just met the man. It wasn't healthy to be so attached to him already, and she knew that if she stayed around, it would only get worse. He was too...everything. Too gorgeous, too intense, too caring, too bossy, too many things that didn't quite fit. It would be better to force herself to leave him while she still had a chance of doing so. A nice, normal little town somewhere, with nice, normal friends, where she could meet a nice, normal guy, one whose very presence didn't terrify her cat...

Pepper's heart clenched, slamming the taste of fear into her mouth. Grabbing hard on the handle, she kicked the door open and jumped from the truck. She was running by the time her feet hit the asphalt. Her keys dropped from her shaking hands twice on the way to the door. She fumbled for the latch in the dark lot, but the door swung under her hands, already open. Sick fear churned in her belly as she cautiously eased it open.

"Bunsen?" Pepper could barely convince her voice to squeak out the name. "Come on, Bun-bun, where are you?"

Trembling fingers searched for the light switch. She managed to flick it on, but no lights answered. Neither did Bunsen. Pepper crept up the rickety step and her voice was tight when she called again for her little black and white cat.

"Bunsen! I'm home, baby. The scary man is outside. You can come out."

Her foot nudged against something. Relief flooded her. Bunsen must have come out of hiding and was rubbing her for comfort. Relieved, she bent to scoop him up, needing the reassurance of his soft, warm fur. Dull, glassy eyes stared back at her, barely visible in the darkness. The ears were gone, and the tiny, bloody teeth showed in a death grimace of terror, but it was unmistakably Bunsen's decapitated head. Pepper stumbled backward, dropping the blood-matted head. Bunsen's ears tumbled off the counter beside the door to land grotesquely across his mutilated face. The oven door banged open, and Pepper screamed as something swung from the handle. The body of a small cat hung by its tail, the black and white fur stained with blood. Pepper pressed her hand over her mouth, as the grotesque scene in front of her filled all her vision.

Chapter Sixteen

Pepper screamed. The sound made Malachi's gut clench with fear. He leaped to the roof of the RV then to the ground on the other side, turning in midair to land facing the door. His claws were fully extended, ghostly white and deadly in the darkness. His jaws reshaped as his teeth grew, strengthened, sharpened to the weapons of an apex predator. The shadow of his stripes showed on his skin as he yanked Pepper out of the doorway so he could step into the darkness of the RV. The scent of blood hit him part way there. It took half a second for the tiger's brain to sort out that it was animal blood, not human blood. Not the blood of his potential mate. That thought held his shift in check, though only barely. His cat-slit eyes lit the interior of the RV, and he could easily see the tiny, furry body hanging from the oven door. The growl rumbled from his chest, vibrating the floor beneath him. Behind him, he heard Pepper, the little creak of the floor as she crawled back to the doorway. Her hands trembled over the mutilated head of her beloved pet as terrible sobs racked her body. Her face was so pale it nearly glowed, the tears bright drops streaming down her cheeks. Her one living link to her past lay brutally destroyed before her eyes. The scent of her anguish and grief swamped him, making his stomach roll in protest. Instinct rose up, sharp and terrible, an undeniable demand that he care for this woman in her unutterable distress. His fury would have to wait its turn. The dark smudges of his stripes receded from the surface of his skin, disappearing entirely within a heartbeat. His teeth and claws retracted just as quickly, and he was fully in human form to turn to his potential mate. Kneeling beside her, so close that her hair brushed his face, he slipped his hand under hers as his arm encircled her shoulders. A soft chuff rolled out of his throat as he rubbed his jaw against the top of her head.

"Come." His voice was very gentle, barely audible, as he slowly stood. His grip was as gentle as his voice as he drew her to her feet beside him. Pepper shook so violently that Malachi was afraid she would be sick, or simply be unable to stand. He angled his body to place his broad shoulders between her and the terrible scene inside her home. He cupped her head to his shoulder, silently encouraging her to lean on him as he took more of her weight, just in case her knees did give out. Pepper's tears soaked his shoulder. With great care, he moved forward, half carrying and half guiding her down the single, rusty step and through the night to the truck. She stumbled blindly along beside him. One-handed, he tugged open the passenger door and lifted her in. Immediately she bent over her lap, face buried in her arms. Malachi stroked his fingers through her hair, seeking only to comfort her, and leaned in to kiss the side of her head.

"Wait here," he said. She didn't acknowledge him. He closed the door, checking his great strength so he didn't slam it. Lifting his face, he inhaled. The sea air filled his lungs, momentarily lessening the obsession of instinct from his mind. His woman was safe, for the moment. The human part of his mind knew that, but the tiger's instincts snarled at him to take her away from that place, immediately. To find her a safe den, clean from the stench of blood. Somewhere that he could guard her properly, where she could rest comfortably and he could ease her great distress.

It took a lifetime of discipline to force himself to walk away from the truck. His instincts roared to the point of pain, and it made him pause for the briefest moment. He wasn't abandoning her. This was simply another part of caring for her. Pepper's entire life was in the RV, and she couldn't afford to lose any of it. He could replace most any items that might be taken, but she'd already lost too much that he could never replace. But he could protect what was left.

Malachi reached for the door. Rough ridges under his fingertips caught his attention: gouges in the thin metal. The beast began to move inside of his mind again, trying to push its way through his skin. He pushed back. Claw marks should not be a surprise. Jensen's scent was heavy in the area, and who else would make such a cruel and vicious threat? Malachi bent to examine the lock. The bolt was bent, as was the plate that should have held it in place, and the door itself was bent. It would have taken a great deal of force to tear the door open, but an easy enough feat for a male Tseng Tse in his prime. Malachi allowed himself the release of a loud growl as he forced the door into place. With one powerful stomp, he broke the step away from its moorings. He braced his foot on one side of the divided step and, gripping the other side, kicked again to tear the thin straps that connected the two halves. He threaded the piece of metal through the door handle and the balance rail beside it. He braced his feet and pushed the two ends toward the middle. The two-inch-wide strip of metal bent, wrapping around the handle and the rail with a groan. Only another Tseng Tse or a very dedicated human with the right equipment would be able to break that open. Pepper's possessions would be safe until he could come back for them. And for Bunsen's body. There was no doubt in his mind that the tiny cousin had attempted to defend the den. The cat deserved the honor of a pyre, and Pepper needed closure to mourn her companion. He would return after he saw his potential mate safely settled, calmed, and comforted.

****

The night closed in around them as Malachi drove. He wanted to put a few miles, at least, between them and the brutal scene at the RV, and he wanted to give Pepper a chance to weep as needed without worrying about anyone else seeing her. The worst of the sobs had spun themselves out before he pulled into the parking lot of a pretty little bed and breakfast on the far side of the small city. The kind glow of a porchlight filtered through a climbing plant and cast a gentle light on Pepper's face. She was pale, and tears tracked down her cheeks now and then, but she was still and silent. Palms pressed together between her knees, she hunkered in the passenger seat, staring into the darkness beyond the windshield. Her only movement was a gentle rocking, back and forth, and he didn't think she was even aware of doing it.

Malachi left the engine running as he stepped from the truck. He considered leaving the door open in case he needed to get to her in a hurry but decided against it.

The air was growing decidedly cool, and he would be able to get to her quickly whether the door was open or not. He made it onto the porch before his instincts dragged at him, slowing his steps away from his potential mate. He stretched his neck as his shoulders bunched up, but he forced them down again. He had been dealing with the tiger's mind since he was a cub, controlling it from adolescence, like all of his kind. He would not give in to the animal's nature now.

He pushed open the door. The man behind the counter was a thin, grandfatherly person, who gave the impression of perpetual generosity and habitual motion.

"I'm glad you caught me in, young man! I was just about to lock the desk for the night," he said warmly. "My inside rooms are all taken, but I've one or two of the bungalows still available. The views are magnificent."

"Thank you, uncle," Malachi said with respect due the man's age, as well as with gratitude. The man seemed startled by the familiar term, but not upset. He laughed quietly, his wrinkled face turning somewhat pink.

"We like to think we run a homey place here, but that's the first time a complete stranger has called me uncle."

Malachi smiled. "Forgive me. I'm afraid I'm losing my American manners in my weariness. I'd like to take one of the bungalows, please."

"With a garden view or an ocean view?"

"Ocean," Malachi answered. It would be easier to defend, and Pepper might find it comforting.

"That one sleeps two, one king-sized bed.

Microfridge unit, bistro seating, garden tub. Lovely little place for two." The older gentleman didn't so much as glance at Malachi as he typed into the computer to one side of the desk, but Malachi couldn't help smiling at his subtle dig for information.

"There will be two adults," he confirmed. "I'll take it for the week, with the possibility to extend, please."

The gray eyebrows rose with mild surprise but lowered again as Malachi pulled out his wallet. He would pay in cash, up front, but that would only raise suspicions. He gave a brief sigh and glanced out the door toward the truck. This was taking too long. He needed to get back to his woman. He handed over a credit card, instead.

"Here you go, young man," the owner said, handing over a large envelope as he returned the credit card. "There are two keys to the door in here, along with the menu for tomorrow, mealtimes, local attractions, and our contact information. Just a moment while I get a flashlight."

The uncle disappeared down a hallway toward the back of the house and Malachi took the opportunity to open the door. Pepper still sat in the passenger seat of the truck, her head back against the headrest. She was so still for so long that he scowled. She scrubbed her face with the inside of one wrist, dragging it over her hair before letting her arm fall again. Even from here, he could see her exhaustion. He wanted to scoop her up and cradle her close, shield her from all harm, discomfort, and upset. It wasn't possible, and he knew it. Asking her to accept him meant accepting his life, and his life was one of danger and brutality. But never for her. Even without the mate-bond, he could not allow harm to come to her, especially not from himself.

With a sigh, Malachi turned back to the desk, running his hands over it. Idly, he picked up a brochure and began looking through it.

"I'm sorry that took so long," the owner said as he hurried back up the hallway. "The darn thing needed new batteries and I had the hardest time finding them."

"Please don't think on it, uncle," Malachi said with a smile. He placed the brochure back on the desk. "Can I still order some of these extras for the room, or is it too late?"

"No, no, you can add them, but some of them won't be available until tomorrow."

"The meat and cheese tray?"

The older man smiled. "You'd be in luck on that. We had a couple order that one earlier and then they had to cancel their reservation. I've got the makings in the kitchen. It wouldn't take me long, if you want it."

"If you would, please. Thank you." Malachi made a mental note to increase the tip to help compensate the older gentleman for the work so late in the evening.

"Just as soon as I get back. Are you ready?"

Malachi gestured for the older gentleman to precede him from the building. The older man laughed silently, shaking his head, but stepped through the door. Malachi went directly to the truck. Pepper's eyes were still haunted, drawing his heart out to her all over again. He opened the truck door and reached inside to offer his hand. She didn't hesitate. Her fingers were cold, though the night was only slightly cool, and he placed her hand on his chest as she popped her seatbelt open. His other hand found her hip to steady her as she stepped off the running board. Malachi tucked her under his shoulder, his arm around her for warmth, for protection, and in a mark of possession. She softened against him, making everything in him tighten.

The older gentleman smiled pleasantly, waiting patiently before continuing on the short walk to the bungalow. Crickets chirped in counterpoint to the waves rolling in nearby, out of sight in the darkness. Malachi refused to let his guard down. His head swiveled constantly, searching by sight, sound, and scent for the slightest trace of Jensen. The scent of the shoreline teased at him. Snakeroot, celosia, and sneezeweed lined the walkways from the main house to the buildings surrounding it, converted outbuildings of a fine old homestead from decades long gone. Sweet alyssum and woolly thyme peeped among the paving stones, adding their fragrances to the myriad around him. A wave of homesickness washed over him, and he tugged Pepper closer to his side.

The landlord slid the key into the lock and started to turn it. Malachi covered the distance in two large strides and covered the older man's hand with his.

"Forgive me, uncle," he said with an apologetic smile. "Allow me."

The older man looked from Malachi's set face to Pepper's pallor and stepped back.

"I'll go get started on that tray," he said simply, and began retracing his steps to the main house. Malachi waited until he was several feet away before he turned the key, positioning himself so he blocked the doorway completely. The door swung open without a sound. Scents of wood and cotton, cleansers and hints of human scents rushed out at him. Only a couple were really recent, and they were unfamiliar, probably belonging to the cleaning crew. Taking Pepper's hand, he drew her just inside the doorway. He flicked on the lights. If Jensen were hiding in the dark, it would blind his shifted night-vision and give Malachi the advantage as he cleared the rooms.

Empty. He turned the water on hot in the large garden tub before he left the bathroom. Pepper had closed the door and removed her shoes. Curled in one of the chairs beside the window, she wept silently as she stared through the glass at the rushing sea. She looked so small and vulnerable, the sight made Malachi's stomach knot.

"I've started a bath for you." He softened his voice to keep from shattering the fragile stillness in the room. Pepper looked up at him slowly, tearstains on her face. Tenderness filled his voice so that he hardly recognized it. "Wash and get warm, Pepper mine. It will help you feel better."

The possessive made Pepper go still. Excitement, pleasure, and uncertainty crashed through the grief in her scent. One foot slid to the floor.

"I can't afford this," she murmured, and he wasn't sure she meant the bungalow.

"I can," Malachi assured her. She shook her head and the other foot found the floor.

"*I* can't." She pushed herself to her feet. She wavered. Malachi was suddenly beside her, his arms around her, supporting her against his own body. She turned her head viciously, away from Malachi.

"You're dangerous." She made it a statement. Malachi was very still but he didn't release her.

"No." The single word was leaden. "I'm deadly."

****

150

Pepper's heart jumped into her throat, only to slam back down into the pit of her stomach. She'd known it. On some level, she had known that Malachi was worse than dangerous. She just hadn't wanted to face it.

A knock sounded on the door. Malachi's arms tightened. Pepper felt the sudden tension thrumming through him, physical proof of a lethal connection to the world around him. He eased her out of his embrace, as if setting aside something precious and fragile to keep it from getting smashed. His hand cupped her cheek, but his gaze was on the door. Pepper wrapped her arms around herself against the sudden chill of his absence.

Malachi stood at the door, his head canted near the wood. He cracked the door, just an inch, and then the tension dropped out of his broad shoulders. He opened it fully, smiling at the landlord, who stood framed by the darkness of the night. In his hands was a large tray with artfully arranged sliced meats, cheeses, and crackers. On his arm hung a paper shopping bag, the raffia handles tied with a green and white ribbon.

"Thank you," Malachi said, sounding grave with the depth of his gratitude, and he took the tray from the older man's hands.

"Of course. There are bottles of water in the fridge. If you need more, or anything else, just call the night contact number." The landlord offered Malachi the bag, as well. "On the house. The young lady looks as if she could use it."

Pepper blinked. Any self-consciousness she may have felt at the landlord noticing her strain was swallowed up in the genuine kindness in his face. She stepped forward to take the bag with an awkward little smile.

"Thank you," she managed to eke out. The landlord smiled more warmly.

"You're welcome. Good night."

"One moment." Malachi easily balanced the tray on one large hand long enough to slide it onto the small bistro table. He took a billfold from his pocket and Pepper did her best not to stare as he pulled out several bills for the landlord, some of them big ones. The older gentleman balked at the amount, as well, shaking his head.

"Please," Malachi said in that low, coaxing tone she knew so well. "It's late, and you've worked hard for our comfort. Allow me to compensate you for your trouble."

"It's my pleasure," the man said firmly. Malachi's eyes shone with amusement as he folded the bills in half and pressed them toward the gentleman again.

"Then allow me to fund the next such generous gesture that your kind heart sees fit to make."

The landlord met his gaze for a moment, then an echoing light lit in his eyes. He accepted the cash.

"All right, then, since you put it that way. Thank you. If you need anything, don't hesitate to call. Good night."

Malachi shut the door. After a brief hesitation, he turned the locks.

"What's in the bag, beauty?" he asked as he turned back toward her. Pepper had forgotten to look. She tugged the ribbons until the bag opened, and almost smiled. Her throat felt tight all over again.

"Bath bombs and electric candles."

Malachi smiled. "Our host is a wise man. Come."

One hand reached for the bag, and the other to smooth her hair. Pepper hesitated; his hand shifted from her hair to the back of her neck. "The bath will overflow if you wait too long."

Pepper shook her head, the movement pure denial. Malachi placed his hands on her arms.

"A hot bath, then water and food, and then sleep. Everything else will wait until tomorrow."

"I told you, Malachi, I can't stay here." She pushed the bag into his chest, pushing against him at the same time.

"You cannot stay at the RV." His tone became grim. "It wouldn't be safe, not even with me staying with you."

"Just what do you think is going to happen tonight?" Pepper challenged, her head tossed back as she eyed him. Her gaze flicked to the one bed in the room and Malachi snorted.

"I think you are going to soak in a hot bath, we're both going to get some food, and you are going to sleep while I keep watch for Jensen."

"That's it?" Malachi couldn't tell if her tone was more wary or disappointed, and her scent didn't give him any clues. He took another deep breath, both of her scent and to calm his suddenly racing imagination. His hands slid to her shoulders, gently angling her against him. His blue eyes were compassionate, but intense.

"I would very much like to kiss you again," he said, his voice low and throaty. His gaze lowered to her mouth for a moment before returning to hers. "I would very much like to hold you as you sleep. But I will not take advantage of your grief, beauty. Even if you did ask me to touch you tonight, I would refuse." Malachi caught his breath at the sudden hurt in her eyes, unprepared for the answering pain in his own chest. His hands cupped her cheeks to bring her gaze to his and hold it there. She had to see the truth of his words. "I am not rejecting you, Pepper. By all the ancestors, there is nothing I want more than you. But not like that, beauty mine. It would break my heart to have your tears on my shoulder after loving you. It would be both honor and pleasure to have the privilege of holding you while you cry, to see you through your grief, but not after sharing your body."

Pepper looked at him steadily for a long moment. The only sounds were the waves and the crickets, and the pounding of her heart. Grief, gratitude, and need shone in her eyes as she softened into him, as if melting. She leaned forward, coming up on her toes as her lips hesitantly sought his.

She needn't have hesitated. Malachi's mouth was warm and firm, eager and caring as he returned the kiss. His thumbs stroked gentle caresses over her cheekbones as he held her face close to his. Arousal suddenly threaded through her scent, and a soft sound came from her throat. Her hands slid around his neck as she fitted her body against his. Malachi groaned, the sound mixed with a growl. His hands sculpted her curves as they slid down her back to rest on her hips. Gentle pressure shifted her away from him, until he could no longer feel the tempting heat of soft curves against him. Malachi rested his forehead against hers as he breathed deeply, in and out through his mouth.

"No." His voice was so quiet, even he wasn't certain if he were speaking to her or to himself. His accent was noticeably heavier. "There will be time. You have need of food, and rest, and comfort. There will be time."

Malachi peeled himself away from Pepper with effort, his body screaming with demands for its mate. It was a little easier to breathe when he wasn't quite so close to her, but her scent saturated the room, calling to him constantly. His instincts stirred, the need to care for her rising in his mind. He fell back on what he had known all of his life: bathe, feed, sleep. It was no cure for distress, but it gave one strength to meet the source, and, in this case, it would give him a little bit of time to get himself under control.

The sound of the bathwater in the next room changed. Malachi hurried to turn it off before it overflowed, taking the bag from the landlord with him. He arranged the candles around the room, some on the edge of the tub, some on the counter near the sink, and a few on the floor. He used one sharp eyetooth to tear the cellophane on a sweet-scented bath bomb and dropped it into the steaming water. Immediately the steam filling the room sweetened with a fresh, floral scent. Already his mind was twining the scent with that of his potential mate. Leaning his head against the wall, he closed his eyes and simply breathed.

Pepper smelled too good. Her scent was a drug, making him crazy with the need for it. It both settled and aroused him. He had been warned—all younglings were—that when he met a potential mate the scent would hit him hard. Malachi had underestimated just what that would mean. The tiger's instincts were suddenly riding him, loud and hard. Even his shift was more difficult to control. He hadn't accidentally slipped fur since he was a youngling, but now his stripes were constantly near the surface. Especially when Pepper was nearby. And when he kissed her...When he kissed her, the changes in her scent and the heat of his own blood made keeping his human form an effort.

His phone rang, echoing on the table in the other room. Malachi roused himself from his thoughts and pulled open the door. His gaze sought Pepper. She had curled up in the chair by the window again. Her face was still pale, but she looked at him as he entered, and looked at his phone, too, reaching to hand it to him. At least she was reacting to the world around her. He took his phone and then her hand, his thumb brushing caresses over her soft skin.

"The bath is ready," he said softly. Gentle pressure on her hand encouraged her to rise. She flashed him a little smile and tucked her hair behind her ear. His fingers longed to follow into those silken strands. He forced his hand to stay on hers. His phone ringing again helped. Malachi canted his head toward the open bathroom door and watched Pepper shamelessly as she slipped to the other side of the door, closing it behind her. Only then did he drop his gaze to his phone and thumb open the touchscreen.

Chapter Seventeen

Malachi stepped away from the bathroom door as he lifted the phone to his ear. He didn't really want Pepper to overhear his conversation. For that matter, he wasn't very happy about it interrupting them at all.

"This had better be good," Malachi said as the bathroom door closed.

"That had better mean I am interrupting something." Israel's voice over the line made Malachi smile as much as the words did, but it was brief.

"Not the time." Briefly, Malachi filled his older brother in on the death of Bunsen and the vandalism of Pepper's RV.

"Jensen destroyed the lock. I had to bend part of the step around the handle and the balance bar next to it to keep the door closed. And the little cousin…" His voice trailed into a soft growl of anger. "He is trying to destroy her, Is. He is systematically chipping away at everything that gives her life meaning."

Israel didn't make a sound. His control was too good, unaffected by the presence of any potential mate. But Malachi knew his brother well enough to hear the lethal coldness in the older tiger's voice.

"I have finished my hunt. I am on my way to the airport."

Malachi exhaled a breath he hadn't even known that he was holding and leaned his hand on the back of the chair. Pepper's scent drifted up from the cushion. He inhaled it, as if holding her scent inside of his lungs could keep her safe.

"Thank you." Malachi's deep voice was low with the strength of his gratitude. "Your timing couldn't be better." His hand tightened on the chair as he struggled to keep his calm. "He's escalated."

"Malachi." The sound of his name was a warning.

"He killed a human. I tracked him to a murder scene. Fresh scent was everywhere. He raped that woman, he killed her, and he enjoyed it. Israel, he's too far gone, even for an aberration. I have no choice."

He would have to come back to Pepper with blood on his hands. The thought hurt, a deep ache blossoming in his chest. She deserved better than that.

"*We* have no choice," Israel corrected. "Do not forget who pronounces sentence." There was a bang on the other end of the line, like a door slamming. "I will be there in a few hours. Your priority is to keep your woman safe. Is that clear?"

Malachi nodded deeply, nearly bowing, simply out of habit. "Yes, Prince."

"Give me your location. I will come to you. Stay in the den, fortify it as best you can, and wait for me."

Malachi gave Israel the address of the bed and breakfast and hung up, sinking into the seat and resting his head in his hands.

****

The steam in the bathroom felt amazing. Pepper inhaled deeply and her shoulders dropped two inches as tension released. Whatever Malachi had put into the bath filled the room, along with the steam. She walked toward the mirror and lifted her hand to wipe down the condensation, then let her hand drop. She didn't want to see. No amount of softening steam or gentle candlelight could make her look good right now. More importantly, she didn't care. Kicking out of her shoes, she peeled off her socks and dropped them in a heap. The rest of her clothing quickly followed. She only shivered once as she climbed the two steps up in order to get into the deep tub and the blessedly hot water. It closed around her comfortingly as she sank into it.

Sharp pain stabbed through her side. Pepper sucked air between her teeth and bit back a grunt of pain as the steaming water washed over the wounds in her side. Tears stung her eyes as her throat closed all over again. The gouges were still there, still hurting, and still unexplained. There was too much about Malachi that was unexplained. He had money, that was undeniable. He wore power like a second skin. He was clearly used to getting his way from everyone, even treating the police like he could order them around. But. She didn't even know where he came from, or what he did for a living. He had a history with this Jensen somehow and was unwilling to involve the police. That made it even more likely that he was involved in something illegal. And obviously violent.

The bathroom door vibrated from the force of the knock. Pepper sat suddenly upright, wincing from the movement. Before she could say anything, the door cracked open.

"Pepper?" Malachi's voice issued through the small opening. He pushed the door open farther without waiting for an invitation. His deep blue eyes glinted in the low lights as he stepped into the room. Every movement flowed like a breeze, like well-sculpted poetry as he crossed the room. His hair brushed over the collar of his shirt to slide over his shoulders, droplets of water clinging to the dark strands, stars on a dark sky. The steam melded his clothing against his body. It moved with him, outlining his hard, muscular shape. Heat washed through her that had nothing to do with the bath. Pepper was suddenly intensely aware of herself as a woman and Malachi as a man as he crossed the floor. She sank down deeper in the water as he sat on the side of the tub.

"Pepper, beauty, you're in pain," he said in that low, sexy voice that always seemed to sink inside her skin. "I'm sorry. I've neglected the wounds in your side. Come. Let me see."

"They're fine," Pepper said hurriedly. "It's just the heat of the water. It stings a little, that's all."

Malachi's gaze settled on hers with such intensity that it was a physical weight, pressing against her chest. His voice was even quieter.

"I need to check your wounds."

Pepper wet her lips. Her entire mouth suddenly felt dry. She couldn't look away. Something in his face and voice was compelling. Carefully covering her breasts with one arm, she propped the other on the tub edge for leverage. Water sloshed as she struggled to lift herself above the surface, grumbling at the pain that shot through her. Malachi slipped his hands under her arms and lifted her to sit on the edge of the tub. Sparks danced from every point where his skin met hers, until Pepper thought she might melt down from the heat. She crossed her other arm over her chest as Malachi slid down a step. His face hovered so close to her that she could feel his breath across her skin. She shivered and tried to pass it off as goosebumps. His large hand slid down her back, absently, but lighting fire in its wake. His other hand splayed over her ribs, gently turning her into the low lights.

"Well?" Pepper tried to sound impatient. His hands—always warm—were scorching her through to her soul.

One fingertip brushed the deep end of the gouges, near her hip. A small, worried sound came from Malachi. Bending even closer, he sniffed. Pepper frowned.

"What are you doing?" This time, it came out as an actual demand.

"The entry points aren't clean. They won't heal right." He straightened. It was a little consolation to Pepper to see that his face was faintly flushed, too. She hoped it wasn't just from the heat of the bathroom.

"I have some healing salve in my bags. I'll treat the marks and bandage them again before you sleep." Malachi sat on the top step, one hand still on her ribs and the other smoothing back her hair. It had already started to gather in damp curls against her skin, but he didn't seem to mind. Pepper found herself leaning into that touch. Her eyelids fluttered briefly as something loosened in her chest, some door that had been shut tight since her father's death. Some place where she kept human connection. Swallowing, she forced her eyes to open again. Malachi was staring at her, hunger and reproach in his very blue eyes. She frowned. So did Malachi.

"What's wrong?"

"I was just about to ask you the same question." Defensiveness colored her tone, covering the wound in her heart. She shifted away, trying to get back into the water. "You don't have to do any of this, you know. You don't owe me anything. And I told you already, I don't want to owe you anything."

"Pepper." There was reproach in his voice. He almost sounded wounded, as well as confused. "What is this?"

"Just now." Pepper turned her face toward the wall. "The way you were looking at me. I didn't do anything wrong."

"Of course not." Malachi took her chin in his palm and turned her face back toward him. His thumb stroked over her chin, the tip wandering up far enough to brush her lower lip. "You were very brave. Jensen is a...a tragic aberration. He would have targeted you as soon as he saw you. I'm not angry with you, beauty. I'm angry with myself, for not getting here sooner, for not stopping Jensen before he ever got to you, for not taking proper care of your wounds and your safety. If I had..."

He shook his head. Pain was etched in his handsome features. Pepper covered his hand with hers. The tears that had been lingering near the surface finally spilled down her cheeks.

"Bunsen—" Her throat closed on the word, making her choke. She coughed to clear her throat and tried again. "Bunsen's death is not your fault."

Malachi's eyes lit with hunger again, with a heat that outstripped even her desire. His gaze dropped to her mouth as his thumb plied her lower lip. Pepper found herself leaning toward him. Her hand slid up his arm, reveling in the heat of his skin and the hard muscle underneath. Her lips sought his. Malachi's mouth descended on hers. The kiss started out gentle, filled with reassurance and care. It didn't stay that way. At the first taste of him, Pepper shifted to get closer to him. She forgot her fears. She forgot her grief. She even forgot her nudity, wanting—*needing*—only to be closer to him.

Malachi's hands slid over her skin, leaving her sensitized and heated in their wake. The change in her body was heady. Heat pooled in intimate places. Blood sang in her ears, surging through her body as Malachi seemed to feast on her. Both hands gripped her hips to pull her against him and one hand fell on the gouges on her side. She shifted closer to him, reveling in the feel of his solid body against her softer one.

Malachi calmed the kiss and, gently, ended it. Pepper's breathing was ragged. Her hand worked against the muscles of his arm, mindless with a desire that was rapidly mounting to desperate.

"You don't have to stop," she managed to gasp out.

"Yes. I do." Malachi groaned the words. "Your grief doesn't allow you to be clear-minded, and you must be absolutely certain I am who you want."

"Of course I'm certain." Pepper clutched at him, trying to drag him against her again, but Malachi kept her in place. One hand cradled her wounds, the tenderness of the gesture striking her right in the heart.

"Are you?" His voice was heavy, weariness warring with sadness for the most prominent emotion. "Even with all the questions I haven't answered?"

"I don't care about that, not right now."

"You will. When the hunger is sated and the heat has burned out of your blood. When you're lying with me in the quiet of dawn, tangled up skin-to-skin, all of

 L. Dawn Jackson

those questions will return to your mind, and you will doubt. You will regret what we have done. I will look into your stunning eyes and I will know it, and it will tear out my heart. No, beauty mine." Malachi exhaled deeply, as if the sound came from the very depths of his soul. "No. You must be certain."

Malachi turned to place one knee on the step. She clung to him as he lowered her back into the water, staring at him. He had actually said no. His hands slid over her skin, sculpting every curve on his way to smooth her hair and making her want to scream with frustration. He leaned to kiss her forehead, his lips lingering.

"Rest, Pepper mine." His voice was rough with some emotion, but so low that it was a part of the steam and the electric candlelight. She could feel the reluctance in his hands as he pulled away from her. He backed across the room, as if he couldn't bear not to see her, not to have that connection with her. She heard the lock click as the door closed behind him.

Pepper sank deeper into the water as she exhaled. Her head dropped back, eyes closed, as tension dropped out of her.

"Well, that sucked," she said to the ceiling.

Her pride was stinging. That was all. And, really, it was for the best that Malachi had told her to wait. She'd only known him for a couple of days. So what if he was too gorgeous to be real? He *was* real, and he was in the next room, waiting for her to be finished in the bath he insisted she take, so he could bandage her side, a side that was wounded by a man from whom he had saved her. He hadn't drawn a bath for her because he wanted her naked. He had done it for *her*. It had been a long

164

time since anyone had cared for her, and no one had cared for her like this before. Malachi acted like his world rotated around her. It was intense. There were times it made her want to run, because it wasn't comfortable. But she wasn't sure it was *bad*.

She wasn't sure if he was bad. He was dangerous. That was obvious from the moment she met him. That didn't make him *bad*. Malachi was determined to protect her, even obsessed with it. And it made him incredibly bossy. She smiled to herself. Beneath the surface of the water, her fingers slid over her hips, retracing the path his hands had taken. Despite the heat of the bath, she could still feel him. Like a brand. Like everywhere he had ever touched her was eternally imprinted on her skin and on her soul. Even deep in her secret heart, he had left his fingerprints.

But Malachi had secrets. Pepper's fingertips hovered over the gashes in her side. He knew exactly what had happened under the bridge that night. He knew why the police hadn't been able to catch Jensen, and he knew, beyond a doubt, that he could. He knew what she was feeling when he shouldn't. He heard things he shouldn't have been able to hear. He was unbelievably sexy, but he was so closed off. Could she live with that? He had said something about having a serious relationship with her—

Wife. Not just a serious relationship with her, but a marriage. His wife. Pepper's heart thudded hard enough her side throbbed in sympathy. Wincing, she shifted, trying to ease it. She could get out of the tub early. Let him bandage the wounds. It would get his hands on her naked body, and from there…A woman could hope, right?

Pepper lifted up enough to sit on the side of the tub. The door rattled with a knock. She'd just opened her mouth when it opened. Again. She frowned.

"You really have to learn to wait for an invitation before opening a closed door," she said with some exasperation. Malachi stepped into the room and closed the door behind him, but not before a gust of chill air hit her bare skin. Pepper curled in on herself. Malachi grabbed a towel from the stack near the door, shaking it open as he crossed to her.

Pepper's breath caught in her throat. The electric candlelight spread over him like liquid gold, highlighting every contour of his powerful frame. The light shone against the depths of his thick hair and tangled in his eyes, making them appear to glow gold and blue. He never looked away from her. Pepper found herself acutely aware of the way the bath water slid over her skin, and the way his hungry gaze traced every movement. She shifted toward the edge of the tub, though she wasn't sure if it was to get back into the water, or to stand to greet him.

"I heard you get out of the water. I don't want you slipping on the steps." Malachi wrapped the towel around her, rubbing briskly to warm it against her skin.

"How? You were on the other side of the door."

"I was listening." His indigo eyes met hers with such naked desire and affection that Pepper was fascinated. "I'm always listening for you, Pepper. Come," he said. His hands cupped her elbows to help her rise and steady her on the steps. She could feel the strength in his hands. He didn't watch her feet, but her eyes. Still, he knew when her wet foot wasn't quite solid on the wooden stair, and easily kept her upright.

He still walked her across the floor, until her bare feet were safely on the woven rug beside the bed. One hand swept through her hair, damp with steam, as the other urged her gently to sit on the bed. He felt enormous, staring down at her, tall and broad and powerfully strong. Muscle rippled against the fabric of his T-shirt, even with so simple a movement as rearranging the towel around her.

"I'm sorry, beauty, I didn't think to grab any of your things before taking you away from there. Our host has brought toiletries. I hope you won't much mind sleeping in one of my shirts."

Pepper bit her lip, hoping to hide her reaction. She liked the idea of wearing his shirt, sleeping in it, having his warmth and scent wrapped around her all night. She liked the idea rather too much. Her gaze traveled over his body as she dragged it back up to his face. The breath was almost knocked from her lungs at the emotions written on his face. Caring, desire, pleasure, and affection all draped themselves unashamedly over the carved lines of his face. Pepper swallowed, wetting her lips as she stalled for the time to find her voice.

"No, that's…that's fine."

Malachi smiled, and her body clenched. She almost blurted out that he was beautiful but stopped herself just in time. His large hand stroked over her hair again, gently laying it behind her shoulder.

"Thank you," he said, as if she'd granted him some great request, instead of simply accepting a necessity. And giving in to temptation. His hand slid off her hair and he crossed to the big deep green duffle bag in front of the door. She watched every movement as he crouched and dug around in the bag for a moment, then returned. He sat beside her on the edge of the bed. One hand held a bunch of cloth: bandage and T-shirt, she guessed. The other cradled a delicate jar. It was white, with an intricate, minimalist painting of bird-of-paradise on it. The yellow and red blossoms almost seemed to jump off the milky surface, they were so vivid. It seemed impossible that Malachi's large hands could open it without breaking it, but it didn't even clink as he undid the golden latch and lifted the lid. He slid to one knee on the floor, making Pepper's breath stutter. His concentration was intense—as was everything about him—as he drew a lavender cream from the jar. The room filled with a wholesome, but slightly pungent, scent. Pepper breathed it in, holding it in her lungs.

Malachi's touch was a brush, a whisper of his fingertips. Pepper inhaled sharply at the sudden coolness pouring into the gashes, her muscles tensing against it. Heat came directly in the wake of cold, a soothing warmth that tingled on her skin and seeped deeply into the flesh inside.

"Easy," he said, a casual command in his voice as he spread the salve over the length of each mark. Sparks danced across her skin and into her blood from every touch. Malachi seemed so focused, so clinical, so calm, that it was almost infuriating. It wasn't fair that she felt so much heat every time she got near him, and he didn't seem to be affected. She hadn't bothered to cover her breasts, this time, leaving her towel casually in her lap, and he was completely focused on tending the wounds in her side.

He wound the bandage around her torso, taking great care not to accidentally touch her. Pepper's mouth firmed. She shifted slightly, just enough to make sure that the back of Malachi's knuckles brushed the underside of her breasts. A shudder ran through her as heat began to rush through her body. Malachi froze. He stayed still for several seconds, the only movement being the rise and fall of his chest as he breathed deeply.

"Be still, please," Malachi finally said before wrapping the bandages again.

Pepper scowled. She wanted his attention, damn it. She wanted him to deal with the desire he sent coursing through her, not just the gouges some other man had left in her side. She lifted one hand, hesitantly at first, then threaded her fingers deep into Malachi's thick hair. He closed his eyes briefly and tipped his head into the touch. One hand held the bandage against Pepper's side. The other grabbed her wrist. His thumb stroked the base of her thumb, gentling the sudden movement.

"That feels too good, beauty," Malachi warned her. "Let me finish with the bandage, and then I will leave you be, that you may eat and get into bed."

"Bed is exactly what I have in mind." Pepper's voice was soft, slightly husky. Malachi raised his head sharply. She wet her lips, catching the lower one between her teeth briefly, but refused to look away from him. His gaze followed the movement of her tongue and lingered on her mouth. She started to lean forward, but Malachi stopped her with a hand splayed across her belly. His fingers stroked against the bandaging as he finished pinning it in place.

"I will not take advantage of your grief, Pepper mine," Malachi repeated. His gaze travelled hungrily over her breasts. Her body reacted to his attention, and he inhaled deeply. For a moment, he seemed to be struggling with his self-control before he spoke again. "Nor your gratitude, nor any indebtedness you may feel from my interference in your life." He lifted his face to hers again, his blue eyes burning. "When you come to me, it will be with joy and love in your heart."

"You don't ask for much, do you." Pepper made it a statement. Rejection chilled through her, and she lifted the towel to cover herself, spreading it more fully over her lap. She started tucking it under her thighs, holding the other end to her collarbone. Malachi stood, lifting the dark T-shirt and shaking out the folds to offer it to her. His expression was somber, bordering on severe.

"I ask for *everything*, and I know it." He waited for her to take the offered shirt. She did, immediately dropping it into her lap with both hands. Her sigh was so deep that they both winced. His hands cupped her cheeks, insisting that she look at him. "Make no mistake, Pepper. I won't be an easy man to live with, but I will be a good man. You will be the center of my world. But my world..." Malachi bent to kiss her tenderly on the forehead, on the eyelids, on each cheek, before finally placing a chaste, adoring kiss on her lips. "My world is a dark and dangerous place. When I make love to you, it will be the seal on my promise to love, protect, and care for you all of your days."

"Malachi." The word was an ache, breathed from the depth of longing he was stirring in her. It was also a complaint. Her eyes closed briefly, as if shutting out the sight of him might help her find the strength to resist him. It didn't work. She couldn't even shut out the sight of him. The image of his face hovered behind her eyelids. His scent surrounded her, fanning the flames inside her blood, and her heart. She tried to sigh it out as she opened her eyes again.

"Malachi, I'm not talking about a lifetime commitment, here. Just you and me, two consenting adults, finding a little bit of...of connection and pleasure in a crazy world. Not a life sentence," Pepper added, dry humor quirking her lips into a crooked smile.

Malachi's eyes flashed. Something dangerous and predatory looked out from his face. Pepper startled backward, but Malachi's hands kept her easily in place. A soft growl sounded from his throat as he swooped down to fasten his mouth on hers. The kiss was hot, claiming, igniting a firestorm that swept up from her toenails. Pepper forgot the towel as sudden need rocked her to her core. Her hands swept into his hair, tugging at him as she lay back on the bed. Malachi followed her down, his body blanketing hers. Even then, he was aware of her wounds, his arm protectively close by as it supported his weight. Pepper felt her heart go liquid, melting to join the fire roaring through her blood. She made an eager sound low in her throat as she moved restlessly against him. Malachi broke the kiss, though his face remained close, so close she could feel his breath on her overly sensitive lips.

"Do not—" His voice was nearly a growl, and only part of it coming from his arousal. His hand gripped the back of her neck as he emphasized the words. "Do not *ever* refer to a lifetime with you as a *life sentence*!" He spat out the words, as if the sounds themselves were filthy, unworthy of being in his mouth.

Pepper blinked...and giggled. She couldn't help it.

The sound just bubbled out of her throat before she could stop it. She was no less surprised by her reaction than Malachi was, though the completely flabbergasted expression on his face only made her laugh harder. Pain stabbed from her side, and she still laughed, until tears streamed down her face. Understanding dawned. Malachi rested his forehead against hers, giving one low chuckle before rising up. Gently, he rolled her to her side—the uninjured one—and tucked the covers around her. Pepper continued to laugh and cry as Malachi lay beside her, drawing her back into his chest as he curled his body protectively around hers. He stroked back her hair and chuffed softly. She sobbed between laughs, and each one of them made her head throb, but she couldn't seem to stop.

"Breathe, beauty mine. Link your breath with mine." He deepened his breathing, making his body move so she could feel each inhale. Pepper did, as much as she was able. She felt him settle around her, and her muscles relaxed in response. Each breath lowered her further and further from hysteria until she finally dropped into an exhausted sleep.

Chapter Eighteen

The muted light filtering through the canopy was gentle on the face of the newborn cub in his arms. He could almost feel her tiny, warm weight against his elbow, and her dark, downy hair in his palm as he shielded her head. She yawned, her mouth drawn into a little pucker as she settled back into sleep.

"She's beautiful, Ana," Malachi murmured. The midday stillness of the First Prince's residence was so complete, it felt almost sacred, and he had no desire to disturb it. Cradled in the roots of an old tamarind tree sprawled an enormous tiger. Dinner plate-sized paws flopped at the wrists as he lay absurdly on his back. Three young cubs—two boys and another girl—draped themselves over him as both bed and pillow, nestling into the fur despite the heat. All of them had their eyes closed. The great cat rumbled with pride.

"It's hard to believe my brother sired her," Malachi continued, watching the tiger. The beast snorted. One paw flexed until the center claw slid into clear view.

"Josiah," the petite woman beside Malachi said with obvious reproach. "Not in front of the cubs. It isn't appropriate for either cubs or the leader of the Tseng Tse. I don't care how Malachi teases you. Put that away."

The tiger grumbled, but the single claw retracted into the velvet pad. First Prince Josiah hooked a paw under a toddler sleeping against his side and scooped the boy onto his broad, furry belly. The cub snuggled without waking, wrapping his chubby arm around the tiger's neck.

A shadow flitted past the edge of the courtyard. Malachi glanced over, but not fast enough; it was gone.

The infant in his arms fussed faintly. He looked at her, tiny face scrunched up behind equally tiny fists, then looked helplessly at Ana. The human woman clucked her tongue.

"You'll never learn if you don't practice, Malachi," she chided gently. She's just too warm. Open the blanket a little more. I thought all of you princes were raised with children underfoot."

Another shadow darted through the edge of his vision. Malachi whipped his head to look, flaring his nostrils. He looked to his elder brother, but Josiah still dozed under the tamarind tree. The tip of the great tiger's tail twitched occasionally in contentment. The scents around him were strange, too cold and salty, with no scent of family. But one scent that intoxicated him. His mind rippled as it struggled to remember something, something vitally important—

The infant in his arms fussed, and he offered the cub again to its mother. "It's been a long time since I worked in the nursery, sister mine," Malachi said. Ana peeled back the light blanket. The chubby face was mottled and brown, like blood on duckweed. He frowned, smoothing his fingertips over the infant's face.

"I'll never get used to the way you Tseng Tse put the noun first and then the possessive," Ana said.

"I'll never get used to the way you humans put the

possessive first," Malachi retorted, somewhat absently. The cub's face. Something wasn't right about the cub's face. "As if my claim of you is more important than *you*."

"Humans don't claim each other the way Tseng Tse do." Ana's voice seemed suddenly far away. The light twisted, casting strange shadows. A dark form crept among them, stalking Pepper through the twisting lights. Malachi frowned. Ana was gone. The cub in his arms was gone. Josiah, the other cubs, even the great old tamarind that had sheltered the First Prince's courtyard for generations was gone. Duckweed tangled his feet, miring him in place.

"Pepper!" he called to her. She turned toward him. Her beautiful face was mottled and bloated, and the front of her throat hung in ragged tatters, as if it had been torn by Tseng Tse teeth. She wore no clothing, only blood. She smiled a death's head grin. Malachi's claws slid from his fingertips as he roared. He tore at the duckweed that bound him. More took its place, wrapping his legs even tighter. More shadowy figures whipped between them, until he struggled even to see her. Duckweed trapped his wrists, drawing them inexorably to his sides despite his great strength. He called on the beast within, trying to shift, but the tiger wouldn't respond. All he could do was watch helplessly as shadows stole Pepper away from him.

****

Malachi jolted awake in the space between one heartbeat and the next. His body was already tensed, rigid with terror and rage. The neat, cozy bedroom of the bed and breakfast settled into his senses, squeezing out the chaos of the nightmare. He breathed. Pepper's scent filled him. His arms tightened, bringing her close against his body. She murmured and sighed in her sleep, nestling her cheek against his shoulder. He inhaled again, lifting a hand to cradle her head. Dark stripes smudged across his skin, showcased against thin, short, white fur. A cold shock rippled through him. It had been decades since he'd popped fur in his sleep. Frantically, he checked his fingertips. No trace of claws or blood. Relief made him drop back onto the pillows. Thank the ancestors he hadn't shown his claws, as well!

Pepper was still asleep, her breathing deep and slow. He could still scent the tears on her face. His heart ached, as if the pain of her loss was his own. His instincts gnawed at him to ease her distress, already rising through the adrenaline of his dream. If this was how he felt already, how much more intense would it become? How could he manage to leave her if she rejected him?

A shadow slid past one window. Malachi's head whipped around, instinctively inhaling to catch any scent of danger. His nose—and mind—filled with Pepper. A muscle twitched in his jaw as he very carefully slid his arm from under her cheek. Pepper whined softly, reaching for him as she frowned in her sleep. His chest physically ached with the sudden rush of emotion that twisted his heart. He tucked the covers around her, trapping as much of his warmth and scent in with her as he could before rolling to the floor beside the bed. He didn't want to alert whoever was outside that he was awake by showing a silhouette on the curtains. Crawling on elbows and knees, belly flat against the floor, he moved to the door and pressed his ear against the crack.

Stealthy steps paused on the tiny porch of the bungalow. Malachi's enhanced hearing could just make out an insistent snuffling, almost directly where his ear was. He pressed his nose to the seam where the door met the wall and inhaled. The only scents were old wood and sneezeweed.

Carefully, very slowly, he turned the locks. His eyes shifted, as did his hands, as he eased to his feet. The large, lethally curved claws slid from his fingertips as he angled himself to block the doorway. One hand yanked open the door as the other shot for the intruder's throat.

A powerful hand knocked his strike away, accompanied by an exasperated growl and a fairly potent Tseng Tse oath.

"Stand down, before you wake the whole community."

Malachi felt his shoulders drop three inches. His claws melted back into his fingers.

"Israel." His voice was pure relief. He reached out to embrace the other tiger, hugging him roughly around the shoulders. "Brother. Thank the ancestors. Be welcome in my den."

Clasping his brother's forearm, Malachi drew Israel through the doorway and into the small building. Israel inclined his head deeply, clasping Malachi's elbow with his free hand. Whatever he was about to say stopped in his throat as he caught sight of Pepper lying in the solitary large bed. One eyebrow raised, he nailed his younger brother with a questioning look. Malachi carefully shut the door, locking it again. Faint warmth rose to his cheeks as he moved around Israel to stand at the foot of the bed, arms folded, as he blocked his brother's view.

"I smell no mate-scent," Israel said, and inhaled deeply, as if checking his initial impression.

"For good reason."

Israel's speculative expression didn't change. He started to move, and a fierce protectiveness surged through Malachi. His teeth were bared and his claws out before conscious thought caught up with him. Israel stood his ground, his amber gaze refusing to retreat.

"I have no interest in your woman." The older man spoke in a very low voice. "Her scent does nothing to me. You bring her to me as a sister and I will care for her as such. Put your weapons away before you wake her. The scent of her distress yet hangs in the air."

Malachi breathed. His human mind wrestled with the tiger's instincts, struggling with a conflict that had been as easy to manage as walking for decades. He sat on the edge of the bed and let one hand rest on Pepper's leg. The sight of his claws so close to her disturbed him, so much so that tiger and man came to an immediate truce. Fully human again, he ran his hand over his face.

"I'm sorry, brother," he murmured. Israel scoffed lightly. Sinking into one of the seats, he crossed one booted foot over the other knee and draped himself against the back.

"For what? For reacting as any male does when another male gets too close to his chosen mate? Fool."

"Potential mate," Malachi corrected. Israel's second eyebrow rose to join the first.

"She rejected you?"

Malachi gently rubbed Pepper's still form through the blankets, his eyes lowered as he shook his head.

"I haven't yet laid that choice before her."

Israel looked sharply at Malachi, his eyes like fire agates. "You have not told her?"

Silence filled the room, underscored by Pepper's soft, deep breathing and the ever-present rhythmic rush of the waves.

"No."

Israel scowled but kept his voice very low.

"Malachi, you cannot put it off, especially if you are already sharing a den with her. It will destroy you. She has to know what she is agreeing to before you bond with her, or you will lose yourself."

"I'm not bedding her." Malachi's protest was equally low. For some reason, it was important to him that Israel understood the truth.

"You have that much sense, at least." Israel's tone made his low opinion of Malachi's sense very plain. "How do you plan to keep protecting her with her scent driving you into your fur every time you get around her? Who will protect her from you when the need of the tiger for his mate finally overwhelms you? The justice of our people will have its due, and you will have earned it."

"Let it destroy me. Let it take my sanity. Let it drive me into fur, or all the way back to the palace, or into the wilds with our cousins, to live out my life as a tiger. I have no desire to be in the world if she isn't."

"We will protect her. There is no doubt about that. No fugitive can long escape two Negrescus, no matter how clever or how tragic," Israel said with a dismissive gesture. "He will not touch her."

"There are other ways to destroy a person." Malachi's hand gripped Pepper's leg for a moment before he remembered himself and released her. "Israel, this is a woman who filmed a rape in progress, fearlessly calling attention to herself in an attempt to end the attack. How well do you think she would fit into our world?"

"Wonderfully well." Israel didn't miss a beat. "Well enough to be the mate of the Third Prince, even, a woman of selflessness, courage, intelligence, quick-thinking, with a sense of justice and a willingness to act." He leaned forward, his elbows on his knees. "You have to tell her, Malachi, or I will."

Malachi's lip half raised in a silent snarl.

"Do not threaten me, Israel. My control is weakened by her presence as it is, and I have yet to get proper control of myself."

"You will not be able to do so until the mate-bond properly forms."

"Or when she is gone from my life long enough." Malachi had to say the words, to throw them into Israel's face, though the thought twisted his soul inside out. Israel gave him a very unamused look.

"Do not be an even bigger idiot than you are already acting. The chances of you ever meeting another potential mate are astonishingly tiny." Israel leveled one forefinger at his younger brother as he eased into the back of the chair again. "You will tell her. Tomorrow. Or." Israel's voice deepened into the tone of absolute command that every Tseng Tse knew, deep in their gut. "Or you walk away from her forever."

Malachi's insides twisted and lurched as the tiger leaped for the surface. He jammed his fist against his mouth and bit down hard on his knuckles. He *would not* roar a challenge at his elder brother. His Prince. The air huffed loudly through his nose as he forced himself to breathe. And keep on breathing through the burning tension in his neck and shoulders. Too tight to move, he could only sit rigidly on the edge of the bed, wrestling himself back under his own control. He nodded once, curtly.

"After the aberration is brought justice." Malachi's voice was very quiet, the words barely audible.

"No." The single word hung in the air. Israel spoke equally quietly. "You will tell this woman, tomorrow, who and what you are, what it is that you do, or by this time tomorrow, you will be on a flight back to the palace, where you will remain until such time as our healers deem you recovered enough to be safe in human society. The hunt will become mine."

Malachi rumbled. Pepper stirred, frowning in her sleep. It quieted him, somewhat, but the effort it took sent him to his feet, pacing the small room.

"This is *my* hunt. Protecting my woman is *my* job."

"It would be," Israel said lazily, though his amber eyes never moved from Malachi's face. "But she is not *your* woman." The voice and look of the Second Prince dropped away, leaving only Israel. "I am protecting *you*. Can you not see that?" He rippled to his feet to grip Malachi's shoulder. "I want this for you, little brother. There are so few potential mates for any of us that it is absolute idiocy to throw away this chance. But you cannot risk mating with her without her full knowledge and consent. I cannot sit by and allow you to endanger your life this way. I will cage you, first."

"I endanger my life, either way," Malachi said. Israel frowned.

"You will not be judged guilty of treason for

revealing our existence to your potential mate. This is
no wanton revelation, no careless act, no brag to gain
favors by showing off. This is your potential mate."

"The law doesn't make an exception."

"You know full well the First Prince will not
condemn you for taking a human mate. Or have you
forgotten that our elder sister is human? From the
outside world, no less, not from the palace." Israel
smirked at Malachi. "You are using an ancient law as
an excuse. You fear that she will reject you."

Something terrible and cold settled in the pit of
Malachi's stomach.

"I place my life between this woman and the risk
of slavery," he said, a lethal quiet to his voice. Israel
regarded him silently for a handful of heartbeats.
Pepper stirred, whimpering in her sleep. Malachi
stroked her arm to soothe her. His face may have been
turned away from Israel, but he held no illusions that he
was hiding anything from his brother.

"I cannot pretend that is not a possibility," Israel
finally said, his voice so low that it barely rippled the
silence. "So make certain she has no reason to reject
you." A teasing note entered Israel's voice. "Do not tell
me that you have so much doubt about your ability to
win a woman."

"Wait until it is your turn, brother." Malachi
regretted the words the instant they left his mouth.
Israel's expression closed, a meticulously sculpted
mask to conceal every thought. Even his scent was
enigmatic.

"I'm sorry," Malachi said. "I spoke thoughtlessly."

Israel smiled, but it had no power to warm his eyes.
"The young often do. I pray to the ancestors that I have

the chance to live out the curse that they just witnessed."

"As do I." Malachi meant it, more fervently than he ever thought that he would.

"You have stumbled upon a very rare gift," Israel said, leaning back in the chair once more. "A gift for which many of our people would give up their ability to hunt. If she really is your potential mate, then she is perfectly suited to you, physically, mentally, and emotionally. She can handle everything you are, the hunter, the prince, the tiger, all of it, or she would not be your potential mate."

Pepper whimpered again, tears shimmering on her lashes as she tossed restlessly. Her arm slipped free of the covers, showing a bare shoulder and back as she settled again. Malachi chuffed softly, smoothing the covers around her again, but not before Israel smirked.

"Are you sure there was no bedding?"

Malachi's hand shot out and smacked Israel up the back of the head, cuffing his brother as he growled in warning. The older tiger ducked from the force of it, doubling slightly over a grin as he rubbed the back of his head.

"Stop batting my tail. I wouldn't risk the mate-bond forming, even by accident."

"You will wake her if you do not settle," Israel said, still grinning. "Though if she wakes to two half-tigers tussling her bedroom, you will have no choice but to explain everything."

Malachi raised his hand in an open threat of cuffing his brother again. Israel's lowered head and small, feral smile told him he was welcome to try, but the older, larger tiger wouldn't give him another easy shot. It would be just like Israel to force Malachi's hand by waking Pepper. Malachi raised his lip in a dismissive gesture and let his hand drop. He stared out the window, but his human eyes couldn't quite pierce the darkness to find the sea beyond.

"She needs more rest. She's been through too much in too short a time. Her body and mind won't be able to keep up, if she doesn't get a chance to recharge." Malachi's expression hardened as he turned to Israel again. "I need to hunt, before she wakes. You'll stay and guard her?"

"And how will this strong, fearless woman of yours react to waking up to a strange man in her den?" Israel's tone was mocking. Malachi scowled.

"You can guard from *outside*."

Israel sobered, though his eyes still shone with teasing humor. His fingers rested on his chin. "Tell me, little brother. If your potential mate wakes to an empty room, how much trouble will it cause for you? From what you have told me, she has lost everything to the aberration. You are her refuge." He shook his head. "You stay. I will hunt Jensen while you guard your woman."

"His *what*?"

Malachi whirled. Pepper was sitting up in the bed, the blankets held to her chest. Her dark hair was beautifully mussed, enticing him to run his fingers through its soft silk, to settle it along her smooth skin, to feel her purring under his hands as he groomed her, touched her...

Israel snickered. Pepper continued to glare at him, far too little sleep left in her eyes. She looked very awake and very irritated. Malachi stepped to the bed, reaching to cup her cheek, but she batted his hand away.

"I think you would be in less trouble if she had woken in an empty room, after all." Israel covered his fist with a flat hand, placed them both on his belly, and bowed. His voice rolled through the room, a physical thing that filled the bungalow from wall to wall and pressed against the ceiling.

"Please pardon my intrusion into your den, woman." The address was laden with deep respect, very different from his earlier teasing. "My name is Israel Negrescu. I am Malachi's elder brother."

Pepper didn't know what to say. She tried to cover herself more completely, shifting the covers up over her shoulders. Malachi reached around her, tucking them behind her back, as well. He sat on the mattress and tugged her back against him.

"You should be sleeping," he said.

"*You* shouldn't be talking so loud." Pepper frowned and tried to move away from him. But he was very warm, and his solid presence at her back made her feel better. Safe. It was easier to face the large stranger in the room with Malachi literally at her back. She gave him another long look.

"Israel?" When he nodded, Pepper continued. "Not to be rude, but what are you doing here?"

Israel's lips twitched, as if he were trying not to laugh. "I have come to help my brother."

Pepper pressed into Malachi, instinctively seeking his protection. His arms immediately wrapped around her, still careful of the wounds in her side. His fingertips stroked her skin, a sensual distraction that sent bits of molten lava through her blood and into her brain.

"The rapist." The words threatened to stick her throat shut and she swallowed hard. Israel inclined his head in acknowledgement. Pepper breathed hard for a moment, then shook herself. "Out. Both of you."

Malachi rumbled low in his throat and even Israel looked thunderous.

"I'm not getting dressed with both of you standing there, and I'm not going to have this conversation naked. Get. Out. And let me get dressed."

Israel pressed his lips together, hard, before turning his face away. He coughed, but Pepper caught enough of his expression to suspect he was covering a laugh. Grabbing the pillow from beside her, she flung it at his head. Israel effortlessly snatched it from mid-air and dropped it into one of the chairs. He didn't bother to hide his grin anymore.

"You have really stuck your nose in it this time, little brother," he said, with a very thorough stretch. His amber eyes included Pepper. "I will be outside, when you have finished."

"Thank you." Pepper didn't move until the door clicked closed behind Israel. Still holding the covers to her chest, she scooted away from Malachi. "Your turn."

"I have seen your body before," Malachi argued, his tone somewhere between amusement and protest. Heat flashed into Pepper's cheeks.

"Yes, and you can't keep your hands off of it. Worse, I don't want you to keep your hands off of it. But this is important, Malachi." She turned to him with vulnerability in her eyes and strength in her jawline. Cupping her cheek, he kissed her, lingering just long enough for her to get a taste of him. His hand swept back through her hair, and he stood. He bent into his duffle bag and pulled out a pair of knit pants.

"They'll be too big, but the drawstring should help. Dress quickly, please." A frown crossed his features as his thumb lingered on her lower lip. "Israel and I will be right outside, but I dislike leaving you alone for very long."

Pepper watched as he backed the short distance across the room and finally stepped outside. The door clicked into place, and she slumped as she dropped her face into her hands. With a sudden, shuddery breath, she drew herself upright. There was no time to fall apart again. All of those questions she had about Malachi wouldn't wait any longer; she'd overheard too much of his conversation with Israel. She needed answers.

Forcing strength she didn't feel into her limbs, she pulled on the pants Malachi had left for her. She may as well have been a child playing in a grown-up's clothes. The waist only cinched in so far, leaving the fabric bunched up and riding low against her hips. At least the shirt should be long enough to cover it. It took her a moment of digging around the bedclothes to find it again. Pepper winced as she tried to dress too fast and a careless movement pulled the gashes in her side. Grinding her teeth, she cried out in pain and frustration, hitting the pillow as hard as she could. Then doing it again and again.

Malachi was going to knock, and then he was going to come right in, whether she invited him or not. She knew it was going to happen before the little rapping sounded on the door.

"Oh, come in!" To her surprise, the words weren't entirely irritable. Part of her wanted to laugh.

Something about his constant vigilance, the way he seemed so attuned to her, warmed her. It loosened something painfully tight and cold in her chest and made her want to reach back for him.

Malachi's head appeared around the door, and she flung another pillow at him. The look of complete surprise on his face was worth the childish act.

"I'm fine. Just mad. Come in." Pepper lifted one foot onto the bed and began rolling up the pant leg. "And tell Israel he's allowed back inside, too."

Malachi turned back and gave a short, sharp whistle, then stepped inside. Before he'd even gotten the door closed, Israel's hand appeared around the edge. He stood in the doorway for a moment, his back to the room. Pepper could hear him sniffing. She paused in between rolling pant legs to stare at his back, completely baffled.

"What are you doing?" she demanded.

"Here, beauty." Malachi stood beside the bed, a bottle of water in his hands. He cracked the top and held it out. Pepper shook her head.

"No, thank you," she said automatically, trying to peer around him to Israel. He shifted to block her view, demanding her focus as he offered the bottled water again. She glared up at him. He simply returned her gaze, unfazed.

"You need to replenish your body," Malachi said. He was like a wall: unruffled, unrufflable, and unmoving.

"Has he always been this bossy?" Pepper asked, ignoring Malachi completely. Israel closed the door and moved to the table, where he was arranging the snack tray. Pepper's stomach rumbled a little in response to the tantalizing smell. Israel turned with a lopsided grin.

"No. He used to listen to me. I think he was five when that ended."

Pepper snorted. "I believe it."

"Drink, beauty mine." Malachi pressed the water on her again. "Tease me later."

Pepper relented. Her fingers brushed his as she took the water from him, sending awareness curling through her body. She downed more than half the bottle without coming up for air, despite Malachi watching her with that unrelenting stare the entire time. She really was depleted, perhaps more so than either of them realized. His hand smoothed over her hair.

"Thank you, Pepper," he said, his low voice sincere. "You need to eat, as well. Please don't try to tell me that you aren't hungry. It would only be an insult to both of us."

Pepper tried to glare up at him, but it didn't work very well. "You haven't eaten, either," she pointed out. Standing, she looked at Israel. "Have you?"

"We will eat when you have had your fill," Malachi interrupted smoothly. Taking her by the hand, he led her to the table, or tried to.

"Seriously? That's rude."

"Perhaps to you," Israel said, his smile coloring his voice. "It is our way. Please. Eat."

Pepper looked from one to the other. Her gaze finally settled on Malachi.

"What are you?" A chill went through her as she said the words, as if she were plunging off the edge of a cliff into a place which she could never leave again, once she had entered. Malachi's expression sobered.

"Please," he said gravely. "Eat."

"Talk and I'll eat."

Israel raised the back of his knuckles to his mouth, but it did nothing to stop the snicker from escaping. Malachi ignored him.

"If you will eat, I'll talk while you do so."

"Fair enough." With a great show of magnanimity that had Israel grinning again, Pepper eased into the other chair at the table. It made a cozy, intimate little picture, just Pepper and Israel at the small bistro table, sharing the light meal between them. Malachi didn't like it. He growled at Israel.

"Move."

Israel raised one eyebrow. He stayed where he was, as if taunting his little brother, before finally peeling himself out of the chair. He shifted to the bed. Deliberately, he settled into the hollow Pepper had left in the blankets when she had gotten up and draped himself over the impression in the blankets.

"Better?" he asked, his gaze never leaving Malachi's.

Malachi only growled louder. Israel chuckled under his breath as he stood again. Pepper felt an absurd urge to giggle as he stepped back, away from both the food and the bed, and bowed to her.

"My apologies, again, for disturbing you, woman," the larger man said elegantly. "I do not think my brother will settle until I am a good distance from both your food and your bed. I will excuse myself."

"You don't have to do that," Pepper hurried to reassure him. Israel's indulgent smile argued without a word, though there was a sad shadow to it.

"It is nothing. I want to take another patrol around the...den, anyway." Israel's features grew cool and impassive, and Pepper suppressed a shiver.

"Den?" she asked. "What den?"

Israel shot that crooked smile at Malachi, who raised a lip in return. Pepper looked back and forth between the two, her confusion mounting. As if seeing it, Israel smiled again, and bowed slightly as he stepped outside once more.

Chapter Nineteen

"Malachi, that was rude," Pepper immediately chastised Malachi. The fierceness in her face made him want to smile, despite the fact that she was defending another male. He shrugged.

"Perhaps, but he was right." Malachi sounded rueful, even to his own ears. He raked a hand over his hair, pacing the small space between the table and the bathroom wall.

"Why?" Pepper demanded. "What are you?"

Malachi hesitated. He'd never felt nerves clawing at his belly quite like this before. He couldn't delay any longer, however he might want to. He gestured to the light snack on the small table. "Eat," he reminded her. "You promised. I'll tell you after."

Malachi watched as Pepper pressed her lips into a stubborn line. Hurriedly tossing a pair of crackers together with some meat and cheese in between, she popped the whole thing into her mouth, staring at him expectantly.

"Thank you." Malachi seated himself on the edge of the bed, where he could watch her every expression.

"My people are called the Tseng Tse. We are an ancient race. We were created by the younger gods when the world was new and full of terrible dangers in order to protect their beloved humans from threats your people couldn't hope to defeat, especially in the infancy of their existence."

Malachi kept his gaze on hers, willing her to believe him. He needed her to see him for what he really was, and to accept him. All of him. Pepper chewed slowly, thoughtfully, her eyes slightly narrowed. At least she was listening. He leaned toward her, his elbows on his knees.

"We're hard-wired to protect humans. It runs counter to all of our instincts to allow any harm to come to your people. To cause it ourselves is…is…" He shook his head as words failed him. Just the thought sent an involuntary shudder running through him as he felt the prickle of fur pushing against the inside of his skin. He breathed. He couldn't afford to lose control, not now. The next few minutes were far too crucial, not just for him, but for her. Everything was for her, now.

"Rarely, something goes wrong, and the consequences of these aberrations are tragic." Malachi shifted his weight, subtly placing himself between Pepper and the door. He breathed deeply, as much to monitor her scent as to calm himself. He made his voice as calm and steady as possible. "Jensen is one such aberration."

Pepper stared. Absently, she reached for another cracker. Her eyes widened as if in slow motion.

"That's why," she said slowly. "That's why you refuse to get the police involved. Jensen isn't human, and neither are you, and if we go to the police…"

Malachi nodded. Very carefully, Pepper placed the cracker in her hand back on the tray. She placed her palms on the tops of her thighs.

"What kind of 'terrible threats' are we talking about here? Like giant, prehistoric bears?"

"I'm sure it happened," Malachi answered. "There are predators in this world that humans only remember in nightmares."

Malachi waited. Pepper had her fingertips at her temples, rubbing in small circles. She looked up again.

"Malachi, you've come this far. You may as well finish, or my imagination will fill in the worst possible ideas. Human brains are like that," she said wryly. Pepper picked up the cracker she'd abandoned earlier and began loading it with meat and cheese. Malachi's heart swelled with pride that neither her hands nor her voice shook, despite the adrenaline in her scent. She was equal to the life he was asking of her as his mate.

"Vampires," he said bluntly. Pepper froze.

"Vampires," she repeated, as if confirming it.

"They're humankind's greatest predator, but there are others." Malachi settled on the edge of the bed nearest the bistro set. "Humans like to think that they have conquered the wild world, that there are no shadows left in the forests or the caves or even the deeps of the seas. It's not true. Worse, humankind's predators—like all predators—have adapted to the habitats of their prey. They're there, in the cities and the towns. They're just camouflaged."

"So there are monsters in the subways besides the human ones. We just don't know it," Pepper said.

"Yes." Malachi couldn't give her any more answer than the single word. There was no way to soften a truth that would surely frighten her. The brutal truth was that humans were not the top of the food chain, as they so desperately wanted to believe. Pepper remained still and quiet. Malachi didn't push her. Her face betrayed little of her thoughts. Even her scent was subdued, a mixture of grief and fear. Finally, she swallowed. Pepper refused to look at him, but she reached one hand toward him. Her fingers trembled. Immediately, he captured her hand in both of his. She stood and he tugged gently, until she sat beside him. Malachi wrapped both arms around her, making himself a cage to keep all others out. Her heart pounded hard enough that he could feel it against his chest.

Malachi tipped up her chin with two fingers and captured her gaze. The fear in her wide eyes made his gut twist. He held her gaze, chuffing openly. Fear faded to wariness and she relaxed beside him, inch by inch. She pushed back her hair with one hand. It still trembled, but not as much.

"What are you doing? And don't—just *don't* blow me off this time, Malachi, or I...I'll bite you or something."

Malachi found himself smiling. "Among the Tseng Tse, that's not necessarily a threat." He continued, "It's called chuffing. We do it to calm each other, or ourselves. It's somewhat an involuntary reaction to strong emotions. Are you able to be calm?"

Pepper hesitated a moment, then nodded. It was much more difficult than Malachi had anticipated to ease himself away from her. The feel of her soft curves against him was far too enticing. His hands continued to wander over her body, tracing every curve and dip. Pepper glared.

"Stop that," she said, batting at his hands. "You aren't done explaining yet, and you are *not* going to distract me."

"Yet," Malachi promised. She scooted away from him, or tried. He refused to let her go, but he did force

195

himself to keep his hands still.

"You were talking about predators. Humanity's predators." Pepper reached for another slice of cheese, seemingly content to stay in his arms.

"Israel and I are hunters." Malachi continued. "We hunt down those creatures that would prey on mankind, including Tseng Tse who have broken our laws, and bring justice to them. Human authorities have no chance against Tseng Tse. We're stronger, faster, tougher." Malachi's jaw tightened. "The police can't protect you from Jensen. They don't know what they're up against. Neither do you." He took her chin in his hand again, bringing her gaze back to his. "You *need* to stay where I can protect you."

Pepper searched his eyes. He allowed it, hiding nothing.

"What, exactly, are the police up against?"

Malachi refused to let her look away. He refused to let *himself* look away. This was far too vital. His chest felt tight, a vise around his heart. There was no way around this, only through it. His thumb stroked along her jaw, needing the connection of even that small touch.

"We turn into tigers."

The words dropped into the room, stones into a pond. He felt the ripples go through her as Pepper grappled with the idea. Her entire body was stiff, tight, like a wire ready to snap. He felt the same tension in himself until her hand tightened on his. He gripped her hand in return as his hand went to her hip, bringing her against him and holding her there.

"You're serious." Pepper's shock filled her voice. Her slender body weaved slightly, and he moved her closer to brace her on his own body.

"Deadly." Placing her hand on his chest, he allowed his fingers to roam through her hair. "The gashes in your side. Jensen began to shift into his tiger form, and his claws wounded you." Anger filled him, down to his fingertips. "It is unforgivable."

"Because he hurt me," Pepper said.

"Yes." Malachi gave in to temptation and kissed her hair, then dragged his jaw over the top of her head. "The law says it is because Jensen harmed a human, but I can't deny that, because he harmed *you,* it's different. It's not just my job as a hunter. He made it personal."

"You're weretigers." Pepper's voice was stilted. "You and Jensen and Israel. You all turn into tigers, sprouting teeth and fur and—" She suddenly tipped her head to one side. "Do you get a tail?"

"Yes." Malachi's lips wandered over her hair and face, and Pepper melted into him a little at a time. He shifted her again, pulling her closer until she sat on his lap. "We prefer the term 'shifter'. Werepersons are ruled by the phases of the moon. The Tseng Tse are not." Pepper turned toward him. Her face was distractingly close to his, her soft breath moving over his mouth in an enticing dance. His hands moved over her, from the silk of her hair to the sweet curves of her body. His voice was deep, roughened. "We're not infected with some disease. We can't turn a human into a Tseng Tse. We're a separate species, though we are compatible with humans, and we are born with the ability to shift. We learn to control our shifts as cubs and through our youngling years."

"Cubs?" Pepper's voice sounded distracted. She gave a tiny laugh. "Children."

"Younglings are our youth, like human teenagers."

Pepper shuddered. From the arousal in her scent, it wasn't entirely due to the conversation. He leaned closer, allowing his fingertips to drift under the hem of her shirt. Her belly trembled faintly as he indulged himself with her satin skin.

"Teenagers that literally turn into tigers. Sounds like a nightmare," Pepper said. Malachi chuckled, as much at the breathiness in her voice as the words themselves. Her body molded to his. His hand threaded upward through her hair and her head dropped back into his palm.

"We are careful with our strength, our speed, all of our abilities. But it does get…lively." His lips wandered over her cheek, down the curve of her jaw to her graceful throat. The air around him was growing thick with the scent of her arousal, and Malachi found himself struggling to keep his mind on the conversation.

"Do you only have those things when you're a tiger, or all the time?" It sounded like Pepper was struggling to form words, as well, and the thought made him rumble with pleasure.

"All of the time. My senses are sharper as a tiger than as a human, but even in human form, they're better than those of a born human. I've been hunting Jensen for weeks, tracking him through his scent, as well as through more prosaic means."

Pepper pulled back a little bit. "That's why you told me to stay in the truck."

Malachi nodded, bunching her hair in his fist as he chuffed. "The area around your RV was saturated in his scent. I was afraid he was still there."

His arms tightened around her as her scent shifted, showing more distress, even creeping toward fear. He much preferred the way she smelled with sleep and arousal.

"He killed Bunsen." She made it a statement. The grief stabbed him in the heart.

"Yes." Malachi had to confirm it. "His scent was heavy around your car, as well, including under the hood. I have no doubts that he took the spark plugs from your engine to force you into walking."

"Why?" Pepper's voice caught in her throat. She was so good-natured. He could only imagine that she was struggling to understand what would make anyone do such a thing. Slaughtering and mutilating an innocent animal, her sweet pet, and leaving the pieces for her to find could only be much, much more difficult. She leaned into Malachi, as if seeking his solid strength and taking comfort in his warmth. His heart soared at the thought as his lips grazed over her temple again. She turned into the touch, and he rubbed his jaw over the top of her head again.

"I believe he wanted to force you into the open. You were much more vulnerable on foot. It's much easier to stalk prey on foot in the dark and the rain than inside a car. Even our speed and strength are challenged by vehicles."

Malachi forced himself to breathe. Slowly. Deeply. Calm the rage. He could feel the tiger demanding its rights to protect its mate, to defend its territory. The man was furious, as well. His control was taxed by Pepper's nearness. It was a potent and almost overpowering combination.

Pepper nestled closer. She slid one hand up his

chest to rub along his jaw as she nuzzled his other cheek. His arms tightened and he inhaled deeply, suddenly, as the tiger soothed at the gesture.

"I'm okay," she whispered, as if seeking to reassure him. His chest felt like it was collapsing in on him. He was always strong, capable, knowing exactly what to do and knowing, without a doubt, that he could do it. He had to. The lives of those humans under his care depended on it, as did the safety of his people. He couldn't remember the last time a woman had tried to reassure him, and it stole his breath. His heart. His very soul. Malachi fought the urge to crush her against him as Pepper continued. "You were there. You've been there, all along."

"And I will continue to be here," Malachi vowed. Even if she rejected him, he wouldn't be able to leave her unprotected. Perhaps he could even manage to watch over her himself, if he could avoid being ordered back to the palace. Little tongues of desire kept surging through his body everywhere their bodies touched, and he soaked in the heat. Pepper turned slightly in his arms. She feathered kisses across his stubbled jaw, and Malachi closed his eyes.

"Pepper." Her name felt like a prayer on his lips. "You're becoming entirely too distracting again."

Those shy little kisses were driving him crazy, making his gut clench with need. With Israel on patrol outside, it was far too tempting to lay her down and explore every centimeter of her satin skin. The tiger demanded he bind her to him, and the tiger brain was getting more aggressive. But she hadn't committed to him yet. She didn't even know what that would fully mean, yet. And the wounds in her side still had to be considered. He exhaled, trying to breathe her out of his system. It didn't work. He only had to inhale again, and her scent was a drug. His hand cradled the back of her neck as he lifted her from his lap and carefully laid her on the bed. His mouth found hers with a small growl of desire. The touch was electric, sending a jolt of pleasure down his spine from his scalp. Heat pooled low and wicked. He meant to be gentle, but his kiss rapidly turned demanding. Pepper mewled softly, shifting against him. He trapped her beneath him, insisting that she give him every reaction he was inspiring in her. Possessiveness curled through him with the heat. *His.* She was his, his to protect, his to please, his to care for. His to see through all the seasons of their lives. He had told his brother that he could, and would, walk away from her, but in his deepest heart, he knew it was already too late. He had to convince her to stay with him, and if that meant using sex to entice her…maybe he was that kind of man, after all.

Chapter Twenty

The door crashed open. Malachi leaped from the bed with a snarl. Before his feet hit the ground, claws erupted from his fingertips and shadowy stripes marked his skin. Pepper backed against the headboard with one kick, groping mindlessly for any kind of weapon. Israel filled the doorway, his massive black shadow spilling into the room. Even in her panic, Pepper could see the silhouettes of long, sharp claws at his fingertips. His hair seemed to stand on end, and both men loomed larger than logic would allow as they faced off for one heart-stopping moment.

Malachi snarled again. Or swore. Pepper couldn't tell for sure. Israel's answer shook the lampshade beside her, sending her heart into her throat. Malachi's head turned half toward her. He looked dangerous. Worse than dangerous, he looked deadly. His lips twitched as the great teeth receded. Israel's amber eyes flicked to her in the semi-darkness, and he seemed to struggle for a moment with his control. When he spoke again, his deep voice was very rough, but understandable.

"Jensen."

The word hung in the air, a poisoned breath. Pepper's heart thudded in her ears as she stared at Malachi. His hands twitched, as did the tightly bunched muscles in his shoulders. Each tiny movement seemed to release a little bit more of the terrifying tension that filled him.

"You," his voice was so rough that Pepper could barely understand him, "have frightened my woman. In my den."

Israel snarled again, more quietly this time. Malachi took two swift steps and slammed his open palm into the center of Israel's chest, knocking the larger man backward onto the tiny stoop.

"Unless the aberration is right behind you, apologize." Only ragged breathing filled the air, a good portion of it Pepper's. Malachi's hand flexed against his brother's chest. It seemed like a threat, though Pepper couldn't have said why. She was still pressed against the headboard, clutching the bedside lamp. Israel looked like a beautiful nightmare, a dark angel daring to walk through the waking world. He peered around the door jamb and inhaled deeply. His head jerked back as if she'd actually hit him with the lamp. It cost him visible effort to lower his shoulders, and when he folded his hands in front of his belly to bow, his claws were short, though still sharp.

"Woman," Israel rumbled, his tone filled with deep respect. "I apologize. Forgive me, please."

Pepper watched him closely. Malachi stayed between them, but the hand on his brother's chest slid away as Israel relaxed. Pepper willed herself to relax, as well, dropping back against the headboard. Her hand ached from gripping the lamp so hard. Opening her fist to set it back on the table was a little bit of a challenge. She pulled the covers up to her chest, arms tucked under for comfort and modesty more than warmth.

"Is he out there?" Her voice scraped out of her

throat. Israel shook his head.

"Not at this time," he answered.

"How fresh is the scent?" Malachi gripped his brother by the forearm to bring him over the threshold again, apparently completely forgiving him for barging in. Pepper forced her brain to work. They had only been at the bungalow for a few hours. Jensen must have followed them from the RV if he found them this fast. She glanced at Malachi. His hands were flexing and stretching, and his face was grim. She found herself holding her breath. She needed him to be calm; she'd come to depend on his strength and centeredness more than she'd realized. As Israel closed the door and planted himself in front of it, Malachi moved back to the bed. One hand sliding around the back of her neck, he drew her into his chest and chuffed into her hair. Everything in her warmed and steadied as she slid her hands around his waist.

"Beauty, you're trembling," he said softly. His lips wandered over her hair. "Nothing will harm you while I guard our den."

Pepper's only answer was to press her cheek against his chest. Malachi's hand strayed into her hair, keeping her close to him, and she didn't protest.

"How fresh is the scent?" Malachi repeated, keeping his voice low. He sounded much calmer.

"I cannot tell." Israel snorted, as if punishing his nose for its inadequacy. "His scent is so bound up with the smell of those colored daisies, it is disorienting."

"Sneezeweed," Pepper said. He blinked questioningly down at her. "It's called sneezeweed." She smiled faintly at the faded memory. "My dad had them by the back door of the house when we lived in

Crescent City. He said the smell kept the insects away."

"I do not know about insects, woman, but it is havoc on a Tseng Tse nose."

"You're allowed to call me Pepper," she said as she loosened her grip on Malachi and settled against the headboard again. Malachi kept his arm around her, holding her close to his side. "It *is* my name."

Israel half bowed. "Your name is one of your most prized possessions. I would not disrespect you by using it without your permission. Thank you, Pepper."

"Of course." Pepper managed not to stumble over the words. Malachi ran his hand along her jaw, encouraging her to turn to him. His indigo eyes were somber.

"I'm afraid that I must leave you." His voice was heavy, echoing the regret in his face. There was a hardness in his eyes and the set of his mouth that made Pepper catch the inside of her lip between her teeth. "Israel will stay with you. You'll be safe here."

"You would rather I stay in your den with your woman than hunt the aberration?" Sarcasm turned the corners of Israel's lips. "Earlier, you could not stand to see us sitting at the same table."

"Stay off the bed," Malachi ordered. The sound was so ferocious that Pepper shivered. Instantly, Malachi turned his attention back to her, and everything about him was gentle. "Not you. You sleep. Israel is as great a hunter as I am—"

"Better," Israel interrupted. Pepper bit her lip against a giggle. Malachi continued as if Israel wasn't there.

"—and you will be safe. You need rest to heal, body and spirit."

A new fear gripped Pepper's heart. She slid her hand into his hair and held on, as if it would keep him with her.

"You're coming back. Right?" When did it become so important to her that Malachi be close by? The idea of him leaving made her slightly ill. She tried to tell herself that it was only because she didn't know Israel, didn't trust him like she did Malachi, but she knew better. It was Malachi, himself. She simply wanted to be with him. "What happens if you find Jensen?"

"Then I will bring him the justice of our people, and your nightmare will be over." Malachi's hand slid over her face, cradling her in their warmth. His focus was on her and only her as he leaned down. Despite Israel's presence in the room, Pepper closed her eyes and guided his mouth to hers. The moment her lips met his, heat surged through her blood. She shifted restlessly but Malachi refused to meet the demand she was making of him. His kiss was filled with care and promise, but he broke the kiss before it could get any more heated. He leaned his forehead against hers without releasing her face, his thumbs feathering over her cheekbones.

"Pepper mine, I need to go. Stay inside. Listen to Israel. I swear on the blood of the ancestors, I *will* come back to you."

He watched her closely, still not moving from the bed, and inhaled deeply. He was waiting for her. Waiting to be certain she was okay before he left. And while he waited, Jensen could be getting farther and farther away. Her heart turned over. She settled back against the headboard and flashed Malachi a little feral grin.

"Go get 'em, tiger."

****

The scent of Pepper's fear clung to his nose as Malachi forced himself away from her, onto the tiny porch. Her scent held arousal, too. It made a potent combination, one that made the tiger rise up, roaring, beneath his skin. He shuddered with the effort to keep control. Israel filled the doorway behind him, and Malachi nailed him with a look.

"I give her to your keeping," he said gravely, a warning edge to his tone. Israel didn't even blink.

"I will keep your den as though it were my own," he replied. Israel clasped Malachi on the shoulder. "Good hunting, brother mine."

Malachi denied himself another look toward Pepper and stepped into the darkness. The night washed over him. The air was heavy with the scent of the colored daisies. Sneezeweed, Pepper had called it. It was an apt name. The feel of it in his nose made him want to sneeze, but he had no choice. Malachi allowed his eyes to change. The world brightened and came into sharp focus at his command. That, alone, would help him to spot Jensen. It was late. The guests at the bed and breakfast were shut up in their dens—such as they were—though many had soft lights glowing beyond warm curtains. He could hear the muffled laughter peculiar to couples drifting on the evening breeze. It did nothing to improve his mood.

He ought to be with Pepper, soothing her fears and making sure she ate, seducing her to sleep beside him. Already the need to ensure her safety, the need to see her comfortable and secure and well cared for, was overwhelming. Malachi knew he would never be free of that thought again, even if he were to leave her. Both the tiger and the man would always need to know, or there would never be any peace in his heart.

The beast was pacing, claws out, demanding release. Malachi needed to hunt like he needed air to breathe. But he couldn't shift. His white coat was too visible in the darkness. With the curtains in the bungalows around him closed, and many of the lights blinking off, he crouched. Malachi had to bend to hands and knees in order to get his nose close enough to the ground, and then drew the scents in, holding them in his mouth to taste them. They were a little cleaner closer to the ground, smelling mostly of wet cement. He let the tiger's mind categorize and name them for him: the gentlemanly landlord, coming and going often; several couples; a dog in need of a vet visit. Pepper's scent jumped out at him. The layer of distress in it was distracting; he had to force it out of his mind.

Malachi swept his head back and forth, like a charmed snake, his eyes half-lidded in concentration though he kept his ears pricked for any shift in sound. He sneezed. Violently. Swearing under his breath, he did his best to clear his nose and bent to the ground once more. Israel hadn't been exaggerating. The scent of the sneezeweed was strong. As strong as his senses were, and as attuned as he was to Jensen's scent, it still took a great deal of concentration for him to catch his prey's stench twining through the omnipresent smell of the flower.

But he found it. It prowled around the bungalow, with traces of anger, desperation, and arousal. Malachi raised his lip in a silent snarl as he lifted his head, a direct challenge to the night. And sneezed. He rose to his feet. His nostrils flared as he worked the scents around in his mouth again, making certain of his course before taking a single step. Once he knew what he was scenting for, he didn't have to put his nose to the ground. It wasn't as if sneezeweed could walk around on its own stems.

He had a few false starts. The landlord had an apparent affinity for sneezeweed, perhaps for the same reason Pepper's father had. The trail led him past quite a bit of the landscaping, but once he reached the parking lot of the bed and breakfast, the scents cleared. The acrid smell of asphalt and gasoline were a distinct contrast to the spicy floral scent. Out here, he could even catch hints of Jensen's scent, despite the sneezeweed.

Tracking went faster. The breeze was blowing toward the ocean, bringing the scents of the town to Malachi's nose. His steps were utterly confident, despite the darkness. The tiger's eyes were born to see clearly by the light of stars and moon. Streetlamps were almost painfully bright to him. Fortunately, they seemed to affect Jensen the same way. The sneezeweed trail wound through the side-streets, taking dimmer routes more comfortable on his eyes. He wasn't so innocent as to believe that was Jensen's reason. The aberration was trying to stay out of the light, to keep from being seen as he hunted.

And he *was* hunting. It showed in his scent. The trail veered from sidewalks to peer in windows, all kinds of windows. Malachi even found traces of him on balconies and garage roofs, places he could crouch to stare into second-story windows. Every house where the aberration stopped had the scent of females. Some were little more than younglings. Malachi's heart hammered against his ribs as his feet picked up pace. The hunt was speeding.

Malachi ran through the darkened streets until he reached a wall of intertwining plants. Malachi lifted his face into the night breeze and coughed. Jensen's scent was strong, and it was vile. Arousal mixed with hunt-scent. Desperation mingled with lust. It took all of Malachi's discipline to force himself closer to that scent. It tangled on the branches, an unseen accompaniment to the death-rattle of the leaves.

The great gate to the seaside botanical gardens was sealed and dark. Malachi leaned his face against the heavy wood. The fugitive had done the same thing. Something had sparked Jensen's interest, and the change in scent made Malachi's gut churn. Backing up, he sized up the gate, and the wall. They were roughly twelve feet high. He could make the jump if he had to, though he might have to scramble a bit over the top. He searched for the scent again, crouching all the way down to the ground. There was no trace of the aberration's scent this far out. Malachi returned to the gate. The mixture of scents went against his every instinct, as well as everything he was raised to be. He drew it in, following it along the perimeter. Jensen's scent pooled slightly, as if he had moved slowly. Hunting something. Stalking something.

Prey.

Malachi prayed to the ancestors that he was wrong. That the fear that clutched his heart was nothing more than the worst-case imagination of a hunter too far from his target. He moved back along the wall, swiftly and silently.

Several yards from the entrance, the wall gave way to a lower fence, only eight feet high. The hedge on either side was thick and tangled, but it would be no barrier to a Tseng Tse raised in the jungle, as he was. As Jensen was. Malachi slowed. There: a break pattern. Something large had pushed through the plants with more speed than care. Small branches were snapped, and the dying leaves had been stripped away to scatter in an incongruous layer on the way to the fence. Heavier branches were broken at the top of the hedge.

Malachi considered his options. He could slip through the gap Jensen had made and jump the fence from standing, but if he did, he risked leaving his scent all over the fence, as well as risked breaking the hedge at the top. He could take a short lead and make a running jump over the fence and hedge together, but he might lose the scent in the process and have to take up more valuable time to find it again.

Malachi shook his head. No. The strength of Jensen's stench should make the trail easy to pick up again. It was worth a few seconds to preserve stealth, as well as the plants. He backed up a handful of paces and, digging in his toes, sprinted toward the barrier to spring over it.

He landed in a silent crouch on the far side, deliberately braced to keep his skin from touching the ground. He needn't have worried about losing the trail. Not only did Jensen's stench permeate the air, but there were footprints in the muddy flowerbed in front of him. He frowned. Jensen had left perfect prints, and his feet were bare. There were too many scent glands on the feet. Every Tseng Tse knew better than to go barefoot. Unless he wanted to be caught. It was possible that some part of Jensen was still Tseng Tse enough that he wanted the hunters to catch him and stop him. That could make things a little easier, if Jensen were fighting himself, as well. It could also make him more unpredictable, and therefore more dangerous.

Malachi didn't have time to think about that right now. There was a second set of footprints in the mud, smaller, more delicate-looking, and wearing shoes. Malachi bent down, so close that his nose was inside the depression of the track.

Female.

Malachi sprang from his crouch straight into a run. There was no time. They weren't far ahead of him, and the woman's scent was so drenched in fear that he could smell nothing else about her. Her terror spurred every instinct inside of him. The gardens blurred as he ran at his top speed. Streaks of muted color flashed by on either side. He couldn't hide his trail now. The paths were soft grass and showed every footprint. If the situation weren't so dire, he would have felt homesick for the palace of his homeland. He had neither time nor leisure as he sped through the darkness, eyes and ears strained to their limits for any sign of the criminal and his terrified prey.

Malachi heard the sobbing first. A wild, broken sound that turned his soul inside out. The need to soothe it hit him hard, a driving force that sent new strength surging through him. Claws slid from his fingertips as his hands shifted, partway between the hands of a man and the enormous paws of a tiger. His teeth elongated as his head changed, taking on the muzzle and fearsome teeth of an apex predator. He barely felt the familiar prickle as fur sprouted through his skin, not quite as long as it would be if he were going to his full tiger form. His ears slid up his head, changing shape to bring in every sound as they swiveled independently. The seams on his shirt strained, then gave out entirely as his torso simply grew, adding layers of thick muscle to his chest and shoulders, especially, as well as protective fur.

He slowed to a more human pace. He placed each foot with care as he sought out the taller plants. If he rushed right up on the attack, he could spook Jensen into killing his prey. The woman was still alive, and Malachi would keep her that way.

Craggy trees twined together near the seaward cliff that marked the western boundary of the gardens. Bodies moved in the deep shadow. He knew Jensen as soon as he saw him. Pinned beneath him was his prey, the young female. Her dark hair tangled around her head, her eyes tightly closed. Jensen gripped her wrists, forcing them over her head in one of his larger hands. His other hand stroked her hair in a grotesque parody of tenderness. His growl was loud and continuous as his mouth assaulted the woman's breasts and belly, but Malachi could still make out her pleas as she sobbed. He caught the glimpse of sharp, shifted teeth in the starlight just as Jensen lowered his mouth toward her throat.

Malachi sprang. He slammed into Jensen with his full weight, as well as all his speed. Jensen snarled in surprise as they tumbled away from the poor woman in a mass of flashing fur, sweat-soaked skin, and teeth. Malachi's blood surged through his veins, burning up reason. His instincts roared, and he roared with them. The sound drove the birds from their roosts and shook the ground. Jensen managed to come out on top, straddling Malachi. His pale eyes were wide as they began to shift. Malachi swiped one clawed hand for Jensen's belly as the other shot for the aberration's throat. Jensen leaped backward to avoid the wicked claws. Malachi drew his legs to his chest for the momentum to spring to his feet.

The woman screamed. Malachi didn't dare look at her, didn't dare to take his eyes from his opponent. Jensen seemed to grow in the darkness. He chose the hybrid form, as well, combining speed, strength, agility, and dexterity. Claws slid from his fingers as his teeth gained their true predator's length. Orange and black rippled over Jensen's naked skin, deepening to nearly a chocolate brown on his limbs, though it wasn't long enough or heavy enough to disguise his reaction to having his prey so close. Malachi snarled, a deep, menacing sound that made the very air tremble. Jensen stepped back. The scent of fear joined those of arousal, lust, and hunt-scent. Malachi refused to look away. He *wanted* Jensen afraid, as afraid as he had made those women. He wanted the aberration to feel every terrified heartbeat, every wound, every ounce of humiliation that he had inflicted upon his prey, and then—only then— would Malachi bring justice and end that miserable excuse for a life. He held Jensen's gaze with a predator's glare, daring the filthy creature to challenge a prince of his people.

Jensen's gaze flicked away. Half a heartbeat when the fugitive admitted Malachi's superiority. Malachi stalked, each step eating up ground. If Jensen were typical of Tseng Tse, he would stay where he was until Malachi reached him and accept justice. Malachi didn't believe it for an instant.

Jensen dove toward the landward side and a woman's scream shredded the air. Malachi twisted, his body moving in a way impossible for human bones as he followed. Catching Jensen low, he slammed the other tiger backward and knocked him to the ground. Before he could pounce, Jensen rolled out of the way and onto his feet. Malachi rushed again. Jensen's darker coat blended into the darkness. Even Malachi's enhanced vision couldn't see the swing coming fast enough. Fire tore through Malachi's body from ribs to hip, slashing across his belly. Malachi's roar was as much fury as pain. He grabbed Jensen's arm, sinking his claws deep into flesh. He hooked in and pulled hard, yanking Jensen into him as he kicked to tangle Jensen's feet. Pain burned through his belly. Blood ran freely through his fur, soaking into what was left of his pants. Jensen twisted inside of his own skin to drive his knee into the gashes over Malachi's belly. Malachi doubled over in pain, his grip loosening on Jensen's arm.

Jensen wrenched out of the hunter's grasp, opening gashes in his own flesh. Dropping to a four-legged run, he sprinted toward his prey. Malachi didn't know if it was shock or injury that had kept the woman from running away, but, whatever the reason, he couldn't allow Jensen to get his claws on her again. He lunged after the aberration, despite the pain and the lightheadedness. He managed to grab Jensen in the upper thigh and drag him down. Using his claws as hooks, he hauled himself over the other tiger's body. Jensen kicked him in the belly, his hind claws gouging as his foot dragged downward. Malachi growled, but Jensen managed to force him off. Malachi dragged himself to his feet, though he was largely bent over, his arm holding his gut. The snarl was much quieter this time, but he glared through the darkness, an implacable challenge in his eyes. He would die for this woman, and he would make Jensen pay dearly for this prey in the process. He would have to go through Malachi to get back to the garden gate. The hunter had him cornered.

Jensen hesitated. His gaze moved between the bent and bloodied Malachi and the naked woman cowering on the far side, and then past, to the gardens and the freedom beyond them. He made a low sound that was half croon. Spinning on his heel, he sprinted for the cliff edge and leaped.

Malachi snarled a Tseng Tse curse and staggered for the cliff edge as fast as he could. A shadow slightly deeper than the others slithered down the cliff-face. He looked back toward the woman. Her fist was stuffed in her mouth, tears gleaming as they saturated her cheeks. She was streaked with mud, leaves and twigs dotting her body. He could make out the scent of blood, but it wasn't enough to be life-threatening. She would survive. Human officials could deal with her injuries. He hated to leave her in such distress, but his presence would likely only make things harder on her. He shook his head, trying to clear the dark fog gathering inside his skull. He needed to not be here when the police arrived. They couldn't pass off two tiger-men fighting as trauma-induced shock if one of them was standing right there. He chuffed softly at the woman, hoping it would soothe and encourage her. Then, turning, he hurled himself off the edge of the cliff.

Powerful legs gave him enough momentum that he missed the cliff itself. The jumbled rocks at the base battered his body as he rolled over the outer edge of them and onto the sand. Jensen was long gone. Malachi never doubted that. His breath came in harsh gasps as he lay on his back. The cold water of the Pacific Ocean lapped at his body, pushing away the blackness in his mind for a moment longer. Pepper. His Pepper, with her strength, her courage, her laughter, her warm heart. He closed his eyes and focused on her face, her scent, the feel of her body against his. The change was agonizing. The pain seemed to go on forever as his mind forced his destroyed body to knit itself back together in a completely different shape. By the time he was human again, Malachi had nothing left to give. He sent a prayer to the ancestors that Israel would keep his Pepper safe, and blackness overtook him.

Chapter Twenty-One

Pepper leaned against the doorway between the kitchen and the back hall. It was empty for the moment. Only Abby was at work this early, and she was in her office. A dull ache throbbed behind Pepper's eyes. She hadn't slept well. She hadn't really slept at all. She'd dozed a bit, tossing in a thin and fitful imitation of sleep. Even wearing Malachi's T-shirt hadn't helped. Every sound, every shift of light had slammed her awake. If Israel hadn't been there to calm and reassure her, she would have lost her mind. He seemed to be in constant motion, on alert either at the windows or the door, occasionally stepping outside for brief periods. She couldn't blame him. His little brother was missing.

Pepper dragged herself off the wall and forced herself to the dining room. Every step felt like lead. Malachi hadn't come back. There had been no word from him that night, nor the next day, nor last night. Instead of wringing her hands with worry, Pepper decided to wring a washcloth. The hot water felt good on her skin, reminding her of the bath Malachi had interrupted. She cleaned the counter first. The room was cool enough that faint wisps of steam curled up from the scrubbed surface, gleaming in the pearly light of a cloud-dimmed dawn.

"I did not think it customary to scrub the surface off the tables when cleaning them, even in the human world."

Israel's soft voice should have startled her, but, after more than twenty-four hours of his constant company, she was used to it. In fact, she was glad of it. She turned to find him standing near the front door, leaning against the jamb with apparent laziness. Pepper was starting to learn, however, and noticed that he was leaning across the door, blocking it, with his shoulder against the hinges. That door wasn't moving without him being instantly aware of it. No one was getting past him. The sight warmed her, and she coughed to clear the sudden tightness out of her throat.

"How did you get in here?" she demanded. Israel only smiled. He was almost as handsome as Malachi, with the same thick, dark hair and clean, masculine features. He was bigger, though. She hadn't thought anyone but pro wrestlers came bigger than Malachi. The family resemblance between the two brothers made her chest ache.

"A man who spends all his money making an unbreakable gate ought to have spent more time on the rest of the walls," Israel said. Pepper blinked. For several seconds, she stared at him with her head tilted to one side, her cleaning cloth dripping into the bucket at her feet.

"Was that supposed to make sense?" she finally asked. Israel shrugged.

"Not especially. It was supposed to get you to think about something besides Malachi, even if only for ten seconds."

Pepper hurled the cloth at his head. Israel unfurled with a casual movement, but he easily caught the cloth in mid-air, long before it was any kind of threat to his face. Smirking, he brought it back to her. Even the way he moved reminded her of Malachi, the same flowing grace, the same absolute confidence. Israel wrapped his arms around her and brought her close in a hug as he chuffed.

"He is going to be fine, little sister," he said, repeating it for the dozenth time since Malachi left the bungalow. "He is hunting. It is not unusual for a hunt to last a few days."

Pepper hugged him hard. She knew she was clinging to him. It just couldn't matter to her right then. Israel was the only real link she had to Malachi, that he actually existed, that he hadn't been the impassioned fantasy of a traumatized mind.

Israel pulled back, his amber eyes kind. "Shall I tell you a story while you work? Perhaps…the time that our Second Healer caught four of us—myself and Malachi included—trying to steal a boat and sneak out of the palace?"

Pepper laughed, as Israel no doubt hoped she would, and took the washcloth from his hand. She dipped it into the bucket and wrung it out, already feeling better just because of Israel's company.

"First tell me what a second healer is."

"Our Second Healer is the second most skilled, most revered healer of our people. She lives at the palace, but, unlike the First Healer, she may travel away from it, and often does, in the course of her duties." Israel began to pull the chairs off the tables, though he managed to constantly keep himself between Pepper and the front door. She shook her head a little, amused and comforted, and started to scrub one of the tables he'd cleared.

"If Abby catches you in here, we're both in trouble," she warned. Israel flashed a grin.

"She will not 'catch' me."

Pepper grunted. "I believe you. Why can't the First Healer leave the palace?" Pepper asked, trying to direct the conversation back to something much more interesting, and almost distracting enough to make her forget the tight ache in her chest.

"It is too dangerous," Israel replied. "The First Healer is the heart of our people. He holds the knowledge and the well-being of all the Tseng Tse inside his head. If we were to lose him, centuries of knowledge would be lost with him. The souls of all Tseng Tse throughout the world would cry out in grief for a long, long time. Our ability to heal each other and to heal others would be catastrophically set back in time."

"Oh." Pepper couldn't think of any other reply to that. "Don't you write books? Get online?"

"We do." Israel's smile was mostly in his voice. "When the First Healer's knowledge began, books were common enough, but the ability to read them was not. The Internet was hundreds of years away. We are an old people, sister mine, old and stubborn, and clinging to tradition in order to survive. For those of us who live in diaspora, it is vital that we know home is still there, safe and intact, with the First Healer, the First Prince, and First Princess safe within."

"Prince and princess?" Pepper looked up quickly. "Like, literal prince and princess?"

"Very like," Israel agreed. A noise on the street attracted his attention, but only briefly. He dismissed it and turned back to her. "I said we are an old people, did

I not? The Tseng Tse are a monarchy, ruled over by a prince or princess, and their mate, if they should be so fortunate as to find one. Josiah did, and it has been an infinite blessing to all of our people since."

Pepper absorbed that for a moment, scrubbing thoughtfully. "They aren't allowed to leave the palace, either." It was a statement, but she hoped Israel would contradict her.

"The First Healer is the heart of the Tseng Tse. The First Prince is our head. Without heart and head, how can we live?" Israel's voice was kind, as if he knew this would be a difficult thing for her and he was trying to make it easier.

"It's archaic," Pepper muttered to the soapy water. Israel heard anyway.

"By *your* standards."

Pepper looked up with an expression that bordered on sarcastic, but the large man was nowhere to be seen. She frowned, turning in a full circle looking for him. The door to the back hallway thudded as Abby pushed her way through, the drawer to the cash register in both hands. Her eyebrows went up as soon as she saw Pepper.

"I was hoping you'd be asleep with your head on the table. Tell me again why you're here two hours early?"

"I didn't tell you the first time," Pepper muttered, then smiled her most charming. "Because I need the hours and you're a phenomenal boss who will let me have them."

Abby snorted as she shoved the cash drawer into place with her hip. A tinge of red covered her cheeks, however, and she looked pleased, in spite of herself.

"You, miss, are a shameless flatterer. I should make you go sleep in my office until your scheduled shift. But," Abby sighed. "Carla's already called in with a hangover. You can switch shifts with her and get off early. Lucky little bird, you."

"Thanks, Abby," Pepper said with a soft smile. Abby disappeared back into the back hallway. Pepper breathed deeply. She couldn't have said if it was a sigh of relief, or a deep breath attempting to control the exhaustion-fueled emotions that lurked just under the hysteria level.

"She cares about you very much," Israel said quietly. This time, he was standing by one of the windows, still looking out at the street. He smiled faintly. "Her face may not show it, but her scent is filled with worry."

"Abby's good people," Pepper said, feeling she needed to say something but not really knowing what. "Where were you hiding?"

Israel only kept smiling. He pushed away from the window to rest his hand on her shoulder. His gaze was level, unblinking. "I will be close. You may not see me, but I will be watching over you. I will hear you if you call. Even if you are only frightened, or worried for your potential mate, call out for me. Yes?"

"Yeah." Pepper nodded with a little smile. "Two days of babysitting. You must be getting tired of it."

"Malachi would bring you to me as a sister. I cannot tire of caring for one of our family."

Pepper opened her mouth to argue—she hadn't promised Malachi anything yet—but before the sounds would come out, Israel laid a finger to his lips for silence and pointed to the door to the back hall. Even

223

Pepper heard Abby's footsteps, this time, or at least heard her struggling with a heavy load. She stepped in front of Israel, either trying to hide him or protect him. There was a very soft chuckle, then a little movement of air across the back of her neck. The door pushed open again, and Abby came through with the load of pastries for the counter. Pepper rushed forward, dropping her washcloth on the way to grab the other side of the large tray.

"Thank you." Abby let Pepper hold the tray and balance it on the counter. Opening the display, she began to shift each piece inside. Pepper's mouth watered as the long tongs passed each one under her nose. It must have shown in her face because Abby gave her an appraising look. "Did you eat this morning?"

"No. I forgot." Her mind had been so absorbed with other things, like getting through a shower with her wounded side and no Malachi to bind it up for her again, that she'd completely forgotten food. At least she could feel hungry again. Israel had been insisting that she eat at regular intervals, and that was the only reason she had managed to eat yesterday. Even then, it had felt a lot like choking down ash.

"There are some turnovers on the shelf over the sink. Grab a couple. I don't need you fainting into the espresso machine from low blood sugar." Abby leveled the tongs at her, a large muffin bobbing threateningly in her face. "But make it quick. Those doors are opening in ten minutes, and I expect you to be ready to work."

"Thanks, Abby. I'll be back in time to finish the tables." Pepper could have hugged her, more for her kindness than for the offer of the turnover. Abby grunted.

"They look ready to me."

Pepper followed the owner's gaze. The chairs had been taken down from every table, and each tabletop gleamed, freshly scrubbed and ready for the day. Pepper suspected Israel, though she couldn't figure out how he'd managed to finish her work for her without being seen or heard.

She didn't offer an excuse, only shrugged and smiled and made an escape to claim a turnover from the kitchen. Abby always set some of the pastries aside, claiming that they weren't fit to sell, but, to Pepper's knowledge, no one had ever found fault with them. The staff suspected the coffee shop owner kept them to feed employees who missed a meal, or anyone else who was hungry.

Pepper grabbed an apple turnover from the shelf. Tearing off pieces with her fingers, she popped them into her mouth as she leaned against the counter. Happy chattering passed by in the hall. That would be the rest of the shift arriving. Pepper breathed a sigh, and this time she knew it was one of relief. The food was warm and comforting—and managed to not taste like ash— and very, very soon the coffee shop would be too busy for her to think about anything but lattes and espressos.

As soon as the doors opened, the morning crowd started the day off bustling. Pepper greeted her regulars by name and prepared their regular drinks…though she got them more mixed up than usual. After the fourth bungled order in a row, Abby threatened to send her home, citing that she was obviously too tired to work and she wasn't going to have an exhausted employee getting burned. Pepper retreated to the corner of the counter for a moment, hiding behind the line of her coworkers until she could get herself under control. Something made her look up. Israel sat at one of the tables. A pretty blonde was obviously trying hard to get his attention, chatting animatedly over insulated paper cups, but his amber eyes were focused completely on Pepper. He didn't wink or nod, or even smile, but something in the unwavering directness of his gaze made her feel steadied, supported. She drew back her shoulders and lifted her chin. Israel's eyes warmed, and one side of his mouth drew upward in a proud, if crooked, little smile. Only then did he turn his gaze to the woman with whom he shared a table and the cup in front of him. Pepper wasn't convinced his attention went with it.

Pepper threw herself into the work. She whirled about the dining room with a brilliant smile. She may have been worried sick, with terror filling her mind, but there was no reason for the customers to know it. She passed Israel several times. He seemed to spend the entire morning just hanging around the coffee shop. No one seemed to notice it. No heads turned when he walked in the door, despite the fact that he was a pretty sexy-looking man. Pepper didn't allow herself much time to think about it. It was too connected to Malachi, and those thoughts would only make things more difficult. The only conclusion she came to was that he was trying to blend in and be invisible, and she just had to leave it at that.

"Pepper," Abby called into the lowered din as Pepper feverishly wiped down tables during a lull. She jerked her head toward the door. "Lunch."

Pepper looked at her watch. The morning had

disappeared. Relief and the morning's practice made it easy for her to force a smile for Abby.

"I'm fine," Pepper said.

"First in, first to lunch." Abby jerked her head toward the door.

"Then you should be taking lunch first."

"I get lunch when I get lunch," Abby replied with a shrug. "The others don't get their lunch until you've taken yours, miss, so get to it before they get too hungry. If they riot, I'm pointing it at you."

"All right, all right," Pepper capitulated. Untying her apron, she stepped back behind the counter, and wished she had a jacket. Not like she could go far for lunch, anyway. Her car was still sitting in the parking lot, completely nonfunctional. So much trouble had come of her filming that attack, interrupting it to get him to focus on her. The attacker was focused on her, all right, and he could turn into a tiger with enhanced speed, strength, and senses at will.

But along with all the trouble had come Malachi.

She pulled the elastic from her hair as she stepped through the back door into the parking lot. At least that would afford her a little bit more warmth on the back of her neck. Parked perpendicular to the lines was a large gray pickup. Pepper's heart jumped into her throat as she sprinted forward.

"Malachi!" she cried.

The passenger door opened. Pepper slowed to a stop as Israel dropped out. Her chest tightened. It shouldn't hurt that much to find that it was Israel driving the truck, not Malachi. She swallowed hard, pressing the back of her hand against her mouth.

"I am sorry, little sister." Israel reached a hand for

her, his face filled with compassion. "It was not my intention to wound you with false hope. Come." Israel added when she hesitated, "Please."

Pepper's throat was so tight that it hurt, but she put her hand in his and allowed him to help her into the seat. Shutting the door, he went around to the other side. In the middle of the bench seat was a large bag from a local restaurant, and it smelled fantastic.

"You need to eat," Israel said in explanation as he settled. "I was remiss enough to allow you to go to work this morning without food. How many more hours are left in your shift?"

"Israel, I'm fine. I promise."

"You do not smell fine," Israel said. Pepper tried not to retreat under his unblinking stare. "Nor should you. You are exhausted. You are hungry. Your heart is aching with fear and loneliness. I can do little against the loneliness, and only so much against the fear. But the hunger and exhaustion are things with which I can aid you. Eat. Human lunch breaks are notoriously short."

Pepper snorted. "And the Tseng Tse have longer ones?"

"Of course." Israel sounded so smug that she was torn between laughing at him and kicking him. "With so much time spent hunting our food, we understand the value of actually tasting it, and then allowing it to digest properly. You humans make a habit of bearing down your food and dashing about. It is little wonder you are so often ill."

Pepper caught the teasing light in Israel's eyes and decided to ignore the disparaging comments about humans. "Bearing down?"

"I believe you say, 'wolfing down', but we get along better with wolf-shifters than bear-shifters. Eat."

Pepper turned to lean back against the truck's door, dropping one knee onto the seat. She watched him carefully for any sign that he was teasing her.

"Let me make sure I'm following you: not only are there tiger-shifters, but there are wolf-shifters and bear-shifters, too?"

"Yes," Israel answered. Pepper wished she had a Tseng Tse nose, just to know for sure he was telling the truth. He looked serious.

"Any others I should know about?" she asked, injecting humor into her tone. It was easier to face if she kept things light. Otherwise the idea was too overwhelming.

"There are many kinds of shifters in the world, little sister, but very few that you need to know about right now," Israel nudged the bag toward her. "Eat."

"So when you say humans 'bear down' our food, you're insulting humans *and* bears. But not wolves. You like wolves."

Israel's lips twitched as if he were fighting a smile. "Yes, and right now, I would prefer that you eat like one."

"And how is that?"

"Eat plenty now, and come back for plenty later."

Pepper pulled a thick paper clamshell out of the bag. Delicious-scented steam issued from inside. She could barely wrap her hands around the sandwich, it was piled so high with meat. Pepper nibbled at it, taking bits of roast beef from between the slices of bread with her fingers.

"Any word from Malachi?"

229

"Not yet."

"Why don't you just go and look for him?" Pepper's tone was heated with frustration. "Your nose is as good as his, isn't it? If he can track someone through rain, can't you just go and find him?"

Israel's expression was somber and filled with compassion. Slowly, he nodded.

"I could. It would not be too difficult. I know his scent very well." Israel smiled slightly, and guilt lanced through Pepper. For a moment, she'd forgotten Malachi was Israel's little brother. Of course he'd be worried, too. Israel continued.

"I do not dare to leave you unprotected, Pepper. I have not seen the fugitive, nor have I smelled him, but, repeatedly, I have smelled...sneezeweed, is it? I have smelled sneezeweed around the coffee shop several times." Israel turned grim. "He is watching you. He is hunting, and waiting only for his chance to pounce."

Pepper's throat tightened, but she shook her head.

"He wouldn't dare," she said with more confidence than she felt. "There are way too many people around."

"Did he not pounce on his prey here once already? Were there fewer people around then?"

Pepper took another bite of her sandwich. It kept her from having to look at him with defeat on her face. The fear that never seemed far away scratched at her heart. She coughed softly in an attempt to clear it away enough to swallow without feeling like she was choking. It didn't work. She coughed in earnest as something stuck in her throat. Israel handed her an enormous plastic cup filled with lemonade. Pepper gulped it down. It cleared the physical blockage but the emotional one still threatened. Dropping her sandwich back into the paper clamshell, she folded her arms on the dash and leaned her forehead against them.

"Pepper." Israel sounded so much like Malachi that she gasped. Warmth flooded through her at the memory of Malachi's low, coaxing tone—so like Israel's—followed quickly by cold. She lifted her head. Israel reached toward her, his hand hovering near her shoulder before retreating. His amber eyes were intent as he spoke clearly.

"He is going to come back," Israel said. Pepper had no doubt that he believed it, and she clung to that conviction. "There is no way that stubborn cat is going to crawl away and die now, not after finding a potential mate." A hint of amusement crept into Israel's tone and lightened his eyes. "If you are not in perfect condition when Malachi returns, he is going to have my hide in front of his fireplace. Please." He picked up the clamshell with Pepper's sandwich and offered it to her. "For my sake. Eat."

"Eat. Sleep. You're obsessed with me eating and sleeping," Pepper groused, but she picked up her sandwich anyway. Israel waited until she took another bite.

"When Malachi returns, he will need to check to be certain that you are unharmed, and he will need to know that you have fed, and slept, and that you are safe and comfortable, or he will not be willing to see to his own needs. Perhaps he will not even be able to."

"Tell me about this potential mate business," Pepper asked after clearing her mouth with another drink of lemonade. "You two sure talk about it a lot."

"It is very important to our people." Israel shifted, trying to stretch out his long frame a little more in the confines of the truck. "Legend has it that, for each Tseng Tse, there are a handful of individuals in the world with whom we are completely compatible, in every way. If ever we manage to meet one, their scent triggers a deep, primal need."

"Sex," Pepper said simply, shrugging it off. Israel was too grave to look offended, but she got the distinct impression she'd crossed a line. Heat crept into her cheeks. "Sorry."

Israel rubbed his thumb over the stubble on his jaw.

"I do not blame you, little sister. You do not...you *cannot* understand. It is something that is foreign to humans. It is far, far more than intense sexual desire. It is an innate need to protect, to care for, to simply be near to them. It is an instinctive reaction, built deep into the parts of us that come directly from the ancestors, one that we can fight little better than standing in the path of a hurricane."

"How many potential mates have you met?" Pepper asked after a moment's shy silence.

"None."

She swallowed, soothing her throat with a drink before trying to speak. "And Malachi?"

"One." Israel stared hard at her, making it very clear who that one person was. The awful knot in her chest loosened a little bit. If it was so rare, then he would fight with all of his strength to get back to her. *If* it wasn't just Israel spouting pretty words to calm the hysterical human.

A terrible thought occurred to her. "What about Jensen?"

"None. If he had, he would never be able to leave

her side. He is far too ill."

"Would he...hurt her?" For the first time in a while, Pepper feared for someone besides herself, as if it was just dawning on her that this creature that hunted her could turn his perverted obsession on someone else, someone who didn't have the protection she did.

"It is very likely." Israel stared out the windows. Pepper wasn't sure if he was gathering his thoughts or if his senses had alerted him to danger that she missed. "It is part of our deepest nature to protect humans. That is why we were created. Something is broken in that deepest part of Jensen, turning him to the tragic and deadly aberration that he is. It goes against everything we are taught. It goes against every instinct that we possess. But," Israel sighed. It was clear he didn't want to say what was coming next. "We believe that he is searching for a mate. He refuses to wait to catch scent. We believe that he is finding a woman that he wants and then convincing himself, somehow, that she is a potential mate. Then he forces himself on her body in an attempt to forge a mate-bond."

"He rapes her," Pepper said bluntly. Israel nodded once with that regal air. She shuddered, hard enough to tug on the wounds on her side. Or maybe she just noticed them because she was thinking about the attack. "But none of them have been potential mates."

"Even if they were, that is not how a mate-bond is formed. Jensen is broken." Israel stated each word separately. His expression made it clear how detestable Jensen's actions were to him. His mouth twitched into something like a snarl and Pepper pressed back against the door of the truck. Israel blinked and cleared his expression. "Forgive me, little sister. I did not mean to

233

frighten you. I will scout a bit and let you eat in peace. Do not leave the truck. I will return for you."

It really wasn't any easier to eat alone, but Pepper managed to get down most of the large sandwich. Israel returned fairly quickly with a grim fire in his eyes. Pepper didn't ask. She had a pretty good idea of what would cause that look, and she didn't want to hear it out loud. He walked her back to the coffee shop, not willing to let her out of his sight for even those few feet. He came in with her, acting just like any other customer, though Pepper was certain that his sniffing was more than appreciating the scents of coffee and pastries.

She tried to shove it out of her mind as she went through the familiar rituals of tying on her apron and washing her hands, and it worked, for a while. The gouges in her side kept burning, dragging her mind back to everything she was trying to forget. She tried to throw herself into the job again, putting all of her focus on the customers. It got a lot harder when the coffee shop emptied. Pepper dived into deep cleaning behind the counter and tried to focus in on what was really upsetting her. Pouring water into the steamer to clean it, she attacked the countertop with a cleaning cloth. She missed Malachi. She was worried about him. The depth of missing him and worrying about him surprised her. She should ask Israel if humans were affected by this potential mates business. It would explain why she had such a strong and sudden reaction to him. But was that really what was making her so miserable?

She picked up a pile of abandoned paper sleeves and stacked them neatly on the shelf, then lifted the kitchen torch to clean the counter under it. No. No, what was bothering her was worry for Malachi. She couldn't put it out of her mind, wondering where he was, if he was all right, wondering why he hadn't been in contact. And it was getting worse. The longer he was gone, the harder it became not to let it turn into a panic.

The bell over the door chimed and Pepper turned, smiling her relief.

"Welcome to—"

The words stuck in her throat. In the empty dining room stood Jensen. Pepper's heart thundered. He stalked her across the floor with a smile on his face.

"At last," he breathed, never taking his eyes from her. He inhaled deeply, then frowned and reached his hand toward her. "Come. I can't scent you properly in this place."

"Hell, no." The words jumped out of Pepper's mouth before she could stop them, though Abby would probably forgive her for swearing on the floor, given the circumstances. Where was Israel? Had Jensen managed to hurt him, or worse? Fear for the Tseng Tse flooded through her, mixing with the fear for herself, until it began to bubble into anger.

"You will leave this place with me, Pepper," Jensen continued. He glided over the floor without so much as blinking, until only the counter separated them. "I'll give you a much better life than waiting tables all day, every day."

"Where's Israel?" Pepper demanded, backing as far away as the narrow space between counters would allow. The edge of the countertop behind her dug into her hips as she sidled against it, heading for the door to the back.

"I've taken care of him. I will not allow anyone to come between us, my love," Jensen crooned.

"I am *not* your love!" Pepper felt sick at the thought of him getting anywhere near her. "Get out, now, before I call the police!"

Jensen's expression turned ugly, as did his voice. "Nothing will keep us apart, not the police, not that animal in your den, not even the great princes. We *will* be together."

Jensen sprang over the counter, clearing it easily. Pepper ran. Strong hands gripped her arms with bruising force, yanking her against him. The reek of his foul breath washed over her as he pressed his nose into her hair and inhaled. He smelled like a slaughterhouse. Nausea rolled through her as she groped along the counter. Her hand closed on the cup under the steamer. Pepper ducked to one side and flung the boiling water over her shoulder. The grip on her arms loosened, though wet fire sparked on her skin as hot drops fell on her. Pepper scrambled forward as Jensen swore. She grabbed the kitchen torch and whirled to face him. If nothing else, she could set him on fire and escape while he was putting himself out. She hoped.

Jensen stopped. He watched the nozzle of the kitchen torch intently, real caution in his eyes.

"Put it down, Pepper," he said. "I will not tolerate my mate threatening me."

"Get out!" Pepper shouted. Jensen made a start toward her. She hit the ignition on the back of the nozzle. A spurt of blue flame spouted from the nozzle and Jensen backed up again. Hope fluttered in her chest. "This will hurt you, won't it? You're afraid. Now get the hell away from me before I melt your face!"

Jensen hesitated a moment longer, and Pepper flicked the switch to turn the torch to continuous flame.

"I. Said." Pepper bit off every syllable. "Get. OUT!"

She lunged at him. Jensen jumped the counter to the dining room. Pepper lifted the counter divider with one hand, the other always aiming the brilliant blue flame at Jensen. It was her turn to be the predator. She stalked him across the dining room, slowly but steadily forcing him toward the door. He raised his lip as he yanked open the door and melted into the crowds on the street by the time the bell finished its chime.

Pepper flicked off the torch and dropped into a nearby chair. Very carefully, she set the torch on the table and simply stared at it. The numbness was slowly wearing off, and she wasn't sure if the bubble in her throat was laughter or tears. Both escaped at the same time. Biting her lip, hand over her mouth, she hurried into the ladies' room. Thankfully, it was empty. Pepper stared into the mirror, at her own red face and wide eyes. The tears spilled over, running down her cheeks in hot splashes as she gulped down air. He was gone. Damn it, she should have brought the kitchen torch with her, just in case. Pepper reached for the door just as it opened. Abby stood framed in the doorway. The coffee shop owner took one look at her face, stepped inside, and locked the door behind her.

"It happened, didn't it?" Abby said with a dark look and a deep sigh. "He's gone and broken your heart. Didn't take that one long!" Abby managed to smear the words into an insult. Pepper shook her head, still trying to swallow the tears.

"It's not like that," Pepper protested. How could she even begin to explain what it was really like, that Malachi was a tiger shifter who was out hunting another tiger shifter who had fixated on her as his mate and was willing to do anything to prove it true? That the shifter rapist had just been in the shop and threatening both of them? Abby had no idea, and there was no way Pepper could tell her.

"You never think it's like that, honey, but it is." Abby sounded like she was trying to be compassionate, but her anger showed through clearly. World-weariness made the lines on her face seem to deepen. "What did he tell you? That he was going out for more condoms? Or that he had an emergency at the office?" Abby snorted. "He probably went back to his wife."

"Abby!" The word was part reprimand and part sob. Her fists clenched at her sides. "You are not helping anything."

The older woman surveyed her face for a moment and softened.

"Sorry, honey." Her tone was much gentler. "Do what you need to do and get cleaned up. Then get back on the floor. Keeping busy will help." Abby gave her a speculative look, along with a little smile. "A very fine-looking fellow came to the counter just before I stepped back here. Tall-dark-handsome type, bit older than you. Seems like your type. Seemed like he was a in a rush, though, so you'd better hurry. Just in case."

Abby turned the lock to let herself out and Pepper choked back a sobbing laugh. Israel. It had to be Israel. Pepper splashed cold water on her face until the front of her shirt was wet, patted it off with a cheap paper towel, and yanked open the door.

If Israel had been in a hurry before, he wasn't now. He stood at the counter, one elbow leaning on it as he chatted with Brett. The young blond man was blushing faintly, glancing away now and then with an adorable shyness. Pepper paused near the pastry display, pretending to work while she looked Israel over. He didn't seem to be hurt. He seemed relaxed, casually winking at Brett before excusing himself to saunter to the pastry case.

"Are you all right?" Pepper murmured as soon as he was within earshot.

"Yes. You are not injured?" Israel pretended to peruse the case, but his expression was forbidding.

"No. I managed to scare him off. What happened to you? He said he took care of you."

Israel snorted, the quiet sound filled with derision. "He only lured me away with a false trail, nothing more."

"He threatened Abby," Pepper hissed between clenched teeth. Israel rumbled under his breath as he swiveled his head, looking for the store owner.

"She is well?"

"Yeah, she's fine." Pepper sighed and rubbed the back of her wrist over her forehead.

"I caught Malachi's scent," Israel said. Pepper fumbled the latch on the pastry case. He continued in a low voice. "He is injured, badly, but he is alive, moving under his own power, and lucid enough to check on you."

Pepper's knees felt weak for a moment. She leaned against the counter. Israel waited, unmoving, not even blinking as he stared at her.

"Give me two minutes," Pepper said as she searched for her apron ties. She had no idea what she'd tell Abby, but she would go, in a heartbeat, even if it cost her job.

"We cannot." Israel's voice was like the slamming of a door, final and inarguable. He finally looked at her. "Malachi is not in human form. To draw attention to him would be to kill him. He was here to assure himself that you are safe and well, and that I am with you. He will return to his den—the place where you are sleeping—and wait for me to bring you there."

Pepper felt as if she were drowning only inches from the surface. Her lungs worked for air, but nothing seemed to go in or out. Malachi was alive! He was close, so close, but she couldn't get to him.

"You must act normally, in case the aberration is watching, as well as for the sake of all the humans around you," Israel said. "You are strong. Breathe. Work. We will go as soon as you are finished."

Chapter Twenty-Two

Time moved in fits and starts, stalling out and then suddenly jumping forward. Two minutes before her shift was over, Pepper was already yanking on her apron strings. Abby just shook her head, saying nothing, and let Pepper run out the back door with knotted apron strings the second her shift was over. Israel was waiting. She ran to the truck and jumped into the passenger side, the Tseng Tse closing the door behind her. He was as eager to see Malachi as she was. He peeled out of the parking lot and ignored the speed limit the whole way. Under the circumstances, Pepper decided not to object, though she was clinging to the crash bar the whole way.

When they reached the bed and breakfast, she barely waited for the truck to stop before she snapped out of her seatbelt and kicked open the door. Israel's hand closed around her arm like an iron band and pulled her back in.

"Shut the door," he snapped. Pepper flipped around to demand he release her, but the words died in her throat. He was angry. She had never imagined that a man could look so terrifying just by staring at her. Without looking away, she closed the door. "Do not do that again. Stay here."

Israel got out of the truck, leaving the keys in the ignition and the engine running. Slowly, he paced around the truck and around the bungalow before coming to open the passenger door for her. Reaching across her, he turned off the vehicle and pocketed the keys. His mood seemed much lighter.

"Jensen may have been close. You must think before you act, little sister. Come." Israel held out his hand to help her from the pickup. Chastised, Pepper took it.

Israel tugged her close beside him. His gaze was everywhere, his entire frame alert and prepared for a fight. His hand on her shoulder kept her still as he carefully scented the area around the door and the small porch. He finally fitted the key into the lock and turned the doorknob. He insisted on stepping in first, his enormous frame blocking the doorway. Pepper fidgeted on the doorstep, trying to crane around him. After what felt like an absurdly long time, Israel finally stepped out of the way. Herding her inside, he shut the door and locked it again.

Pepper's heart leaped. Malachi sprawled naked on the bed. A large bandage wound around his midsection. For one, horrible instant, Pepper thought he was dead. Then he sighed, shifting in his sleep. She rushed to the side of the bed and grabbed at his arm.

"Malachi!" He barely stirred, and Pepper frowned. "Malachi?"

Israel stalked across the floor. Pulling back one hand, he slammed it down onto Malachi's naked backside with an echoing slap. Malachi woke with a roar that left Pepper's ears ringing and the dust floating from the ceiling. He jolted to his back, trying to get to his feet. Israel pinned him to the bed with a hand on his shoulder and Malachi showed his teeth in a snarl. Israel snarled right back. With his other hand, he caught Pepper gently around the shoulders and brought her into Malachi's line of sight. Malachi settled instantly. He wrapped a hand around her wrist and tugged her onto the bed. Pepper wrapped both arms around his neck as he pulled her into his lap. He inhaled deeply as he dragged his jaw over her hair and face. His stubble was long enough that it scratched her a bit, but Pepper didn't care. Catching her face between his hands, Malachi stared into her eyes for a moment, inhaling again. He claimed her mouth in a searing kiss, joy, possession, and love mingling into one. Pepper kissed him back, completely absorbed in him. The rest of the world faded away as she melted into his warmth, his strength. He was alive, and he was back with her. She shifted, trying to get closer to him, until she felt him wince. With a gasp, she pulled back. Her hand splayed over the bandage covering him from hips to ribs.

"You're hurt!"

Malachi smiled, his hand stroking from her cheek into her hair.

"I'm fine, beauty mine." He eased back onto the bed, stretching out carefully as he twitched the bedclothes over his hips. Keeping Pepper tight to his side, he pressed her head into his shoulder and turned his head toward her, to kiss her face and surround himself with her scent. It calmed him, more than he had been in days. He nuzzled her head. "You haven't slept." The words were concerned, though the glare he shot at Israel was accusatory.

"Your woman was worried for you. There is little I can do about that." Israel had remained quiet and still in front of the door. His gaze raked over Malachi, worry plain in his amber eyes. "You are not 'fine', brother mine. You have had two days to heal, and your scent is still filled with blood and pain. How badly did the aberration hurt you?"

Malachi hesitated for a brief moment as his arm tightened around Pepper.

"Badly," he confessed. His eyes darkened with worry. "Did the woman survive? Was she found?"

"I have not heard. I have been a bit busy," he said dryly. "What happened?"

Malachi gave Israel a brief report of the fight at the garden. He chose his words carefully, always aware of the soft, slender woman pressed close to his side. Pepper seemed content to rest against him, slowly relaxing toward sleep. He kept his voice pitched low and steady to lull her. If she could sleep through the rest of his reports, it would be best. Israel growled with quiet menace, more eloquent than any swear words could be.

"I will go to the beach and search for the scent." The older Tseng Tse made it a declaration. "Pray to the ancestors that there is something left to find."

His gaze flicked from Malachi to Pepper and back again. Malachi understood and gave a tiny nod as he rubbed his jaw over Pepper's hair. She needed him as much as he needed to be with her. Her eyes were closed, her breathing slowed, her hand in a fist on his chest.

"You must find him," Malachi spoke quietly, hoping not to disturb her. "He has killed once already, and I'm certain he would have killed again if I hadn't driven him away. Perhaps...it might be best if we were to call in the nearest streak. We may need an entire group of our hunters, as well as a healer, before this is over."

Israel's hands flexed as he choked back a snarl. Malachi shifted to place himself between his brother and his woman, adrenaline flooding him. Israel nodded, as if he didn't trust himself to speak. The door to the bungalow groaned in protest as Israel flung it open. It crashed into the wall and bounced back to slam against the latch without catching. Malachi caught a glimpse of Israel sprinting away before he was out of sight among the landscaping.

Malachi considered staying right where he was, only partly because of pain. He had no desire to disturb Pepper. In reality, the door would be little protection from Jensen, anyway. Any of his people could go right through even a solid-core door. But the wind was picking up. Debris would start to blow in. More importantly, Pepper wouldn't be comfortable with the door standing open, and he would never be comfortable unless she was. With another kiss to her hair, he carefully slid his arm from under her head.

"You stay there." Her voice wasn't even muddled with sleep. She stretched against him then peeled herself from his side. One hand rubbed her face as the other helped to push her to the edge of the bed. Malachi rumbled with pleasure at the sight of her, hair mussed, clothing wrinkled, looking sweet and kittenish as she shook herself to stand.

"How is your side, beauty? Come and let me see." He pushed himself to his elbows, one hand reaching for her as she closed and locked the door.

"Don't worry about my side. I'm fine. You need to worry about *your* side, and front, and other side."

Pepper glanced out the windows, trying to hide a worried frown. "What is it with this guy and sides?"

"Bellies, actually." Malachi worked to get himself fully to sitting, wincing as he went. "Bellies, throats, spines. It's how we hunt."

"Do you need to get up?" Pepper hurried across the small space to wrap her arm around his waist, ducking under his arm to support his weight. Malachi simply brought her against him, both arms around her to hold her tightly.

"Only because you were refusing to come back to the bed." There was humor in his tone, as well as relief. Malachi convinced himself to let go of her enough to cup her chin in his palm, tipping her face up to him. He knew much of what she was feeling from her scent, but what she was thinking would be only in her eyes. His thumb stroked absent caresses from the corner of her mouth to her jaw as he studied her. Her eyes were filled with worry, with weariness, and yet there was still fire there. Strength sat in the way she held her shoulders back, and courage in the lift of her chin. She was frightened, but she was not beaten. His thumb drifted to the center of her lower lip. Her tiny intake of breath was enough to start a fire inside of him. She felt it. He knew she did, in the subtle shift of her body into his, in the way her gaze suddenly dropped to his mouth as she wet her lips. Malachi leaned slowly toward her to cover her mouth with his. He tried to keep the kiss gentle, affirming, assuring her that he was really there, and assuring himself that she was really there. Pepper's hands slid around the back of his neck, pulling him closer to her. He groaned into the kiss.

"Pepper…beauty," he murmured, his forehead

against hers. "You cannot know how much I have needed you these past days. How much I still need you."

Pepper choked back a sound suspiciously like a giggle as color filled her cheeks.

"You're still naked, Malachi. I can take a pretty good guess."

Malachi smiled, his heart lifting. Everything about her charmed him, from the soft blush in her face to the way her scent wrapped around his soul. He kissed the tip of her nose.

"That isn't what I meant, though I won't try to deny that, either." Malachi leaned down to claim her mouth again, but Pepper placed both hands on his chest and pushed gently against him.

"You should be resting. I'll find you some pants. Just go lie down again," she said. "And food. When was the last time you ate? Can you eat? You should be at the hospital."

"No," Malachi said. He captured her wrist in his hand and tugged her toward the bed. Lying down again did sound good, but he needed her beside him. "No hospitals. No doctors. If there were a healer nearby, I would happily take their aid, but the nearest one is hundreds of miles away, in San Francisco. I'm well enough to eat, and I do need to, soon. Right now, I need to hold you a little longer."

"Pants." Pepper dragged her feet but allowed Malachi to draw her back to the bed. She pulled against his grip, looking around for his duffle bag. Malachi chuckled and drew her up against him. His hand threaded into her hair to lift her face toward his. His breath brushed over her lips, and he felt the sudden

247

thrumming in her body as her scent changed.

"Why?" He was so close, he could feel the vibration of his voice against her body. Heat flared through him as his hands slipped under the hem of her shirt, finding skin. "I'd prefer to be skin-to-skin with you."

"What did Israel mean, about having two days to heal?" Pepper's voice was breathless as she allowed Malachi to lead her onto the bed and pull her down into it with him. His mind skittered off into other circumstances where he could make her breathless. Her body pressed against his, soft and yielding, and every touch sent her intoxicating scent into the air. His skin trembled with the need to find hers.

"It's a part of being what we are," Malachi murmured. He smoothed her hair back from her face and tucked his fingertip into the elastic that held her ponytail. "I think I prefer your hair down, beauty. It gives off your scent better that way."

"It doesn't make sense for work, and stop changing the subject." Pepper shook her hair out, anyway, fighting a smile with little success. Immediately, he buried his fingers into the loose strands with a gentle massage. He was getting drunk off her scent and didn't even care.

"Tseng Tse heal quickly." Malachi leaned into Pepper, dropping a trail of light kisses across her hair between words. "We have to, in order to be able to change forms. The fact that I've had two days to heal, and I'm still in this bad of shape, tells Israel just how badly the aberration was able to injure me."

Malachi bunched her hair in his hand, leaning down to inhale deeply, and felt her muscles relax as she leaned into him.

"Why do you keep doing that?" she asked, her voice soft.

"It's a long story," Malachi said. Pepper pulled her hair away from the stubble on his chin and leaned back to consider him.

"It's because I'm your potential mate," she answered, watching him as if waiting for a reaction. He raised his brows slightly, more curious than alarmed.

"Where did you hear that term, beauty?"

"From Israel. He said I'm your potential mate, the only one you've ever met. That's why you keep sniffing me, isn't it?"

"Israel talks too much," Malachi snorted.

"Were you going to tell me?"

He tipped her chin up toward him. "Yes," he said firmly. "When the justice of our people was delivered to Jensen, and when you'd had a chance to recover from your shock and fright and grief. When you would be at liberty to think clearly, I would have told you everything. Did Israel tell you what being my potential mate means?"

"It means that I'm supposedly perfectly compatible with you."

"It means that I am obsessed with you," Malachi confessed with a crooked smile. Pepper seemed surprised. "Your scent is a drug. *You* are my drug." His expression sobered as he slid his fingers through her hair, fascinated by the way the strands caressed his skin, as smooth as water, but warmer, and so much more alive. "I need to know that you are safe and comfortable. Like I need air to breathe. I can't think about my wounds until I know that yours are seen to. I can't stand the thought of eating until I know that you are fed. Yes, I am exhausted, and I am in pain, but your scent is filled with weariness and hunger and distress. I'm too tired to fight my instincts. I need to care for you, and then, when you are settled, I can care for myself."

"That isn't fair, Malachi," Pepper protested after a moment's silence. "You can't put all of that on one person. How could I possibly care for you, then?"

"If you are taken care of, then my instincts will be at ease and I can revel and rejoice in your care of me." His smile was echoed in his voice. "Mates manage it all the time, and do quite well at it, when they are willing to put in the work."

"Oh, so even being perfectly compatible means work?" Pepper fussed with the covers, as if trying half-heartedly to pull them over him. Her brows were lowered in thought, and the worry in her scent increased. Her heart rate was increasing, and Malachi wasn't sure it was for the right reasons. He regarded her steadily.

"Of course. Once the mate-bond forms, if mates don't work at caring for and adapting to each other, they'll drive each other insane."

Pepper snorted. "It's not so different from humans."

"Humans always have the choice of separating from each other. A mated pair doesn't." Malachi leaned back against the headboard. He allowed Pepper to pull the blankets over him, then drew her tight against his side. Her elbow caught him in his wounded belly, forcing out a grunt of pain. Instantly she struggled to sit up. Malachi rumbled reassuringly and guided her to lie against his chest, facing him.

"When the mate-bond forms, we become acutely aware of each other, automatically checking each other's state through scent, heart rate, breath rate. We become acutely sensitive to each other's distress, reacting on a deep, primal level to that distress. A Tseng Tse can't be away from their mate for very long without feeling like a part of themselves is missing. If a mate-bonded pair doesn't work on the relationship, and they can't be away from each other, then they will, quite literally, drive each other insane."

Pepper drew back and looked at him for a long moment. Her dark velvet eyes shone with wonder, and more than a hint of suspicion. He stroked her back, urging her to stay against him.

"I told you, Pepper mine. I don't mess around. If you agree to be my mate, then I will spend my entire life working to make you happy, safe, and comfortable, but there is no escape clause with a Tseng Tse. It is for life."

Pepper shook her head. Malachi's gut clenched painfully. If she was going to reject him, it would be in this moment. He found every muscle tensing and his own pulse racing for the wrong reasons as he feigned a patience he didn't feel. Pepper inhaled, holding the air in her lungs as she pushed away from Malachi to stand up.

"Show me."

Malachi blinked. One corner of his mouth pulled up in a crooked smile to belie the rolling in his stomach.

"I was showing you, beauty mine. You're the one who insisted on covering me up."

Color rushed into Pepper's cheeks, though she

didn't take her gaze from his.

"You've spent all this time saying you're a...a Tseng Tse or whatever. A part-time tiger. Before this goes any further, show me. If you can turn into a tiger, prove it. Do it."

"Are you certain this is what you want, Pepper?" Malachi's voice was low, his gaze riveted on her. She wet her lips. Even under these circumstances, it was a struggle to keep his focus off of her invitingly glistening mouth.

Finally, she nodded, the movement determined and decisive.

"Yes." Pepper's voice was steady, but her scent was filled with caution.

Malachi unfurled from the bed. He tried to hide the effort it cost him to draw himself up to his full height, but from the sudden frown on Pepper's face, he didn't entirely succeed. He inhaled deeply.

The change was slow. He was still worn, his body taxed by his injuries. Then shadows began to show on his skin, faint patterns that slowly darkened to nearly black, stripes all over his body. White fur showed underneath, then in the stripes, as well. He grew. Simply grew until the room seemed too small to hold him. Bandages popped free, unwinding themselves from his mid-section. Pain popped through him as torn flesh was forced to knit itself together too quickly with too little rest and too little protein. Pepper backed toward the door, her eyes wide, as his face extended into a muzzle. Enormous teeth showed in the sunset lights shining through the windows, sharp and powerful. His hands and feet became paws the size of dinner plates, his claws carefully drawn into silken fingers. His long, graceful tail flowed behind him as he took one step toward her, then another. He chuffed. A shiver ran through her at the sound. It was the same sound he made as a human. She knew it. But he was no longer a man. He was a tiger, an enormous tiger slowly padding toward her, staring at her with that unwavering predator's gaze. One hand groped for the doorknob, despite it being several feet behind her. Her voice trembled.

"You...you really are a tiger. A tiger, seeking a mate. Just like him. You're no different." Her scent was suddenly drenched with distress. Malachi made a soft sound in his throat. His chest was tight, as if the very life was being squeezed out of his heart.

"Don't!" Pepper's voice was sharp. She held up one hand, palm out. "Just...don't. Not right now. My God, I've actually fallen in love with a tiger."

Pepper stumbled backward, her hand outstretched. Malachi sailed over the bed to shove himself under her hand and keep her from falling. Her fingers found his fur. He leaned into the touch, rubbing against her in imitation of a housecat. Perhaps the gesture would comfort her when he couldn't give her words. Her fingers flexed in his fur, as if she were getting a good feel for it, or maybe just reflecting her heightened emotions. Her hands tightened, tugging his fur almost to the point of discomfort before she pulled her hands off of him. Her distress tore at him. He tried again to comfort her, chuffing and moving to lean against her, but Pepper shook her head.

"I need to *think*, Malachi, and that means...means a space without you in it."

The fur along his spine rose as the tiger mind

roared. His skin rippled and his claws slipped free of their velvet pads as panic filled him. Pain flared in his chest. He clamped his jaws against the primal reaction to roar and dug his claws into the carpet to keep his paws safely away from her. He wanted to pull her close to him and refuse to release her until she was calm. Every instinct in him demanded that he claim his mate, to keep her with him, safe and loved. But it had to be her choice.

"I have to go," Pepper said, inching toward the door. "I need to clear my head." A soft plea crept into her voice. "You can't ask me to make this decision under these circumstances, and you clearly can't go out there. You need to move. Let me out."

She was right. He couldn't cage her here without causing her further distress. He couldn't shift back to human, either. The tiger's mind was too panicked at the thought of losing his mate, and Malachi was barely keeping control of the beast as it was. He was too tired to force his form back to that of a human. He couldn't force her to accept him; he couldn't force her to mate with him. Cold rippled through him as he made the only choice he could.

He couldn't tolerate being the source of her distress. Malachi forced one foot away from the floor, then another. His claws felt like daggers inside his paws as he dragged himself to the bathroom doorway, but sheer force of will kept them from showing. His fur stood on end, and his tail lashed so hard the sound echoed through the building as it crashed into the walls on either side.

Pepper paused, like prey poised to run. Malachi had to tear his mind away from the thought. Sorrow edged into Pepper's scent. He growled low, the sound tinged with pain. Her hand gripped the doorknob until her knuckles turned white.

"Malachi, I—" Pepper stopped, swallowing hard. Her voice was a rough whisper. "Thank you."

Chapter Twenty-Three

Pepper stumbled out of the bungalow, her fists tight at her sides. The sun was going down, sparking bright lights from the sea behind her and sending the long shadows into stark relief. Tears slurred light into darkness and made it hard to navigate through the narrow paths between the bungalows. The scent of sneezeweed was a cloud, and she pushed her way through it. Malachi's truck was still in the parking lot. She trailed her fingers over the tailgate, still cool from the recent rain.

This was ridiculous. Instead of caressing his car, she should be inside caressing him. She could almost feel his rough stubble in her palms, or the solid heat of powerful shoulders. Her lips tingled with longing just at the thought of him. She could be inside, curled beside him, safe and warm and dreaming of long nights filled with skin and satin.

"But for some reason, I'd rather be outside in the cold rain!" She struck out at branches unfortunate enough to get in her path as she left the parking lot. The streets were quiet, between the darkness and the lingering rain. The occasional streetlight reflected in the standing puddles dotting the streets. Pepper shattered the reflection as she broke into a run. She needed to push her body so she could drown out her brain. And her heart. Her brain was panicking over having been so close to a tiger for days—two tigers, including Israel. Three, with her attacker so close. Yet Malachi and Israel had kept her safe. They had both done their best to comfort and care for her. And Malachi...

She screamed her frustration and sped around the corner into another street. She didn't know where she was, but since she didn't care where she was going, it didn't matter. She was thinking of spending a lifetime with a man who spent half his life as a tiger. Not just thinking about it, but *wanting* it. Somehow, when she wasn't looking, she'd fallen in love.

No one had ever put her first the way Malachi did. He was so focused on her, on her needs and desires. That kind of devotion was hard to resist. On top of that, he was incredibly sexy. Just the way he looked at her made her feel alive down to her toes. She wanted him, and she wanted to be with him.

Pepper paused in the halo of a corner streetlamp, resting one hand on the cool metal to catch her breath. When her father had died so suddenly, she'd decided to live as safely as possible, and this situation was anything but safe. Since the moment she'd met him, Malachi had been helping her, protecting her, keeping Jensen at bay. Living with a tiger shifter who hunted the dangerous creatures would never be safe.

But it would be worth it. She had no doubts about that, not now. The thought of leaving him to face his dangerous life alone when she could stand with him as his mate was entirely unacceptable. She'd learn how to help him, how to be his mate, just as he'd learn how to be hers.

Pepper turned back the way she'd come, retracing her steps with a light and fluttering heart. Headlights struck her eyes in the early darkness, making her squint and look away. It pulled to a stop and Pepper moved to the far side of the walk to make room. Her eyes adjusted to see a familiar pickup. Her heart leaped. He came after her, after all, and part of her mind was already celebrating going back with him. The other part of her mind was already starting the lecture. She strode toward the truck as the passenger door opened.

"There is absolutely no way you should be driving—!" she started.

A blurred figure launched from the truck, slamming into her with enough force to knock her into the garden wall behind her. Breath whooshed from her lungs as her head cracked on the stone. She would have bounced from the wall and fallen except for a tall, strong figure pinning her against it. He inhaled deeply, a long, drawn-out sound near her face as he slid up her body. The face so near hers was a little too thin, his hair shaggy. Several days' growth hid the lower part of his face. Deep brown eyes peered at her from far too close by and her breath stopped in her throat.

Jensen.

"Pepper." Her name was an obscene caress, a corrupted prayer. Jensen stroked her hair. The touch sent horror shuddering through her. "Pepper, lovely one. My clever lovely one, you have escaped them. Well done."

Her heart slammed so hard it made her stomach roll. Her throat was so tight she could barely breathe, let alone scream. Jensen's rough fingertips continued their steady caress along her hair and cheek. They slid down to her throat, resting on the rapid pulse until she felt her heartbeat against his fingers. He leaned close, until she could feel his hot breath on her cheek. The scent of blood surrounded her.

"Run."

Pepper's lungs stuttered, unable to fully expand. A tiny sound managed to squeeze past the block in her throat, a scream throttled into a whimper. Jensen chuffed, sending a wave of sickness through her.

"Shhh, lovely one. It's all right, now. Now we will take our chance." His fingers took her chin and turned her face toward him. Even in the low lights, she could see something wild in his eyes. "You will run. I will hunt you. When I find you, I will claim you as my mate, and no one will be able to take you away from me, not even the great Prince Malachi. I will erase his scent from you, and we will be one, lovely one, for all time."

Pepper retched. Her mind couldn't even hold onto a thought. It was too absorbed in Jensen's hands stroking her skin, his fingertips delving inside the collar of her polo shirt. Her entire body trembled with disgust and fear as she pressed back against the wall, trying to gain even a little distance from him. He followed. His entire frame pressed tightly against hers, she couldn't miss his arousal. His hand bunched in her hair, inhaling deeply, before sliding down her throat, over her breast, down to her waist to grab her hip. Jensen stepped back, dragging her away from the wall.

"Run," he repeated, his voice barely above a whisper. Nausea flooded through her as she took only a few steps. Part of her mind rebelled against doing anything he said, though running was the thing she most wanted to do.

"Run!" Jensen roared, the sound shaking the

branches around them and frightening roosting birds into the air.

Pepper ran. She didn't know where she was going and didn't care, as long as it was away. The dark streets swallowed her. Fences, trees, cars, buildings, all passed by in a dizzying smear of gray. Pepper leaped off a curb, stumbling in the uneven asphalt at the gutter's edge. Her foot rolled out from under her, dropping her into the jagged pavement. She went down hard, and her skin burned where it dragged over the asphalt. Shock jarred up her arm all the way into her skull as she caught herself on one hand.

"Carefully, lovely mine." Jensen's voice issued from somewhere in the darkness behind her, singsong and soft. He wasn't even breathing hard, but she gasped for every breath. "It wouldn't do for you to break what belongs to me."

Pepper pushed herself back up to sitting, setting her hand down on something hard and jagged. The blurred lights of a streetlamp shone on a large chunk of cement. She wrapped her hand around it. The rough edges dug into her stinging palm, but the solid weight was reassuring. A rock wasn't much protection against a tiger, but it was better than an empty hand.

She scrambled back up to her feet, ignoring the sharp spike of pain shooting up her leg. She didn't have time to be hurt. Pepper took the first left, dashing down a well-lit street. If she was lucky, it would buy her a little bit of time. She didn't put much faith in it. If Israel could sneak in and out of the locked coffee shop without anyone being the wiser, and if Malachi could leap over her RV from standing, there was nothing to keep Jensen from snatching her between the halos of the lamps. If he was willing to attempt to force a woman into her car in a parking lot filled with sunlight, what would stop him from attacking her right in the light?

Her lungs burned and her head throbbed as she pounded one foot after the other against the pavement. A car door slammed a little distance ahead of her, followed by the sound of laughing voices. Pepper zigzagged across the street toward it. A snarl rippled through the night as a large figure flowed out of the darkness to run beside her. Jensen showed too-sharp teeth.

"This is between you and me, lovely one." His voice carried through the darkness. "A male and his mate, no one else. I will kill them before I allow them to interfere with our joining."

He snapped his teeth in blatant warning. Pepper leaped away, dashing back across the street. She could hear him breathing behind her, sometimes behind her right shoulder, sometimes behind her left, but always behind her, and always far too close. He was toying with her, playing with his prey like a cat. She turned into the parking lot of a large apartment complex and ducked down between the cars. Dropping onto her stomach, she crawled under several of them before leaning against the side of an SUV. She had to rest, for just a moment. Gasping against the back of her hand, she fought down the need to cough. If he could hear her, it wouldn't help her hide. Rain began to fall in fat drops, still faintly warm from the heat of the day. Maybe the rain would help hide her scent. At the very least, it would help cool her sweat. Pepper lifted her face to it. Jensen's bearded face peered down at her.

Screaming, she dove under the SUV again and slithered out from under the back bumper. Her legs and back shrieked a protest as she forced them back into a sprint, and she coughed hard, choking, as she covered the parking lot.

"Pity about the rain," Jensen said amicably. His voice was so distorted by bouncing off buildings that she couldn't tell where he was. "I can't leave you out in this cold and wet, not naked and sweat-soaked. I will have to end our hunt early. Pity."

Pepper dove into a stand of trees on the far side of the lot. She ducked between trees, weaving and zagging as much as possible. Some part of her mind still clung to the hope that she had some kind of chance to escape him, and that was the part that kept on running. Another part of her mind, however, had realized that it was hopeless, and that part of her mind was growing ever larger. Jensen was going to catch her. He was going to rape her. And when that failed to create the mate-bond he sought, he was going to kill her.

Boughs shook over her head, showering rain and dead leaves down on her head. Pepper flung up her arms to protect herself, glancing up. Jensen leaped from branch to branch, easily keeping pace with her through the trees even as she dodged between them. He smiled, the lascivious expression showing far too many sharp teeth. Bile rose in her throat, sharp and acid. Retching, she forced herself to keep moving forward. No more weaving or zigzagging. Her fatigued muscles and straining lungs couldn't handle any more. The only remaining thought was to run. Just run. She clung to her chunk of cement as if it were her very life.

The rain hit her full in the face as the trees dropped

away. Pepper stumbled as half-decayed leaves and earth gave way to the hard surface of another parking lot. It was empty, except for a single small hatchback a few dozen yards away, parked under a streetlight. Disorientation crashed through her like a wave. The whole scene was familiar. Her panicked mind took another two heartbeats to realize that she was at the coffee shop. The small blue car parked under the light was her car, still abandoned and immobile.

She dove for it, anyway. The sudden burst of hope gave her strength, and she powered across the distance. One hand still gripped the rock, but the other grabbed at the handle of the door, pulling desperately. It was locked. She patted her pockets for her keys, but she'd run out of the bungalow without them. The trees over the edge of the parking lot rustled. Cold terror speared through her as Jensen strode from the deeper darkness under the boughs. He flowed with a predator's grace, and primal fear rose up in her throat to choke her. She scrambled around the back of the sedan, trying to put something between her and the predator openly stalking her.

The contents of the emergency kit were still strewn across the back seat. A wild cry tore from her throat as she swung her arm, hard, slamming the chunk of cement into the back window as hard as she could. The glass cracked. Pepper grabbed her makeshift weapon in both hands and, hefting it over her head, slammed it down again and again. On the first blow, the cracks spread. On the second, the window shattered. She hit it once more to knock the safety glass free of the frame, and then launched herself into the space. The sill caught her on the hips. The sharp points of broken glass overlaid the deeper pain of her healing gashes but she barely felt it. She clawed at the seat and the junk still spread over it in order to drag herself inside.

Hands closed on her hips with enormous strength. Pepper screamed a denial as he dragged her back through the window. She grabbed onto the seatbelt, clinging desperately. Her feet found the ground as a hand slid under her shirt, up over her back, holding her in place. Behind her, Jensen rumbled, a sound of pleasure and lust.

"Mm...my perfect little mate," he crooned. It burrowed under her skin like insects, gnawing and biting at her soul. His hands roamed over her hips and buttocks without allowing her to move. Glass dug into her stomach, each shard a razor-slash of burning pain. His hands felt hard enough to bruise. "Already presenting for me, even though you are only human."

Pepper kicked behind her like a mule. Her foot connected with his upper thigh, hard. He snarled. A new pain flared through her as his hand slammed into her backside, making her cry out through the terror. She clawed to get away from him.

"No," he said firmly, as if correcting a dog. He slapped her hard on the other side. "My mate will not strike out at me. This mate-hunt is over. It is time."

His fingers curled into the waistband of her jeans. She heard the fabric tear as cold rain poured down onto her legs, soaking her underwear. Pepper shrieked, as furious as she was frightened. She kicked out again, her hands dropping onto the seat for leverage. One hand closed on the emergency road flare. She latched onto it. Hands pushed up her shirt, caressing her belly and sides as she tore off the cap. Cold-numbed fingers pulled desperately at the scratch pad cover. It tore in two pieces when she finally got it free. Pepper threw her hips back, slamming into Jensen with every ounce of strength adrenaline could give her. Sharp pain lanced down her arm as Jensen stumbled back a step or two, reaching out to steady himself. He dragged her with him only to slam her hips against the car again. She could feel his excitement against her backside as he ground against her, pinning her to the side of the car. She could hear him inhale as he slid up her body. Pepper struggled to strike the cap against the top of the flare. The damp surface didn't want to catch. Her arms were trapped inside the car, the only place there was any kind of room to work. Jensen's lips found the back of her neck as he nuzzled her hair aside. He kissed her gently, running his tongue over her skin as if tasting her. Revulsion ran down her spine into her stomach, making her retch. Pain flared through the back of her neck as he sunk his teeth into her. Pepper fought a scream, forcing her trembling hands to keep working. She struck the cap again and again, praying for the spark to catch as Jensen growled low. His teeth left her neck as he dragged her out of the back seat. Steel hands turned her by the hips, keeping her pinned against the car.

The spark caught.

Bright flames tore the night. Jensen snarled, squinting against the sudden brilliance. Sparks showered both of them as Pepper raked the flare across his eyes. Jensen roared. The scream of a human man in agony laced the sound as she drove him back, shoving the flare into his face again. He covered his face with his hands as he stumbled backward. Small flames licked around his fingers as his eyebrows and facial hair burned.

Pepper gripped the flare until her knuckles were white. She didn't dare let it go as she sped away from the car. There was a chance the coffee shop was still open. She dashed for the door, straining for the sound of pursuing feet the entire way. She pounded on the back door with both fists, scattering more sparks down on herself. Screaming, she kicked on the door, anything to attract the attention of someone inside. The menacing growl was behind her again and closing fast. Without pausing to look back, she groped for the roof access ladder with her free hand and jumped up to the second rung. Clawed hands dug into her hips before she could get a grip on the slick metal rungs. Jensen dragged her from the ladder with effortless ease, his claws piercing into her hips, raking her skin as he threw her onto the asphalt. Beyond the meager protection of the road flare, he loomed too large, a creature that was half man, half tiger, and entirely crazed with fury and lust. Raw, yellow flesh glistened through the blackened patches on his cheeks and nose where the flare had burned his skin. The fuel from the flare dribbled down his face and neck to fall on his chest, sparks dancing in its wake. He stared down at her from scorched and useless eyes, then dropped to hands and knees on top of her and roared.

Chapter Twenty-Four

Malachi watched Pepper stumble off into the night.
Pain tore at his heart, overwhelming the pain from his
wounds. Instinct roared, demanding he chase after her
and bring her back to him, but a lifetime of practice
kept his human mind in control. She turned out of sight
into the parking lot. He stood in the doorway a moment
more, lifting his nose to the breeze to catch her scent,
but he could barely find it amidst all the sneezeweed.
He snorted the scent from his nostrils and eased the
door closed with his face, leaning his forehead against it
for several seconds. Every movement an effort, he
turned and sat with his back against the door. His heart
beat too hard and his limbs felt leaden with the exertion
of the shift. He should rest. Israel was hunting the
aberration, well-rested, uninjured, and without the
weight of loss dragging on his heart. He closed his eyes,
letting his head sag until his nose drooped between his
front paws. She was gone. It echoed through his mind
as he struggled against the tiger's instincts. The tiger
couldn't accept her choice so easily. His instincts
gnawed at him, the fear and worry, the anger and need,
until he shuddered with it. Maybe if he shifted back to
his human form, it would be a bit easier.

The change didn't come easily. He was sweating
by the time he settled back against the door again, one
hand on his injured stomach as he just rested. It would

be better if he could weep, but he was too numb. It was better to stay numb until he had a bit more strength and could more easily control the beast. He wasn't so far gone as to commit suicide-by-treason and go running through the streets of the city. Especially as it would be Israel who would have to bring the justice of their people. He wouldn't do that to his elder brother.

His fingers drew lightly over his wounds. The exhaustion was slowing his healing, as well. Sleep, and food, were the best things he could do for himself and his people right now, but he couldn't bring himself to that point. His mind refused to leave Pepper, brave and foolish and wandering out there. If Israel weren't out tracking the aberration, there would be no way he could have let her get even this far away from him. If Israel was watching Jensen, then he could protect Pepper if Jensen got too near, at least until Malachi could get there himself.

Malachi inhaled. He dragged himself from the floor, using the door as support. He dug in his bag for more bandaging. He'd have to buy more, or go to San Francisco to find the nearest healer. He might just do that, anyway. The thought of a healer was soothing. It might be the best thing for him, after leaving this city—and Pepper—behind him. He wound what bandaging he had around the deep claw marks and tied it off, then pulled on a pair of dark-colored jeans. Grabbing up a navy button-down shirt, he headed out of the bungalow. He was still pulling it over his shoulders when a figure blurred out of the shadows, striding toward him. His heart rate increased as he inhaled deeply...then sighed: Israel. He frowned and his brother echoed it.

"What are you doing here? Where is your truck?"

the older tiger demanded without pleasantry or preamble. Malachi glanced toward the parking lot, though it wasn't visible through the gardens. He slid a hand through his hair.

"Pepper must have taken it. Good." Malachi's voice was hollow, weary, even to his own ears. "Very good. That's much better than her being on foot."

Israel inhaled and his eyes narrowed. A soft growl started in his throat, a low sound of deep concern.

"Where is Pepper?"

Malachi looked up sharply. He focused on his brother's face for the first time.

"Where is the aberration?" he demanded. Israel shook his head.

"I lost his trail. I came back to find the scent again. Where is your woman?" Israel repeated.

Malachi swore. He launched into a run only to slam into Israel as the older tiger shoved him back. Malachi snarled viciously. Israel didn't even growl as he stared his brother straight in the face. Malachi's shoulders bunched, his hands working his claws toward the surface. Israel gripped him by the front of his shirt, his forearm tight against his younger brother's collarbone. He didn't blink, didn't push, but he didn't allow Malachi to move, either to retreat or to advance. Malachi continued to show his teeth for a moment, then his shoulders dropped. Only then did Israel relax his grip. Clapping him on the chest in approbation, he stepped aside.

"How long has she been gone?" he asked. Malachi shook his head.

"I don't know. I lost track of time." Malachi was barely listening as he swung his head from side to side,

269

drawing the air deep into his lungs. Coughing, he cursed. "I will burn this sneezeweed to the ground!"

"Focus." Israel's voice remained absolutely calm. "She is your potential mate. Your woman. She has shared your den and even your bed. You know her scent above all others. The sneezeweed is irrelevant. All other scents are irrelevant."

Malachi breathed, deep and evenly, allowing Israel's calm to lead him. His brother was right. He knew her scent, like he knew the feel of his own heart beating. He eased up the pressure on the tiger's mind, allowing it to come forward a bit more and sort scents for him. The ever-present scent of sneezeweed; Israel's scent, comforting in its familiarity; the landlord had passed by recently; someone had ordered kung pao beef; and Pepper. He inhaled again, and again, drugging himself on her scent. She was upset. Eyes closed, he began to walk. Israel stayed at his shoulder, occasionally nudging him one way or another.

"Why did you allow her outside of your den alone?" Israel asked, so quietly that his voice barely intruded on the night.

"I couldn't force her to stay." Malachi spoke absently. His intense focus on following Pepper's scent dulled the pain in his heart. Adrenaline helped to dull the pain of his wounds, as well, pushing both back until they didn't matter anymore. Finding Pepper and stopping Jensen mattered.

"Certainly you could," Israel said in the same calm voice.

"Not in the human world."

"You are not human. Your woman will not live in the human world."

"That's why she ran." If Malachi had his tail, it would be lashing. "She doesn't want me. I am not enough to offset our world."

"She has hardly seen our world. Calm," Israel reminded him. His hand touched Malachi's shoulder, a connecting gesture as well as one to steer him. "You are starting to show stripes."

"My potential mate is out there with a lethal aberration that would rape her, then kill her. Even when we find her, I will have to leave her life and return to the palace. Of course I'm showing stripes," Malachi snapped, quite literally. Israel growled a soft warning.

"You are giving up? You, one of the princes of our people, you have the chance at a mate, and you will give up so easily? Run back home with your tail tucked and hide in the palace with the cubs and the elders?"

Malachi snarled. He whirled on Israel, hands already turning to claws as he tore into the front of his brother's shirt to slam him against a car. The alarm blared against the night as the head and tail lights flashed. Israel's head snapped back against the hood from the force of it. He dug his feet in under the car to push back. Grabbing Malachi around the waist, he dragged him into a run, covering the parking lot and getting out onto the streets as fast as he could drag his brother to go. He kept his voice even, but the intensity of it was a physical pressure against Malachi's skin.

"You are not in control. You have not made the decision in your heart to give her up. Do not pretend that you have. It will impede our hunt."

"Do you think I want to give her up?" Malachi rubbed his face, his own claws tracing lightly over his skin. "I can't force or frighten her into it. She has to

271

choose it. If you had seen her face...If you had caught her scent—!" Malachi shook his head. "When it happens to you, you'll understand."

Israel regarded him steadily, his amber eyes cat-slit and his voice a deep growl.

"It will never be my turn, little brother. Out of all the billions of people on this planet, a scant handful might be a potential mate. In all of my decades of traveling, I have yet to meet one. Not among those of our own kind in diaspora, and not among the humans whom we protect. You have a priceless gift within your reach. I have spent time with this woman. She is your match, a fine and great woman who will be an excellent princess for our people. You are not willing to give her up. You are only dulling her loss with your human mind. Do not. Let the tiger's mind lead. He will find his mate. Feel that need of her. We need it. She needs it."

Malachi raised his lip in a silent snarl. His belly tightened as he willed himself to face the tiger's pain, his loss, his need. The beast roared up inside of him. Israel gripped the back of his neck, chuffing and rumbling to him as he began to tremble. The roar burst out of him, shredding the night with the primal sound of loss and fury. Malachi's spine bowed with the force of it. Israel steadied him as he roared to the stars.

Malachi sucked in air, deep breaths to fill his straining lungs. Pepper's scent flooded him. He fought to keep his human form but allowed instinct to take his mind. Snarling under his breath, he took off into the night with Israel at his shoulder. Her scent was a beacon, drawing him to her. She hadn't taken his truck; her trail was too heavy. She didn't even have that protection.

Anyone looking out their windows would have seen two men out for a run in the cool night air. They wouldn't see the tiger-slit eyes or the ferocity in their faces. Pepper's trail wound through the small city at random, and that worried him. She was in too much distress to be aware of her surroundings. It was a perfect state for Jensen to prey upon her. He should have tried harder to follow her right away, to ensure her safety, even in spite of herself.

The criminal's scent flared up from the path before him, so strongly that Malachi showed his teeth and whirled, searching for the hated creature that threatened his mate. His chest heaved as he dragged in scent, always scent. His woman's scent changed. There was a sudden flare of hope and joy, but it was very brief.

"Little brother." Israel's voice was a call to his human mind. It stirred, prodding cautiously against the tiger's instincts. Malachi focused on Israel, his prince, his brother, at least enough to focus on his face. Israel gestured to a truck parked by the curb. Both of them moved forward cautiously. The cab was dark, and there was no heat rising from the under the hood of the big pickup. Malachi reached it first. It was his truck, the one he'd been driving since his arrival in California. It reeked of the fugitive.

"Jensen." The word was so badly snarled, it was barely understandable. Malachi swiped his claws at the driver's door just to vent his feelings. "It is filled with the stench of his lust and…triumph."

Israel didn't answer. Malachi turned to find the other Tseng Tse with his nose against a garden wall. Israel inched his way along the stone, quartering it in every direction. His brother's hair stood on end as the shadow of stripes flickered in and out of sight on his skin. He smelled of fury.

Two strides took Malachi to his side. He leaned close to the wall. Pepper...and Jensen. Her terror and his lust, all mixed up with the scent of a hunt. Malachi's already tenuous control snapped. His hands were already halfway to paws as he slammed them into the wall. Wickedly curved claws dug into the stone, gouging shallow furrows through the bricks where the aberration had trapped his woman. Where he had held her against her will and touched her. His teeth elongated as he opened his mouth to taste the scents. He would hunt. He would kill. He would protect what was his, his territory and his mate. He would claim her and take her to his real den, where she would be safe, cared for and protected all of her days, never to roam and be exposed to such awful danger again.

Something hit him hard on the back of his neck. It gripped him tightly, like powerful jaws without teeth. His head flung back as he spun to fight. There was another male—strong and in his prime—in *his* territory, another threat to his mate that he must destroy. The strength of the grip only increased. It shook him, rattling him like a cub in its mother's mouth. Amber eyes stared him down, daring him, holding him with power...and compassion. He became aware of his breathing, how rapid and shallow it was. He became aware of the night wind on his ears, of the pressure of broken mortar between his claws. Of rain dropping onto his fur.

Israel leaned his forehead against his as Malachi's mind began to clear. The older tiger chuffed. The sound trickled down his spine, inside of his skin, making it ripple. Israel never released the back of Malachi's neck, even as Malachi gripped his older brother's forearms. The rain stung Malachi's throat as he gasped for air. Shock threatened to rob him of the strength adrenaline had given him, nearly knocking his knees from under him. Israel tightened his grip on his neck, as well as grabbed onto his shoulder.

"Stay human." The words mixed command and compassion. "You cannot help your woman if you are feral. Nor if you are unconscious. You are Tseng Tse. You are a prince of our people. You will hold your shape and finish your hunt."

Malachi focused on Israel's voice and scent. Shivers tripped down his spine, one after another, both comforting and uncomfortable at the same time. Israel watched him closely, rain pouring down between them. He nodded. Malachi returned it. Israel peeled his hand from the back of his brother's neck and lifted his forehead, caution in the back of his eyes. Malachi straightened fully as he filled his lungs. One final shudder threw off most of the discomfort of his brother's grip.

He wasted no breath on words. Pepper's trail was easy to follow, her sweet, spicy scent made acrid with terror. Both Tseng Tse raced through the streets, no longer concerned with keeping up appearances. The scent was too stale; they needed speed. Pain clutched at Malachi with every step. He drove through it. Every moment was a battle against his instincts as Pepper's scent tore at him. He had no choice but to run, to hunt, to find her and protect her. He had to stay human. Another shift would take too much out of him, making him useless to her. He forced his slower, weaker human form to keep going, knowing it was taking too long. Jensen had too much head start. He would rape her, and kill her, and Malachi would have only a body to mourn.

Light flared in the darkness ahead. For a moment, he thought his eyes were playing tricks on him. A fire, even so small a fire, in the middle of the city? The scent of oil and smoke hit him at the same time a roar of agony and fury ripped the night. Malachi abandoned the scent trail and simply ran. Rain and blood soaked his shirt. A woman's terrified scream slammed past his ears, past his mind, into his very soul, and every thought fled. Only Pepper.

He burst from the stand of trees and into the parking lot of Turtle Creek Coffee. Every sense he had tuned to search for her. His woman. His potential mate. His entire world condensed into one strong, beautiful woman.

In the painfully orange lights at the back door of Turtle Creek, a slender figure struggled up the roof access ladder with the small torch in one hand. A much larger figure—half tiger, half human—reached up after her, his claws clearly visible as he dug hands into her hips. He dragged her off the ladder and threw her onto the ground. She slid several inches. Both hands held the small torch in front of her, scant protection against the aberration as he stood over her. Smoke lifted from his head and even from across the lot, the scent of singed fur and skin was unmistakable.

Malachi was already on the move when Jensen dropped to the ground on top of Pepper. Sparks chewed at the aberration's blackened face, his red eyes streaming. Pepper kicked up at Jensen with all of her strength, fighting like a tigress to keep him off of her.

Pride in his woman shone in his heart, helping to keep the beast within him at bay. His wounds pulled and bled, making him far too slow. He swore in his native language, calling on the ancestors to burn Jensen in his tracks. Malachi could see his hands groping over Pepper and hear the revulsion in her sobs. She swung the small flare at him, shoving it into his chest and forcing him back by a few inches.

A bright streak bounded past him. He knew the stripe pattern: Israel. His brother's enormous tiger form swallowed up ground with each stretch of the powerful cat's body. He must have hung back long enough to shift. Israel had barely worked up to full speed when he leaped on Jensen. He hit the fugitive hard, knocking him into the back wall of the coffee shop. Jensen's snarl filled the air as he lashed out at Israel. The prince danced away from him, keeping his own body between Jensen and Pepper. Jensen showed his teeth, growling and grumbling as he turned his head one way then the other. His nose worked furiously over the long whiskers and thin lips pulled back over his teeth. He made no move to attack, and Malachi realized that Pepper had managed to blind Jensen with the road flare she still gripped in both hands.

Israel was still pacing in a half-moon in front of Pepper, keeping Jensen off-guard by growling from one place and then another without exposing the human woman to another attack. Malachi dropped heavily to one knee beside her, wrapping his hand over both of hers. Pepper's eyes were enormous as she tried to jerk away from him. Soot and tears marked her face, and he could smell burned flesh on her as well. Recognition dawned in her eyes. She sobbed. Malachi pulled the flare from her hands and flung it into the open parking lot. His other arm wrapped around her, he half dragged, half carried her back from where Israel paced.

The brilliant orange tiger flicked one ear back at him, listening. So was Jensen. The aberration launched himself from the wall, following their sounds. Israel rose up to meet him, claws outstretched as he snapped at Jensen's face. Jensen pulled back just in time to avoid the jaws. Israel's claws sunk deep into Jensen's heavily muscled chest, latching into flesh mercilessly. The fugitive swiped his claws at Israel's face and belly. Israel snapped once and Jensen roared in pain, his hand-paw crushed in the prince's powerful jaws. Jensen's other hand-paw scored deep through Israel's belly. Fur flew as blood erupted through the deep lacerations. Jensen must have felt the drag of tissue; he tightened into a fist. Pepper stoppered a scream with her fist. Malachi dragged to his feet, claws bursting through his fingertips. Israel leaped. He slammed his back feet into Jensen's stomach as he released his holds, trying to kick the aberration away from him. Jensen dropped forward. Malachi heard an ugly crunch as Israel's spine hit the ground, and the tiger went still.

Pain ripped through Malachi, but it was familiar. The beast within leaped for the surface with power like he had never felt. He shot up as layer after layer of thick muscle added to his body. Razor teeth popped from his suddenly massive jaws. The roar came from the depths of his soul to shake the stars, leaving him panting.

The aberration had gone still. So had Pepper. She stared up at him with those beautiful dark eyes, eyes he could lose himself in, and filled with absolute trust.

Like she knew he could never lose this fight. Like she knew he would never let any harm or evil touch her again. Blood soaked her ragged shirt but there was no fear in her beautiful face. Only trust, and strength, and love.

It was her. Malachi's heart thundered as power poured through him. Not his power, but *hers*. The pain didn't matter anymore. The weakness of recovery, even the exhaustion of shifting so often in succession were all gone. Strength filled every cell in his body. Pepper still lay on the asphalt, one hand over her bloodied shirt. Too much of her blood had been spilled, not to mention the blood and tears of the other women Jensen had attacked. Israel still lay where he'd fallen, his sides heaving with each breath.

Malachi spun and launched himself at Jensen. He hit the fugitive square in the chest, driving him away from Israel. They slammed into the brick wall at the back of the coffee shop. Jensen roared. He swung wildly at Malachi with claws fully extended. Malachi ducked, and Jensen's claws sailed over his head. He slashed at Jensen's thighs, aiming for the big arteries at the inside of the leg. Malachi's claws struck deep, and he raked upward. Jensen howled in agony. Malachi's other hand caught the criminal by the throat, pinning him against the wall.

"I am Malachi Negrescu, Third Prince of the Tseng Tse," he snarled. "I deliver to you the justice of the Tseng Tse."

Malachi removed his claws from Jensen. The fugitive slid down the wall, leaving a trail of blood down the bricks. Malachi gripped Jensen's head in both hands, and twisted. There was a sickening snap, and the aberration went limp.

Chapter Twenty-Five

The sound of rain woke him. It battered against the windows hard enough to pull him from the deep sleep of healing, but not enough to shock him fully awake. That came from the large, masculine form sprawled in one of the chairs, cleanly silhouetted against the soft light filtering through the window. The roar started as he shifted to sit up, struggling to free his arm from under his woman.

"Be still, you fool," a familiar voice spoke, quiet but clear. "The healer will not thank you if he has to stitch you up again, or if you wake your woman in a panic."

Malachi dropped back into the bed. "Israel." He rubbed the disorientation from his face.

"Who else would be babysitting your idiot self? Anyone else would let you simply throw everything away, including your life." The chair creaked as Israel pulled himself out of it. Coming to the bedside, the older tiger pushed hair from Malachi's face to lightly grip the back of his neck before resting a hand on his shoulder. Malachi felt the worry in the gesture. He reached to clasp his brother's forearm, using decent strength. Relief and pride filled Israel's face. "You are all right."

"Yes." Malachi released Israel's arm and turned toward Pepper. He inhaled deeply, closing his eyes.

Instinct made him rumble softly, chuffing into her hair as he nuzzled his jaw against the top of her head. "How is she?"

"She will recover." Israel let his hand slide from Malachi's shoulder. Going back to his chair, he picked up his half-finished sandwich without taking his amber gaze from his brother.

"How bad is it?"

"Her wounds? Yours? Mine? The situation in general?" Humor filled Israel's voice as he took a large bite of sandwich. Malachi wasn't very amused, but the fact that Israel was teasing him was comforting. His brother wouldn't have been so flippant if anything were terribly wrong. Malachi felt himself start to relax again, though shot Israel an unamused look.

"How bad are my woman's wounds?"

"Not nearly as bad as they could have been." Israel chewed placidly, then continued. "It was clever of her to think of the road flare. She is very strong, brother mine, more than I would have expected of a human."

"Don't let Ana or Josiah hear you say things like that." Malachi curled around Pepper, protective, sheltering, as he drew her closer against his body.

"Our sister has heard me say such things, more than once." Israel smiled crookedly. "She and our brother have cuffed me for it more than once, as well."

"They aren't cuffing you hard enough," Malachi muttered without turning from Pepper. "How badly are you injured? I'm glad you're walking. From the way Jensen slammed you into the ground, I wasn't sure."

"Neither was the healer, for a day or so." Malachi frowned. From Israel, it was a concession, flippant as it was. He must have really been hurt. "A few days of rest and food, and I am well enough to finish the record-keeping for you on this hunt." Israel finished the sandwich he'd been eating and picked up another, just as thick. He contemplated it a moment before taking a bite. "These sandwiches made by your host are quite good. He understands the necessity of meat very well…for a human."

Malachi snorted as Israel baited him. Pain shot through him, but it wasn't nearly as bad as he expected.

"And the other woman Jensen attacked? In the garden?" he asked.

"The healer has spoken with her several times. It is still unclear how much of the attack she remembers. We have arranged for her to be placed in a hospital in San Francisco, where our healers will watch over her, and intervene if necessary."

Malachi nodded. "Good. She may need it." His arms tightened around Pepper. "How long have I slept?"

"Three days and the nights in between, and most of this day, as well."

"She's still here?" Malachi's voice was a breath of wonder. He cradled her head close to him. The touch sent a wave of scent from her, fear and sweat and fire and blood…and Jensen. Malachi's gut clenched hard. He had to fight to keep from holding her too tightly and snarling.

"She has hardly left your side," Israel said softly, as close to soothing as he generally got. "Indeed, she's barely waked herself."

Malachi frowned. "That isn't normal for humans."

"It is when a Tseng Tse healer wishes it for them, and the Second Prince sanctions the action."

"You said her injuries weren't that bad." Malachi's heart pounded, that strange, new fear rising in his throat. It was rare for a healer to suggest sedating a human to heal, and even more rare for a prince to approve it. His hands smoothed over Pepper's curves, needing to know how badly she was injured.

"I said her injuries were not nearly as bad as they could have been." Israel paused to take a long drink of water. Grabbing up another bottle, he cracked the top and leaned over to nudge Malachi in the back with it. "Drink."

"Tell me," Malachi demanded. Israel refused to respond, simply looking at Malachi until he took the bottle of water. He knew he needed it in order to heal, as much as he needed food and sleep, but his instincts fought it. They gnawed at him, demanding he leave the water for his woman, despite the fact that there were half a dozen bottles still on the table and he had no idea when Pepper would wake.

"There is plenty of water and food for your woman, as well as for you. Drink." Israel stretched out his frame and helped himself to another sandwich. "The healer called it an avulsion fracture. Part of the bone tore away from her ankle. Jordan says that, from the extent of the damage, she must have kept running on it for some time after injuring it. He also needed to clean out the older wounds Jensen left in her. He spent two hours picking glass from her belly and arms, and that does not include the stitches. There are burns on her hands and arms, as well, from holding onto the flare so long. There is also concern that there may be some damage to her vision from the flare. Jordan wished to sedate her in order to keep her still and quiet so that she would have a chance to heal. It is not yet her time to join the ancestors."

"You may spend your life among humans, but you don't know much about them." Malachi kissed Pepper's face. His heart ached as she made a soft sound and nuzzled closer to him, still clearly asleep. She was inside his heart. He could almost feel her there, warming and calming him. The beast within was quiet, content to rest and keep watch over his female, and Malachi basked in the peace inside of his mind. He could only pray she felt the same as he did.

"I know enough to know that it is I who am taking responsibility for that decision. Let Pepper be angry with me for curbing her freedom, not you, and not the healer."

"Thank you," Malachi said quietly. "You have kept my den as if it were your own."

"Of course, little brother. We are family. I would see you whole and happy." Israel smiled, small and lopsided and filled with a tenderness the older tiger rarely showed. "I have grown fond of Pepper. I would see her as your mate, for her sake as well as yours. I can do no less than to see to her wellbeing, until you can see to it yourself."

Eyes closed, he rested his forehead against Pepper's temple. She turned toward him in her sleep. "What of the aberration?"

"There is no body left to find." Israel's tone was emotionless, as if he spoke of ants instead of one of their own, and Malachi sighed faintly. It had been that way with Israel more and more over the last several years, a divorce from emotion in order to fulfill his role for their people.

"You won't tell me what happened to it, will you?" he said, already knowing the answer.

"My burden, brother mine, not yours."

"Does Pepper know?"

Israel shook his head. "Not about the body, no. It took her only a few moments to slip unconscious. You were both out by the time I was able to shift and heal enough to get us all under cover."

"You didn't dispose of it then?" Malachi was appalled. "The risk—! He was hybrid!"

Israel took another bite of sandwich and chewed leisurely. "The risk to our family was greater. Jordan arrived shortly after, accompanied by the Tenth Streak. With so many of our hunters present, I allowed us to rest while the others dealt with cleanup. The leader reports the body was undisturbed. Drink." Israel nudged the bottle of water still in Malachi's hand. "You cannot care for her if you are still weak, and she needs care. She stinks."

Malachi raised his lip instantly, even knowing he was being baited. Pepper shifted, stirred, rubbed her cheek against his arm. A sound like a mewl came from her throat. All of Malachi's attention riveted on her. He barely heard Israel murmur something about going to find Jordan as he let himself from the bungalow. His brother wouldn't go far, and neither would the healer. Malachi was too vulnerable, right now, and that left Pepper too vulnerable, as well. They would guard the den. He could focus on Pepper.

She seemed so small, tucked into the curve of his body. One foot was wrapped in a bandage, stabilizing it. Very carefully, Malachi slid his legs under Pepper's to elevate her foot, his hand stroking over her hair. His scent on her was recent, and that comforted and calmed him, but Israel was right: she did stink. It twisted his gut. He had resolved to let her go, to give her her freedom without argument, but after what had happened at the coffee shop, he wasn't sure he could, anymore.

"I'm sorry, beauty. I'm not that strong of a man."

Pepper stirred, warm against his heart. The soft sounds slipped inside Malachi's skin to wrap around his soul. She raised a hand to rub at her eyes, and he caught it in his own. Bringing her knuckles to his mouth, he pressed kisses against her skin. This close, he could smell the burns, the phosphorus, and the balm Jordan had used under the bandages. He chuffed.

"Peace, Pepper mine. Be still." He kept his tone low and crooning, sending his heart through his voice to coax her to him. His hands traced the contours of her body, gently caressing as he sought to soothe her. She shifted, stretched, winced faintly as the small movements tugged on painful places. "Does it hurt much, beauty?"

Pepper squeezed her eyes tightly shut before fluttering her lashes open. Her dark eyes were slightly unfocused, hopefully only with sleep or with the remnants of whatever Jordan had used to sedate her. She frowned. Her eyes suddenly flew wide as she tensed to sit up.

"Jensen!"

Malachi held her easily, his arms a gentle cage as he chuffed.

"He's gone. Try not to move much. The healer has yet to release you, and you took some hurt."

"Gone?" Pepper clung to that one word as if to a lifeline. "What do you mean 'gone'?"

"Permanently gone." Malachi nuzzled against her hair, bunching it in one hand just to feel it. "I told you, the only sentence possible for him was death. Justice has been delivered. You're safe."

Pepper gasped, deeper and deeper as the word ricocheted in her mind. Safe. She was safe. Jensen was dead, and he was never coming after her again. Sobs bubbled up from deep in her chest until she felt like she was nearly convulsing. Pain stabbed from her belly and arms, even on her face. Her lungs burned as air raked in and out. Malachi held her tightly, keeping her close as the tears broke the surface. She clutched for him, her hands scraping over his bare skin into fists, over and over again. Hot tears poured down her face as the strain and horror of the last several days overflowed. Malachi murmured softly, chuffing occasionally. She couldn't find words in the quiet little rumbles and growls that came from his throat, but there was comfort in the sounds, anyway. She felt the kisses he dropped on her hair, lifting her wet face into them. He kissed her tearstained face without hesitation, finally allowing his lips to settle on hers. She clung to the kiss, wrapping her arms around his neck to bring him closer to her. He shifted carefully, bringing her half onto his body. Hands in her hair, he gently ended the kiss.

"I'm so sorry, beauty mine." His voice nearly broke in the tightness of his throat. Pepper frowned in confusion. "I couldn't protect you."

"I'm alive, Malachi. Without you, and Israel…" Pepper shook her head. She couldn't even think it without feeling the hysteria welling up again.

"I'm alive," she repeated. She opened her mouth to say something more, but only a rough cough came out.

She gasped for breath, and Malachi propped her upright.

"I'll get the healer. He has to be close." Malachi started to rise but Pepper clutched him.

"No, please," she said hurriedly, her voice worn by the cough.

"Pepper, you need the healer."

"Please, Malachi. Just for a little longer, I want it to be just you and me. Then I'll see him. I promise." Pepper's hand tightened against his arm. Her voice was almost a whisper. "Please."

Malachi regarded her steadily. Growling, he lay back down beside her and pulled her into his arms.

"Ten minutes more," he conceded, as if he was granting her a favor.

"Thank you." Pepper snuggled against the hollow of his shoulder, settling as comfortably as her injuries would allow. "Malachi?"

"Hm?"

"What would happen if I were to agree to be your mate?"

Malachi's heart thudded under her ear, but the rest of him went very still.

"The mate-bond would form. I would tune to you, learning your biorhythms as a second instinct. Your well-being would become the most important thing in the world to me, more, even, than it is now." Malachi sighed, but she could still hear the longing in his voice. "It would be my right and privilege to care for and protect you, and to accept the same from you. I would take you to my home to share my family with you, and to rejoice with them and my people that I have found a mate."

"Your people. Your family." Pepper's voice was quiet, thoughtful, until she scoffed. "Your *royal* family? *Prince* Malachi, is it?"

"Did Israel tell you?"

Pepper shook her head without lifting it from his shoulder. "Jensen did. He said…he said no one would be able to separate us, not even the great Prince Malachi. He was telling the truth?"

"Yes."

"You said you were a hunter." Pepper's tone hovered between accusatory and plaintive.

"I'm both. Prince is what I was born into and raised to be. Hunter is what I chose for myself."

"Were you going to tell me?"

Malachi nodded. "Yes, beauty mine, after you'd had a chance to meet us as people, and you wouldn't be intimidated by titles, or tigers."

Pepper finally lifted her head to blink at him. Malachi cupped his hand against her head and urged her to put it back on his shoulder, as if he didn't like the cold spot left behind. She refused.

"Just how many titles do you have?"

"Two. The rest are epithets." He brushed his fingers through her hair as if she were made of the finest porcelain. "Each of us only has one noble title."

"Every one of your people has a noble title?"

"I'm not explaining this well. Forgive me." He inhaled deeply. "I think explanations will have to wait until the healer has seen us both."

Pepper instantly shifted away from him, but Malachi's arm around her brought her back against his side.

"You're hurt! I've been crawling all over you!"

He rumbled a laugh. Threading his hand into her hair, he brought her lips to his for another long, leisurely kiss.

"I like you crawling all over me, beauty mine," he said. "I'd love to have you crawling all over me every night for the rest of our lives, and occasionally during the days, as well. I want…I *need* to have the care and protection of you, to see that you are safe and comfortable, always." He pulled back enough to find her gaze, his own earnest, as if his world hinged on her. His thumb grazed over her jaw. "Accept me, Pepper. Allow me to give my life to you. I cannot promise that it will be easy, but I swear by all that I hold most dear that I will spend every thought in making it worth it."

Pepper blinked up at him. Her difficulty in breathing had nothing to do with the burning in her lungs. Emotion swelled in her throat, making it impossible to speak. A laugh tried to force its way through, along with tears. She nodded. A brilliant light flared in Malachi's deep blue eyes. His arm tightened around her.

"Say it, beauty, Pepper mine. I need the words," he whispered. Pepper laughed as two little tears escaped.

"Yes, Malachi. I…I accept you as my mate. I'll be your mate. What do I need to say?"

"That will do it." Malachi rolled Pepper beneath him, carefully guarding her ankle with his own legs. He sealed his mouth to hers, joy and gratitude fueling the passion in his kiss. Pepper returned it, meeting his heat with her own. Little hungry sounds came from her throat. Malachi growled low with his hunger, his hand sliding over her side, including the bandages. He fanned the heat of the kiss for a little longer, then eased it back, leaning his forehead against hers. Both of them were breathing harder, and she could feel the scraping in her lungs that shouldn't be there.

"Mine," he whispered, as if reveling in the right to say the word. "Are you feeling up to a bath, Pepper mine?"

"Will actual bathing be involved?" Pepper tried to make her tone suggestive—or at least saucy—and she must have succeeded: Malachi laughed and kissed the tip of her nose.

"Yes. You need to heal. I would wait, but..." He sobered. "You still smell of fear, and pain, and fire."

"And Jensen." Pepper held Malachi's gaze as she said the words. He nodded.

"And Jensen."

"And this bothers you?"

Malachi nodded again. "I don't like another male's scent on you, not like that, on an instinctive level as well as an intellectual one. My chosen mate needs to be comfortable, safe, and well. I can't tell how your current pain level is if you still smell of old pain." He smiled, even white teeth in a three-day shadow of growth on his jaw and cheeks. "Smelling like me will afford you some protection in my world."

"You're going to have to teach me how to live in your world." Pepper shifted. "I can't get up with you lying on me."

Malachi moved, however reluctantly, and helped her to sit. He stood and brought her up to him, steadying her as she stood on one foot. "I've got you." He brushed his thumb over the back of her knuckles. "Of course I'll teach you how to live in my world. We all will."

"Who is 'we all'?"

"All of the Tseng Tse, but especially my brothers and sister." Malachi grabbed his phone from where Israel had left it on the nightstand and sent off a quick text. Somewhere outside, a celebratory roar—mostly human—echoed between the buildings, quickly followed by a loud cheer. Pepper looked at the windows with concern, but Malachi laughed. Supporting her weight with an arm around her waist, he led her toward the bathroom. "Israel and our healer are celebrating your decision to join our family. It will be much louder at the palace when Israel passes on the news. My brothers alone will roar enough to rouse the ancestors."

"How many do you have?" Pepper leaned on the counter as he helped her sit on the edge of the tub. "Brothers, not ancestors."

"Twelve." Pepper's jaw dropped and Malachi grinned. "One is mated, giving me my sister, and she is close to delivering her sixth cub."

Pepper almost felt dizzy. "That…is a lot of family."

"Don't worry about that now. First, wash. Then see the healer and eat, and then more rest. There is time for you to learn of us."

The door to the bungalow opened. Malachi turned and inhaled.

"The healer is here," he told her. Her gaze darted to the doorway and her hands closed on his wrists.

"Please don't leave me alone with him," Pepper whispered fiercely. She felt safe with Malachi, and even with Israel, but the thought of being left alone with a strange man and a tiger, no less, made her want to run. Malachi knelt to press his forehead against hers, his hand on the back of her neck.

"My precious chosen mate." His voice was hardly more than a whisper. "It will be a very, *very* long time before I leave your side, and you will never be alone again."

****

Sunlight streamed down on the blacktop and Pepper turned her face toward it. It had been easy enough to stay inside and rest while the storm system had hovered over the small coastal city, but the string of sunny days had been much harder. Malachi hadn't helped. She laughed under her breath. He'd been so anxious to get outside with his brother and the healer, but he'd refused to leave her. She'd finally had to conspire with the other two Tseng Tse to get him out for a run with Jordan while Israel stayed with her. Even then he'd had to give her a thorough going over with eyes, nose, and hands to assure himself that she was as well as he'd left her.

"What has my chosen mate laughing at the sunlight?" Familiar strong hands slid around her, always so careful of her wounds. "You aren't tired by the crutches, are you?"

"I'm fine, you great worrywart." She grinned as she turned to catch his kiss on her lips instead of her cheek. He rumbled with pleasure. "You know you're going to have to stop fussing so much eventually."

"No, he will not." Israel jumped from the top of the RV, landing as if he'd jumped from only a few feet. His expression was typically sober, but his amber eyes were as warm as the sunlight. "It is the fate of our mates. Accept it."

"We'll see." Pepper held back the laughter. This

was only the latest iteration of an ongoing conversation. "Do you know what's wrong with the air conditioning?"

"Nothing. One of the hoses had come loose. It should work fine now."

Israel stepped back, opening the door as he did. A new—and better—set of locks shone incongruously new against the door. He'd replaced the step, as well while Pepper and Malachi had healed, but he didn't pull it down. He held out his hand for her crutches. Pepper didn't argue, but she did turn slightly pink. She knew what was coming.

As soon as she handed her crutches over to Israel, Malachi scooped Pepper into his arms, cradling her close to his chest. She tucked her face against his neck, partly to hide the blush and partly to keep her head from getting bashed against the narrow doorframe.

"Does this count as being carried over the threshold?" she joked.

"Practice," Malachi and Israel chorused. Malachi continued. "My den is at the palace."

"What if I don't want to live at your palace?" Pepper said as Malachi stepped up into the RV.

"Then we will discuss it and create a proper den somewhere we can both be happy and you will be safe."

"Because this is *not* a *proper* den," Pepper teased both brothers with their own words, including the haughty emphases. "Neither is the bed and breakfast."

"Now you begin to understand," Israel said, so blandly that she wasn't sure if he was joining in the teasing or if he was completely serious. That was a common question with Israel.

"Wow," Pepper said as she looked around the place that had been her only home for so long. "Israel, it looks great. You've really put some work into it. Thank you so much."

"I had to do something to keep from going cage-crazy while my young fool brother healed."

"So you took on my old RV."

Over the last several days, Israel had replaced the tires on the RV, and overhauled the engine, and had the windows all replaced, as well as had the weatherizing updated. He'd replaced the cabinets and fixed the bathroom fan so it didn't rattle and whine every time it turned on. Pepper swallowed as she glanced over the oven door, and the new table, and the new carpet throughout the RV. There was no trace of Bunsen's murder, now, but the changes only seemed to highlight his absence. Malachi seemed to guess her thoughts, or maybe her scent changed. He leaned close, kissing her hair before sliding past Israel, out the door. She turned her face back to Israel with a warm smile.

"It's amazing. I hate to just...leave it somewhere while we're gone. What if something happens to it?"

"There is a family of Tseng Tse near Eureka who has a significant property. I am certain they would happily keep an eye on it for you. I can drop it there before I move on."

"Why don't you just take it to Nevada? You've put all this work and money into it, you ought to enjoy it."

"I would do no less for any of our people, let alone my sister."

Pepper's smile deepened, still caught off-guard by the Tseng Tse tradition of dropping the 'in-law' from the title.

"Then I am allowed to insist that my brother take my RV as transportation and shelter as he travels to check up on and take care of our people." Pepper lifted her chin as she mimicked Israel's speech. The tiger gave one of his rare laughs.

"You are learning to be the Third Princess already. Well done, little sister." Leaning forward, he cupped the back of her neck and kissed her forehead. "Very well, then. I accept, and with thanks. It may not be a *proper* den, but it is better than motels and diners for weeks on end."

"Why don't you stay with the Tseng Tse—" she still struggled with pronouncing the words, but Israel smiled his approval, "—that you're visiting?"

"I have no wish to burden them with the visit of a Prince. There are few who would be comfortable with such a thing, and those who are, are rarely at their own dens, anyway."

Pepper's phone chimed. She jumped. She wasn't used to having a phone on her anymore. Malachi and Israel had given her a new one only two days before, insisting that she needed it for her safety as well as their sanity. The first call to come through had been from the First Prince with an official invitation to visit the Tseng Tse palace. The second call had been from Abby. Israel had, of course, informed the coffee shop owner that Pepper had been attacked and needed significant time away from work to heal, but Abby had insisted on speaking with Pepper as soon as possible. She wouldn't believe any other assurance that her employee was fine. It had taken Pepper two phone calls plus a visit in person to calm her boss's fears that she was really okay, and the brothers weren't holding her prisoner somewhere or something. She was going to miss Abby. The woman had assured her she had a job to come back to, whenever she was well, but Pepper had relinquished her position for the good of the shop. Let Abby get someone on the payroll who could work and take the extra pressure from the others. Pepper had no idea when, or if, she might be back.

"We'd better get going," she said as she turned off the phone's reminder.

"I will take you both to the airport. It may be years before I see either of you again." A shadow slipped through Israel's eyes.

"It will be only months," Malachi said from the doorway. "The world can spare you for a few days to attend your little brother's wedding."

A loud and demanding meow interrupted Israel's answer. The color drained from Pepper's face, and she reached for the table to steady herself. She looked desperately at both brothers' faces, searching for any sign that they heard it, too. Israel looked as if he were trying not to smile. Malachi stooped for a moment, straightening with an armful of orange fur. Pepper gasped as an enormous purr started up.

"He may be the largest cat I have ever seen, but he isn't afraid of my scent, nor Israel's, nor Jordan's." The giant tabby rubbed his face against Malachi's chin, making the tiger laugh. "Indeed, he seems to like it."

Israel hovered to steady Pepper as she reached for the cat. He came to her easily, trilling as he rubbed his head against her face.

"Oh! He's perfect!" She stared in wonder at Malachi as he climbed into the RV and closed the door behind him. "When did you have time to find him?"

"The healer found him, once we told him you had lost your little companion. Jordan visited several animal shelters and rescues before he returned to San Francisco."

"And he can come with us? He'll be safe at the palace?"

Malachi wrapped his arms around her.

"Yes, Pepper mine. He's cleared to fly with us, and his papers are all in order to clear customs at home. He's yours, if you want him."

Pepper couldn't have answered if she'd wanted to. Happiness choked off her voice. Balancing the cat on her hip, she made a fist in the collar of Malachi's shirt and pulled him down to her. She filled the kiss with all the love and promise in her heart. Words would never have sufficed, anyway.

A word about the author...

L. Dawn Jackson began writing stories as soon as they put a pencil in her chubby baby hand. She was a 2021 and 2022 finalist in the San Francisco Writers Contest. She was also selected as a mentee in the inaugural 2021 Romance Authors Mentorship Program through Romance Writers of America. She lives at the top of the American Rocky Mountains with two miracle children, her amazing husband, a lupus diagnosis, and an ever-increasing knitting stash. https://www.ldawnjackson.com